DATE DUE

A *FIXER* NOVEL

THE

LONG GAME

Also by Jennifer Lynn Barnes

The Fixer

A *FIXER* NOVEL

Fixer #2

THE

LONG
GAM

JENNIFER
LYNN
BARNES

BLOOMSBURY
NEW YORK   LONDON   OXFORD   NEW DELHI   SYDNEY

First published in the United States of America in June 2016
by Bloomsbury Children's Books
www.bloomsbury.com

Bloomsbury is a registered trademark of Bloomsbury Publishing Plc

For information about permission to reproduce selections from this book, write to
Permissions, Bloomsbury Children's Books, 1385 Broadway, New York, New York 10018
Bloomsbury books may be purchased for business or promotional use. For information on
bulk purchases please contact Macmillan Corporate and Premium Sales Department at
specialmarkets@macmillan.com

Library of Congress Cataloging-in-Publication Data
Names: Barnes, Jennifer (Jennifer Lynn) author.
Title: The long game : a Fixer novel / by Jennifer Lynn Barnes.
Description: New York : Bloomsbury Children's Books, 2016.
Summary: Tess Kendrick, a junior at the elite Hardwicke School in Washington, DC,
can fix just about any problem her classmates—or their power-wielding parents—might
have, but when terrorism, assassination, and murder strike, she soon finds herself
wrapped up in an intricate plot that may end up hitting closer
to home than she could have ever imagined.
Identifiers: LCCN 2015025288
ISBN 978-1-61963-596-8 (hardcover) • ISBN 978-1-61963-597-5 (e-book)
Subjects: | CYAC: Families—Fiction. | High schools—Fiction. | Schools—Fiction. |
Wealth—Fiction. | Washington (D.C.)—Fiction. | Mystery and detective stories. |
BISAC: JUVENILE FICTION/Family/Siblings. | JUVENILE FICTION/Mysteries &
Detective Stories. | JUVENILE FICTION/Law & Crime.
Classification: LCC PZ7.B26225 Lo 2016 | DDC [Fic]—dc23
LC record available at http://lccn.loc.gov/2015025288

Book design by Amanda Bartlett/Andrea Tsurumi
Typeset by Newgen Knowledge Works (P) Ltd., Chennai, India
Printed and bound in the U.S.A. by Berryville Graphics Inc., Berryville, Virginia
2 4 6 8 10 9 7 5 3 1

All papers used by Bloomsbury Publishing, Inc., are natural, recyclable products
made from wood grown in well-managed forests. The manufacturing processes
conform to the environmental regulations of the country of origin.

For Jeana

A *FIXER* NOVEL

THE

LONG
GAME

CHAPTER 1

"Tess, has anyone ever told you that you're an absolute vision when you're plotting something?" Asher Rhodes shot a lazy grin in my direction.

I ignored Asher and kept my gaze fixed on the street in front of the Roosevelt Hotel. A man named Charles Bancroft had a reservation at the Roosevelt's five-star restaurant for lunch—pricey, considering Mr. Bancroft had recently convinced a judge that his child support and alimony payments should be kept to a minimum.

"Asking for a friend," Asher clarified. Then he nudged his best friend. "Henry, my good man, tell Tess she's pretty as a picture when she's preparing to unleash her wrath on the delightfully unsuspecting father of one of our classmates."

"Kendrick?" Henry Marquette said.

"Yes?" I replied without taking my eyes away from the street.

"You are utterly *terrifying* when you are plotting something."

A dark car pulled up to the curb. I smiled. "Thank you," I told Henry. Then I turned to Asher. "Get Vivvie on the phone," I instructed. "Tell her we're a go."

Vivvie and her aunt had lived at the Roosevelt Hotel for almost a month until they'd found a DC apartment. That was plenty of time for friendly-to-a-fault Vivvie Bharani to have endeared herself to the staff.

Convenient, that, I thought as I watched Charles Bancroft climb out of the backseat of his luxury sedan. Asher relayed my message to Vivvie, then put the phone on speaker.

"The eagle has landed," Vivvie said from the other end. "The bird is in the bush."

Few things in life gave Vivvie and Asher as much joy as talking in code. I didn't bother translating. One of the bellhops wheeled a cart of luggage out in front of Bancroft's car. Bancroft disappeared into the restaurant, but his driver wasn't going anywhere.

That was my cue.

I took a step forward. Henry caught my elbow. "No bloodshed," he said. "No blackmail. No obstruction of justice."

"You drive a hard bargain," I told him, stepping away from his grasp. "What are your thoughts on extortion?" Without waiting for an answer, I headed for Bancroft's car.

Henry and Asher followed on my heels.

"The cat is dancing in the catnip," Asher reported back to Vivvie. "Grumpy lion is grumpy."

"Did you just refer to me as a grumpy lion?" Henry asked Asher.

"Absolutely not," Asher promised. Then he took the phone off speaker and lowered his voice. "*Suspicious lion is suspicious*," he stage-whispered to Vivvie.

With one last glance back at Henry and Asher, I approached Bancroft's car and knocked on the window. The driver rolled it down.

"Can I help you?" he asked.

"I'm a friend of Jeremy's," I said. "I'd like to talk."

Jeremy Bancroft was a senior at the Hardwicke School, due to graduate in the spring. Or at least he had been due to graduate from Hardwicke in the spring until his father stopped payment on his tuition. From what I'd gathered, Mr. Bancroft's sole focus was making his ex-wife suffer for daring to divorce him, and he had no qualms whatsoever about using his own children to do it.

I had no qualms about lying in wait in the man's car. An hour later, I was rewarded.

"I'm telling you right now," Bancroft said, shifting his phone from one ear to the other as he situated himself in the backseat of the car, "they'll be signed on with the firm by the end of business day tomorrow. Guaranteed."

The car pulled away from the curb. I sat silently in the front passenger seat until we'd merged into traffic. Then I turned around.

"What the . . ." Bancroft hung up the phone and started barking out orders to his driver. "Mick, pull over."

"Mick had to step out," I told Jeremy's father. "Right about now, he's probably wondering where you and your car are."

In reality, Bancroft's driver had agreed to take a very conveniently timed bathroom break. He was, as it turned out, fonder of his boss's son than of his boss.

"I don't know who you are," Bancroft gritted out, "or what you want—"

"I'd like for you to stop using your children as pawns in what-ever sick game you have going on with your ex-wife," I said. "But I'll settle for a rather large transfer of funds."

Bancroft stared at me in disbelief. "Who put you up to this?"

"A better question might be what I'm going to do if you don't transfer those funds."

"Do?" Bancroft sputtered. "You can't *do* anything. You're a kid."

"I'm Tess Kendrick," I said. "Keyes." The second last name was an afterthought. The combination of the two had the man in the backseat paling. "I go to Hardwicke with your son. Jeremy seems fairly convinced that you're hiding money in an offshore account to keep your child support payments to a minimum."

Bancroft showed not even a trace of emotion at the mention of his son. "Prove it," he spat out.

"I don't have to." I took my time explaining those words. "Either you *have* been hiding assets," I said, "which makes you a felon, or you're actually as broke as you claim to be, which makes you the very last person in the world whom anyone in DC should trust to invest their money." I paused. "I wonder how long it would take for news of your financial difficulties to spread."

Bancroft snorted, but his eyes gave him away. He was looking nervous. *Good.* "You think my ex-wife wants DC society to real-ize how broke *she* is?" the man countered. "If she was going to go public with this, she would have already."

True.

"I'm not your ex-wife." I picked up my phone and brought up the contact information for the *Washington Post*. "And as it turns out, *I* don't have a vested interest in whether people think she's broke or not." I turned the phone toward Bancroft just long enough for him to see who I was calling, then hit the *call* button, setting the phone to speaker.

It rang once.

Twice.

"Stop," Bancroft said.

I hit the button to end the call just as someone picked up. I held out the paperwork Henry had asked his family attorney to draw up. "In an ideal world," I said, "you'd amend the divorce settlement you made with your ex-wife."

A muscle in Bancroft's jaw ticked. He'd take his chances weathering damaging rumors before he'd give his ex anything she wanted.

"However," I continued, "I thought you might prefer making an anonymous donation to your children's school."

I held out the papers again. Bancroft took them. Reading them, he frowned. "A scholarship fund?"

"Donors can put whatever stipulations they would like on a donation. Your stipulations are very specific."

Jeremy and his little sister would be the recipients of scholarships that would pay their Hardwicke tuition through graduation.

"I only have two children." Bancroft looked up from the pages and glowered at me. "Why am I funding three scholarships?"

I offered him a tight-lipped smile. "Price of doing business."

A vein in Bancroft's forehead throbbed. "And if I tear up these papers, call the police, and have you arrested for stealing my car?"

I shrugged. "Technically," I said, "*I* didn't steal your car."

The car slowed to a stop at the curb of the Roosevelt, having circled the block. In the driver's seat, Henry turned around. "Technically," he said, "I did."

"Henry Marquette," I clarified for the man in the back-seat. "His mother is Pamela Abellard." My smile took on a cat-eating-canary glint. "Correct me if I'm wrong, but aren't the Abellards your firm's biggest client?"

Bancroft's grip tightened over his phone, his knuckles turning white.

"We both know you're not making that call," I said. I nodded toward the paperwork in his hands.

The man's eyes went back to Henry's.

"Normally," Henry told him conversationally, "when someone asks me to commit grand theft auto, my answer is a firm no. But I have a sister." Henry's expression was perfectly polite, but his mint-green eyes flashed, striking against his dark brown skin. "My little sister," Henry continued, "is your daughter's age. Nine years old."

Bancroft signed the papers. He made a call and authorized the transfer of funds.

As I exited the car, I glanced over at Henry. "Should I call Asher and tell him we won't be needing that getaway distraction?"

Before Henry could reply, pop music reverberated off the building. Asher jogged into the middle of a large crowd and struck a dramatic pose.

"You say 'distraction,'" Henry deadpanned, "Asher hears 'flash mob.'"

Five seconds later, Vivvie danced wildly past and gave me a questioning look. I nodded.

"The possum has fallen on the nun!" Vivvie called to Asher.

Asher didn't miss a beat of choreography. He shimmied and punched a fist into the air. "Long live the possum!"

CHAPTER 2

I had exactly three hours to recover from my confrontation with Jeremy Bancroft's father before I found myself facing off against a very different opponent.

"What do you know about the War of the Roses?" My paternal grandfather closed his fingers around a black knight and then used it to remove my rook from the chessboard.

No mercy. No hesitation.

"*Wars* of the Roses," I said, countering his move. "Plural."

The edges of the old man's lips quirked upward. He inclined his head slightly—both an acknowledgment of my point and a command to continue.

"Bunch of guys in the fifteenth century fighting for the throne of England."

I kept my summary short and to the point. As in chess, every move in a conversation with William Keyes came with consequences, either immediate or down the line. He was grooming me as his heir, attempting to mold me in his own image. If I gave an inch, he'd take a mile, and I had no desire to be either molded or groomed.

Especially by a man who may or may not have conspired to assassinate the chief justice of the United States Supreme Court.

"The Wars of the Roses were a series of lethal confrontations and political maneuverings between the house of Lancaster and the house of York," Keyes corrected, sliding his bishop across the board as he lectured. "Political unrest tends to be unkind to weak and strategically impotent kings."

His gaze settled on the chessboard—on *my* king—but I knew he was thinking about another ruler and another throne.

Weekly Sunday night dinners at the Keyes mansion had cemented my understanding of my paternal grandfather as a man with many allies and many enemies. More often than not, he considered President Nolan the latter. Every bump in the road for the Nolan administration was taken as incontrovertible evidence that Peter Nolan had never been the right man for the job.

I picked up my bishop and plunked it back down. "Check."

"Bloodthirsty girl," Keyes commented. "You get that from your mother. Patience," he continued, eyeing the board, "is a Keyes trait."

This was the way it was with him, drawing lines between the Kendrick blood in me and the Keyes.

"Did you know that the term *kingmaker* was first used to refer to the role the Earl of Warwick played in the struggle between Lancaster and York?" My grandfather resumed his lecture, but I knew his eyes missed nothing—not the effect that hearing Ivy referred to as my *mother* still had on me, not the positions of the pieces on the board. "During the Wars of the Roses, Warwick deposed not one but two kings."

Kingmaker was what people called William Keyes. He wielded tremendous power and influence behind the scenes in the American political game.

"Warwick wasn't just wealthy and powerful," Keyes continued. "He was *strategic.*"

Power. Politics. Game theory. This was what passed for casual conversation in this house. William Keyes had two sons. One of them was dead; the other was estranged. I was his only grandchild. In his eyes, that meant his legacy rested on me.

"I'd like to see you showing a bit more initiative about becoming a part of the Hardwicke community, Tess."

From the Wars of the Roses to high school extracurriculars in two seconds flat.

"I'm not really much of a joiner," I said. That was an understatement.

"The debate club, a sport or two," William Keyes continued, as if I hadn't spoken. "It's high time you started making your mark."

The prestigious Hardwicke School was a microcosm of Washington. The mark I'd made there, up to and including what I'd done for Jeremy Bancroft a few hours earlier, wasn't the kind you could put on a résumé—or the kind my newfound grandfather would have approved of.

"The queen," Keyes told me, returning his attention to our game, "is the most dangerous piece on the board." His index finger trailed the edge of the black queen for a moment, before moving it forward. "Check."

He was boxing me in.

I could see, already, how this was going to end. "You'll have checkmate in three moves."

The old man's lips parted in a dangerous smile. "Will I?"

He'd gone into this game fully expecting to win it, just like he fully expected me to yield to his decrees about Hardwicke.

"Luckily for me," I told him, my fingers closing around my own queen, "I'll have checkmate in two."

CHAPTER 3

Shockingly, I made it through my Monday classes without developing the slightest inclination to sign up for the debate team.

"Hypothetically speaking," Asher said as he took the seat beside mine in our last class of the day, "if I told Carmen Seville that you could take care of a little problem involving a vengeful ex–best friend on the yearbook staff and some aggressively unflattering photo angles . . . would that be a bad thing or a good thing?"

Asher smiled when he said the words *good thing*. It was implied that I should find that smile persuasive.

Sliding into the seat behind him, Vivvie took one look at my face. "Bad thing," she told Asher, correctly interpreting my facial expression. "That would be a very bad thing."

"Allow me to rephrase," Asher said. "If I had, by chance, volunteered your most excellent services—"

I stopped him there. "I don't have services." Seeing the skepticism clear on their faces, I clarified, "Yesterday, with Jeremy's father? That was a onetime thing."

Asher raised one eyebrow to ridiculous heights. "So when one of the seniors on the lacrosse team was hazing the freshmen and you surreptitiously recorded said hazing and uploaded it as an attachment to his college applications, that was . . . what, exactly?"

I shrugged. No one had been able to prove that was me.

"What about that rumor you squelched about Meredith Sutton going to rehab?" Vivvie asked.

That hadn't been a rumor. It had been the truth—and no one's business but Meredith's.

"And that time that Lindsay Li's boyfriend was threatening to tell her parents exactly how far they'd gone if she broke up with him?" Asher raised his other eyebrow. "Correct me if I'm wrong, but didn't he end up in military school?"

"Your point?" I asked.

"Their point is that you are a meddler." Henry helped himself to the seat behind me. "An incurable, insatiable *meddler*. You simply cannot help yourself, Kendrick."

And who was right there beside me yesterday? I refrained from pointing that out and turned around to face him. "I don't *meddle*," I said.

Unfortunately, all that did was set Vivvie and Asher up to chorus, "You fix!"

During my first week at Hardwicke, I'd inadvertently come to the rescue of the vice president's daughter. At the time, I'd had no idea who she was—all I'd known was that she'd been humiliated by an older boy who'd talked her into taking some very *intimate* photos. When I'd heard the jerk was flaunting those photos, I'd lost my temper, stolen his phone, and issued a couple of pointed threats.

Anna Hayden had been very grateful. She'd deemed me a miracle worker, and just like that, the Hardwicke student body had collectively decided that I was to them what my sister was to their parents.

A professional problem solver. Someone who excelled at crisis management. A *fixer*.

I'm not a fixer. I'd given up making that particular objection out loud. *And*, a persistent voice continued in the back of my head, *Ivy isn't my sister*.

As I'd recently found out, she was my mother.

The sound of the bell broke through my thoughts, saving me from going down the rabbit hole of trying to figure out what Ivy really was to me now that I knew the truth.

"I know how much you all love Mondays," Dr. Clark said from the front of the room. "And the only thing that makes Mondays better is pop quizzes, am I right?"

That elicited audible groans.

"Paper and pencils," Dr. Clark decreed, ignoring the groans. On the whiteboard, she wrote a single question in all capital letters: *WHAT ISSUE DO YOU THINK WILL MOST AFFECT THE RESULTS OF MIDTERM ELECTIONS?*

Instead of history, Hardwicke juniors took Contemporary World Issues. Theoretically, this class was supposed to turn us into global citizens, informed about a wide variety of issues playing out on the international stage. In reality, there were enough of us in this class with political connections that "world issues" all too often struck close to home.

"Your answers to this question will form the basis for today's discussion." Dr. Clark leaned back against her desk. "Since I'm not *actually* cruel enough to give you a Monday quiz, feel free to leave your names off your papers."

As my classmates started scribbling down their answers, I turned the question over in my head. I was enough of a Kendrick—and enough of a Keyes—to know that the midterm elections were shaping up to be brutal. If the president lost control of Congress, his chances of getting a second term in the White House were next to nothing. Ivy was currently working for no fewer than three congressmen up for reelection at midterms. I had no idea what exactly she was doing for them, but a person didn't come to Ivy Kendrick unless there was a problem—or a secret that needed to stay buried.

Slowly, I put my pen to the page and jotted down my answer, letter by letter. What factor did I expect to play a role in the midterm elections?

C – O – R – R – U – P – T – I – O – N.

As my pen formed the letters, I thought less about what Ivy was doing *now* than about the secrets I carried, in part, because of her. My first few weeks at Hardwicke had been *very* eventful— the kind of eventful that involved assassinations, cover-ups, and being kidnapped by a rogue Secret Service agent.

"Answers in," Dr. Clark called.

I folded my paper in half, then turned and met Henry's eyes as he passed his to me. He held my gaze, and I wondered what he'd written down.

I wondered if Henry was thinking about the political conspiracy we'd uncovered together.

As Dr. Clark collected our answers, she started lecturing. "Right now, the Nolan administration has the benefit of a majority in both the House and the Senate. But—as I'm sure many of you are aware—that could change in a heartbeat with what is shaping up to be one of the closest midterm elections in recent memory."

Beside me, Asher withdrew a roll of duct tape from his bag. Henry made a slight choking sound, which I translated to mean, *Dear God, who gave Asher that duct tape and what is he planning on doing with it?*

At the front of the room, Dr. Clark resumed her perch on the edge of her desk. "So," she continued, "let's see what factors you foresee affecting the very balance of power in this country." She unfolded the answers, one by one. "Jobs. Health care. Immigration." She sorted the answers as she read them, pulling out and saving a few for later. "Jobs again. Terrorism. The economy. Terrorism. Defense.

"And now things get interesting." Dr. Clark went on to the slips she'd pulled out of sequence. "Ideology. Religion. Voter turnout." She paused. "Not exactly what I meant by *issue*, but undoubtedly true, Ms. Rhodes."

Near the front of the room, Asher's twin sister tossed her strawberry-blond ponytail over one shoulder. Somehow, I wasn't surprised she'd written her name on her answer. Emilia Rhodes believed in giving credit where credit was due—particularly if it was due to her.

"Last three," Dr. Clark announced. "Presidential approval rating." Her gaze flickered briefly toward my side of the room—to Henry. "Transparency." She moved on to the next-to-last sheet, then ended with mine. "And corruption." She paused. "Mr. Rhodes, while I'm sure you do a passable Houdini impression, I would prefer you not duct-tape your hands together during class."

Asher gave her his most charming smile. "Your wish is my command." He did a good job of pretending his hands weren't half taped together already.

Only Asher, I thought. But there was another part of my brain—the part where instinct and emotion blended together, where *fight* and *flight* lived in wait—that couldn't help remembering a time when I'd been bound hand and foot.

I felt a light touch on my shoulder. *Henry*. I didn't turn to look at him, but my gut said that he knew exactly where I'd been a moment before. *I was held hostage by a rogue Secret Service agent.* Thinking the words sapped the memory of some of its power. *That rogue agent helped murder the chief justice of the Supreme Court. And the American public will never know.*

Transparency wasn't President Nolan's strong suit.

The rest of the class period passed in a blur. When the final bell rang, I stood.

"About that grudge-holding yearbook editor—" Asher started to say, but before he could recommence wheedling, he was summarily cut off.

"You owe me a favor." Emilia Rhodes wasn't a person who bothered with words as mundane as *hello*. She was as intense as Asher was laid-back—and she was, unfortunately, correct.

I *did* owe her a favor.

"What do you want?" I asked Emilia.

She hooked an arm through mine. "Walk with me." She didn't speak again until we'd made it to the hallway. "Tomorrow during chapel, they'll be taking student council nominations."

"In November?" I asked.

"Student council elections take place on Election Day." Emilia executed a delicate little shrug. "Hardwicke tradition."

Hardwicke wasn't a normal school. Most days, it didn't even pretend to be.

"The next student council term begins in January," Emilia continued. "I intend to be president. You have a certain amount of . . . *influence*"—it pained Emilia to say that word—"at this school, particularly among freshmen and miscellaneous social misfit types. When the headmaster calls for nominations tomorrow morning, I want you to nominate me. Maya will second your nomination."

I waited for the catch. "That's it?" I said, when none was forthcoming. "Nominate you for student council president, and we're even?"

Emilia gave a roll of her blue-green eyes. "No. You'll nominate me, and then you'll make sure I win, and *then* we'll be even."

I narrowed my eyes at her. "And how am I supposed to make sure you win?"

"How do you do anything?" Emilia shot back. "I'm not asking for a miracle here, Tess. I'm qualified for the job. I'm in good social standing. I have the right connections. And you know I'll do a better job than John Thomas Wilcox."

John Thomas was the horrible excuse for a human being who'd coerced the vice president's daughter into taking those pictures. After I'd stopped him from sharing them, he'd zeroed in on me as a target.

He was a predator and a coward, and even the sound of his name set my teeth on edge.

"John Thomas is your opponent?" I couldn't keep my features from working their way into a scowl.

"One of them," Emilia confirmed, thrusting out her chin. "In the past decade, Hardwicke has had only one female student council president. My parents are dentists. His father is the minority whip." Emilia stopped walking and turned to face me head-on. "I intend to win this, Tess."

The last time Emilia had attempted to hire me, it was to keep Asher out of trouble. Putting her in office over John Thomas Wilcox seemed like a less Herculean task—not to mention more *enjoyable*.

"Fine," I said. "I help you win this election, and then we're even."

Emilia's lips parted in a small smile. "Welcome to the campaign."

CHAPTER 4

It took Bodie less than ten minutes after he picked me up to ferret out the finer details of my day. For someone I was fairly certain had committed his share of felonies, Ivy's driver could do an impressive soccer mom impression when it came to pumping information out of me on the way to and from school.

"I doubt 'student council campaign manager' was what Keyes had in mind when he told you to get more involved at school." Bodie flashed a smile at me.

"I agreed to Sunday night dinners and allowing him to publically acknowledge me as a Keyes," I retorted. "Field hockey and debate were never a part of the deal."

Bodie studied me for a moment, the way he always did when the subject of William Keyes came up. "If the old man starts to make noise about it," he said, trying to mask the fact that he was taking mental notes on my well-being for Ivy, "you can always tell him you're taking a page from the Keyes playbook and trying your hand at calling the shots behind the scenes."

I grimaced. The last thing I needed was for the Hardwicke populace to decide that I was some sort of kingmaker-in-the-making.

"It's a favor for a friend," I said. "That's it."

"You're a Kendrick," Bodie told me, taking the turn toward Ivy's house. "Favors for friends have a way of complicating themselves."

Bodie slowed the car as we approached the driveway. In addition to being Ivy's chauffeur, he was also her bodyguard—and mine. With casual efficiency, he surveyed the street in front of Ivy's house, his gaze coming to rest on a car at the curb.

Since Ivy worked out of the bottom floor of our sprawling DC home, clients came and went with a fairly high frequency, but this car didn't fit the profile of Ivy's typical client. Beneath the grime, the vehicle was burnt orange—and clearly used. The windows weren't bulletproof. I doubted its owner had ever even considered hiring a driver.

I glanced over at Bodie, trying to get a read on him. Did he recognize the car?

As he pulled into the driveway, his phone buzzed. *A text, almost certainly from Ivy.* Bodie read the message. A second passed. He put on his best poker face, then glanced back up at me. "How would you feel about ice cream?"

Bodie kept me out all afternoon. By the time we got back to Ivy's house, it was dark outside, and the orange car had been joined by another vehicle. This one, I recognized.

"Adam's here," I said.

"So he is," Bodie replied evenly.

If I wasn't already wondering about my newfound uncle's presence at the house, the fact that Bodie had missed an opportunity to refer to him as "Captain Pentagon" or "Mr. America" would have tipped me off that this wasn't just business as usual. Bodie had no shortage of nicknames for anyone—and he considered mocking by-the-books Adam Keyes to be one of life's finer pleasures.

Ivy called Adam in. She texted Bodie and told him to keep me away from the house. As I climbed out of the car and made my way into the foyer, I turned that over in my head.

Bodie slanted his gaze toward me as he shut the front door behind us. "If I told you to go upstairs and forget about all of this, you'd end up ignoring me, so do us both a favor, kitten, and just try not to let Ivy catch you down here."

With that advice imparted, Bodie made for Ivy's office himself. I heard the door open and close—and then, nothing.

First Adam, now Bodie.

Whatever was going down, it had Ivy calling in the troops.

CHAPTER 5

I didn't go upstairs. I stood in the hallway just outside of Ivy's office, staring at the door. I could hear the murmur of voices behind it, but couldn't make out what they were saying.

Ivy's job—her clients, the things she did on their behalf, the lines she was willing to cross—that was a portion of her life she kept from me, as best she could.

Logically, I understood that Ivy's line of work required a guarantee of confidentiality and discretion. I also understood—*logically*—that she wanted to protect me. The last time I'd been involved in one of her cases, I'd been kidnapped.

But no amount of logical understanding could mute the sharp ache in my chest that I felt staring at a closed door, knowing that Ivy was the one who'd locked me out.

Some days, it felt like my whole life had been a series of doors I'd never had a choice about closing.

Ivy had shut the door on being my mother when she'd given me to her parents to raise as their own. She'd locked that door when she'd agreed to lie to me and thrown the deadbolt for good measure when I was four years old and she'd handed me—tears streaming down her cheeks in the wake of our parents' funeral—to Gramps.

She'd cracked the door open when I was thirteen and then slammed it in my face.

Ivy had chosen to leave me. She'd chosen to shut me out of her life. She'd thrown up walls between us, because living the lie that she was my *sister* was too hard.

Logical or not, fair or not, that was what I thought of every time Ivy locked herself in her office and locked me out. I couldn't push down the violent feeling roiling inside of me that said she'd lost the right to have secrets when she'd kept the biggest one from me.

Grow up, Tess. I forced myself to turn away from the office door, but instead of going upstairs to the apartment Ivy and I shared, I turned and walked toward the conference room. Like Ivy's office, it was technically off-limits.

I wasn't a person who paid much attention to technicalities.

I tested the knob, then pushed the conference room door inward, stepping over the threshold. Weeks ago, Ivy and I had stood in this room, looking at a trio of photographs she'd tacked onto the walls.

Three men—including a Secret Service agent and the White House physician—had conspired to kill Henry's grandfather, Supreme Court Chief Justice Theodore Marquette. It was in this conference room that Ivy had told me she thought there was a fourth person involved, a conspirator who was still out there and whose identity we did not know. For one night, Ivy had let me in. She'd stopped trying to lock away the parts of herself she thought weren't safe for me to know. She'd recognized that whether she liked it or not, the two of us were the same.

I wasn't any more capable of sitting by and watching something bad happen than she was.

Walking over to the conference table, I closed my eyes, trying to remember exactly where Ivy had been sitting when we'd had that late-night discussion. I tried to picture the list of suspects on the table beside her—a dozen or so names, among them *William Keyes*.

No one—not Asher, not Henry, not Vivvie, whose father was the White House physician who'd helped kill Justice Marquette—knew that Ivy suspected there was a fourth player, one who'd engineered the attack on Justice Marquette and gotten away from the whole ordeal unscathed. I hadn't mentioned Ivy's theory to my friends. For their own protection, I'd kept them—and would continue to keep them—in the dark.

"You're not supposed to be in here."

I turned to see Adam standing in the doorway. My brain automatically searched for similarities—between Adam and me, between the kingmaker and his firstborn son.

"I've never really excelled at doing what I'm supposed to," I said.

Adam gave me a look. If he'd been protective before I'd learned that he was my uncle, he was worse now that I knew the truth. "Try harder," he ordered.

Adam was the type who played by the rules. I'd gathered that my father—his younger brother—had not been.

"Ivy has all her secrets locked away," I said, turning back to the bare walls. "What does it matter if I come in here if there's nothing left to see?"

Adam must have heard something in my voice, because he softened his own. "Tess—"

"I had dinner with your father last night." Nothing shut Adam up faster than mentioning William Keyes. "He wants me to get more involved at Hardwicke."

Adam gave me a long, considering look. "Do you want to get more involved at Hardwicke?"

"I want to know who Ivy's talking to in there."

"Tess." This time, there was an edge in Adam's voice—a warning. "Ivy isn't the only one who wants you kept out of this."

This as in her current case, or *this* as in the massive chunk of Ivy's life from which I'd been barred?

"Tommy wasn't a person who knew when to quit." My uncle's blue eyes held mine. "He wasn't the type to sit back and think things through."

"If he had been," I pointed out quietly, "I wouldn't be here." I meant the words to sound flippant. They came out sounding rough.

"I loved my brother. And I see so much of him in you." Adam's voice was as rough as mine now. "I'll be damned before I let you get tangled up in anything dangerous ever again."

I tamped down on the rush of emotion those words provoked. "Dangerous?"

Silence.

"Who's in there with Ivy?" I asked again.

Adam kneaded his temple. "Like talking to a wall," he muttered.

"I can hear you," I told him. "I'm standing right here."

He crossed the room until he was toe-to-toe with me. He placed two fingers under my chin, angling my face up toward his. "Don't push me on this," he said quietly. "You won't like the result."

I'd never met my biological father, but I couldn't help wondering—if he were alive, if he were here, would he be saying those same words to me, that same quiet warning in his voice?

"Tell me you understand," Adam ordered.

I understood that if my uncle was this serious about my steering clear, then whoever Ivy was meeting with, whatever she was on the verge of doing—it was *big*.

"I'm waiting, Tess."

I held out a moment longer before saying what he wanted to hear. "I understand."

Adam removed his hand from my chin, trailing it lightly over the back of my head for a moment before stepping back. At his direction, I made my way out of the conference room. Just as I stepped into the hallway, the door to Ivy's office opened.

Adam was behind me in an instant, his hands resting lightly on each of my shoulders. If he'd had time, he probably would have steered me back out of the hall, but within a heartbeat, Ivy's gaze landed on me. To an outside observer, her expression and posture would have seemed perfectly relaxed, but I could feel her struggling to hold on to that composure.

She thought I was upstairs.

Bodie appeared behind Ivy and mouthed four words at me: *You had one job.*

"Adam already read me the riot act," I told Ivy. Before she could reply, I turned my attention to the man standing next to her. He was in his late twenties. His blond hair was just long enough to be a little messy. His skin was suntanned. There was something familiar about the set of his features.

"It's fine," the man told Ivy. "I don't bite." The dark circles under his eyes spoke of sleepless nights, but his voice was wry.

Ivy's not afraid of you, I thought, studying the way that she stiffened at his words. *But she is afraid of something.*

"I'm Tess," I said, since no one seemed inclined to introduce me. After a beat, the man held out a hand.

Adam's grip tightened slightly on my shoulders.

"Walker," the man said.

The name triggered something in my brain, and I realized why he looked familiar—and who he resembled.

His mother.

I took his hand. "Walker," I repeated. "As in Walker Nolan."

The president's youngest son.

CHAPTER 6

Ivy refused to say a word about Walker Nolan's visit. She left shortly after he did and still wasn't home when I woke up the next morning.

What could the president's son have said that would send Ivy straight to DEFCON 1?

Before Bodie dropped me off at Hardwicke, he put the obvious into words. "Don't tell anyone—"

"That the president's youngest son is in some kind of trouble?" I filled in. "My lips are sealed."

The night before, I'd stayed up late reading everything I could find online about Walker Nolan. Of the three Nolan sons, Walker was the only one to decline Secret Service protection. He was twenty-nine, stayed more or less out of the limelight, and had spent two years with Doctors Without Borders before his father had taken office. I didn't need to be a political genius to guess that any scandal involving the president's son would dominate the news cycle going into midterm elections.

Whatever Walker's problem was, it had even Bodie on edge. "Not joking, kiddo." Bodie turned in his seat and fixed me with a stare. "No matter what you see, no matter what you hear—you say nothing."

Dangerous. The word Adam had used the day before echoed in my mind.

My stomach tightened. "I won't."

After two or three seconds, Ivy's driver gave a slight nod. "Get out of here," he said, jerking his head toward the school. "And good luck with the campaign."

"We'll begin with nominations for class presidents and then proceed to the school-wide offices." The Hardwicke headmaster was a small man with glasses, a finely tuned sense of his own importance, and a voice that carried. "Are there nominations for freshman class president?"

The nominations began to trickle in, and I leaned back in my seat. Once a month, the entire Hardwicke Upper School was shuffled into the chapel for an all-school meeting. Today's meeting, as Emilia had indicated, was devoted to the upcoming student council elections.

It was hard to bring myself to care about student council when my gut said that Ivy was on the verge of something big— something awful.

No matter what you see, no matter what you hear—you say nothing.

Bodie's warning lingered in my head. Each time I went back over the words, they were more chilling. What exactly did Bodie think I might see or hear that would cause me to say something about Walker Nolan's visit to our house?

Why does the president's son need Ivy's services?

Adam worked for the Pentagon. Since I'd moved to DC, he'd only consulted with Ivy on one other case: the assassination of Justice Marquette.

No matter what you see, no matter what you hear—

"And now we'll open up nominations for student-body president." Headmaster Raleigh's voice broke through my thoughts. My whole body felt stiff, and I wondered how long I'd been sitting there, playing Bodie's warning over and over in my head.

"The office of student-body president is open to any junior in good academic standing," the headmaster continued with the solemnity of a jury foreman delivering a verdict. "I encourage you to think long and hard about who will best represent both you as a student body and the principles of the Hardwicke School."

There was a moment of silence, broken by Asher rising to his feet and calling out, "Hear ye, hear ye!"

The headmaster did a good impression of someone who was developing a migraine. "Mr. Rhodes," he acknowledged. "A bit less with the dramatics, if you please."

In response, Asher placed one hand over his heart. "I, Asher Rhodes, being of reasonably sound body and mind, do hereby nominate the honorable—and, I might add, ridiculously good-looking—Henry Marquette."

Asher really didn't know the meaning of the word *less*.

"Who among you stands with me?" he asked, punching both fists into the air.

It occurred to me then that Emilia had told me that John Thomas would be *one* of her opponents.

As Henry's nomination was seconded, Emilia caught my eyes and gave a small shrug. Clearly, she still expected me to hold up my end of the bargain.

"Do you accept this nomination?" the headmaster asked Henry.

"I'll accept," Henry said, "if and only if Asher agrees to never refer to me as good-looking again."

I snorted.

"I regret nothing!" Asher yelled.

A second later, someone called out, "I nominate John Thomas Wilcox."

The lacrosse player who'd been so fond of hazing—until I'd shut him down—seconded the nomination.

"I am John Thomas Wilcox," John Thomas said, with what passed as a good-natured grin, "and I accept this nomination."

That got a few snickers.

"The floor remains open," the headmaster declared. "Do we have a third nomination?"

Emilia shot laser eyes at me. After returning her glare, I stood up.

"Ms. Kendrick," the headmaster said. "Err . . . Keyes," he corrected himself. "Tess."

My last name was still a matter of some contention.

"Do you have a nomination?" Raleigh asked me.

I avoided looking at Henry as I answered, "I nominate Emilia Rhodes."

CHAPTER 7

"Blackmail or bribe?" Asher caught up to me on the way back to the main building after chapel let out.

I didn't answer.

"Blackmail or bribe?" Asher repeated. "Because I have some serious doubts that you were overcome by a swell of civic admiration for my twin, lovely though she may be."

Right now, *lovely* wasn't a word I would have used to describe Emilia Rhodes.

"My dearest, darling sister didn't happen to mention she was running against Henry, did she?" Asher asked.

"She left that tidbit out," I said dryly.

Vivvie popped up on my other side. "Henry's been our class president since kindergarten. Everyone figured he was a shoo-in for student-body president this year."

"You guys had a class president in kindergarten?" I asked incredulously.

Asher nodded. "Henry was the only five-year-old to run on a three-pronged platform."

I honestly couldn't tell if Asher was joking or not.

"The third prong," Asher continued, "was cookies."

We hit the door to the main building a second before the art teacher came striding out. "Inside," he called. "Get to class, everyone." The teacher's whole body was as tight as a rubber band on the verge of snapping.

We crossed the threshold into the building. All up and down the main corridor, teachers were ushering students into classrooms. A feeling of unease slithered down my spine.

No matter what you see, no matter what you hear—

Henry appeared beside me. From the expression on his face, it was clear that student council elections were the last thing on his mind. His jaw muscles were tensed, brown skin pulled taut across his cheekbones, his full lips set into a grim line.

"What's going on?" I asked him as we stepped into the classroom. I could hear murmurs all around me, was vaguely aware of the teacher telling us to take our seats—but my attention was focused on Henry.

Wordlessly, he passed his cell phone to me. I forced myself to look at the screen.

BOMB DETONATES IN DC HOSPITAL

The headline froze the air in my lungs. I couldn't inhale. I couldn't exhale.

No matter what you see, Bodie had told me, *no matter what you hear—you say nothing.*

CHAPTER 8

I had no way of knowing if Walker Nolan's problem had anything to do with what the media were calling an act of terrorism. I texted Ivy with shaky hands. I needed her to tell me she was okay. *Ivy called Adam in on this one. Adam works for the Pentagon. Bodie told me not to say anything—*

Ivy texted back less than a minute after I'd texted her. *I'm fine. Can you get a ride home from school today?*

In other words: she needed Bodie with her.

What's going on? I texted back.

The reply came an instant later. *Can you get a ride home from school today?*

My Spanish teacher saw the cell phone in my hand but said nothing. I wasn't the only one texting my parents.

Yes. I typed in my reply, pressing down on the urge to repeat my question to Ivy the way she'd repeated hers to me. Henry had a car. So did Emilia—and Asher was pretty liberal about "borrowing" it. I could manage a ride home from school.

I'd just spend the next six hours wondering what Ivy was doing that she needed Bodie with her.

Spanish class flew by, then physics. Since chapel had replaced my first-period English class, fifth period—the only class I shared with John Thomas Wilcox—came quickly.

"Word on the street is that you're helping Emilia Rhodes with her campaign." John Thomas clearly wasn't having any trouble shaking off the news of the bombing. The rest of the school was on edge, a pallor cast over the student body at the reminder that bad things could and did happen close to home. The expression on John Thomas's face was appropriately somber, but mismatched to the glint in his eyes.

"Just like your sister helped President Nolan with his campaign," John Thomas continued. "And look how well that turned out. Nolan has made a mess of national security. Whatever casualties there are today, that blood is on your precious president's hands—and your sister's."

No matter what you see, no matter what you hear—you say nothing.

"Class is starting." Henry took the seat in front of me and leveled a stare at John Thomas. "Eyes to the front, Wilcox."

"Protective, isn't he?" John Thomas asked me. "You do have a way with the opposite sex."

Among the limited tricks in John Thomas's repertoire was suggesting that I'd cemented my position at Hardwicke by sleeping my way through the junior class. He'd never managed to get a rise out of me on the topic, but that didn't keep him from trying.

Mr. Wesley—who taught Speaking of Words, the Hardwicke version of "speech"—seemed to sense that today wasn't a good day to even attempt a lecture. He put on a video of a poetry slam and turned off the lights.

"Girls like you, women like your sister—they're only good for one thing," John Thomas whispered. "And it's not running campaigns."

"Mr. Wilcox," the teacher called out. "Watch the video."

John Thomas let his eyes linger on me. "I'm watching."

CHAPTER 9

"Sources are reporting that there were no casualties in today's bombing—thanks, in large part, to an anonymous tip that Homeland Security received last night about this woman."

The moment World Issues had started, Dr. Clark had dimmed the lights and turned on the news. In sharp contrast to the video in Speaking of Words, everyone's attention was focused on the screen now.

This woman. The picture that accompanied the anchor's words was a profile shot, taken from a distance. The woman was young—dark hair, fair skin, athletic build.

"While the Nolan administration has issued no confirmation of the woman's identity, documents leaked to the press suggest she was a medical researcher living in Bethesda under the name Daniela Nicolae. It is unclear at this time whether or not that is her actual name."

At the front of the classroom, Dr. Clark watched us watching the news report. I glanced at Henry, whose eyes were locked on the screen, then at Asher, who was sitting as still as I'd ever seen him. Beside me, Vivvie's fingers worried at the sleeve of her blazer, her dark brown eyes cast downward.

"No casualties. A suspect in custody. I don't see how this is anything other than a victory for the current administration."

While I'd been assessing my friends, the program had switched to a "he said, she said" format. Pundits sat to either side of the anchor. *He* had no sooner given his opinion than *she* chimed in.

"Who is this Daniela Nicolae? How did she get into the country? And why is an anonymous tip the only thing standing between us and a terrorist attack on American soil?" The female pundit was a redhead in her early forties. She was girl-next-door pretty and utterly without mercy. "Under the Nolan administration," she continued, letting loose at rapid fire and not giving her opponent an opportunity to interject, "our intelligence agencies have become more concerned with spying on American citizens and policing *our* private communications than in tracking foreign nationals like Nicolae."

An argument erupted between the two pundits. When the anchor took over again, he addressed the camera, his voice solemn. "This is what we know: according to her passport, Daniela Nicolae is twenty-eight years old, with dual citizenship in Venezuela and Belarus. She was educated in England and graduated from Oxford with a degree in medicine at the age of twenty-four. She spent three years with Doctors Without Borders before beginning a research fellowship here in the States."

"And the only reason we know any of that," the female pundit said when the floor was hers once more, "the only reason we even know this woman's name, is because of a security leak. Quite frankly, I don't know whether to be more concerned that we still haven't heard from the president on any of this, or about the fact that under his watch, our national security is springing leaks."

Dr. Clark lifted the remote and hit the power button. As the screen went black, she said something about us breaking into small groups to discuss our own reactions to the day's events, but I barely heard her.

I was still stuck on three words, buried between the female pundit's diatribes.

Doctors Without Borders.

CHAPTER 10

Walker Nolan had volunteered his medical services overseas for two years under the Doctors Without Borders banner. I wanted to believe that it was a coincidence that Daniela Nicolae had worked for the same group.

I wanted to, but I didn't.

Homeland Security apprehended her based on an anonymous tip, my brain kept reminding me.

Ivy solved problems. Walker Nolan had one—and his problem had required the help of Ivy's contact at the Pentagon.

"You are being suspiciously quiet." Henry had volunteered to drive me home. Until now, both of us had passed the ride in silence. Henry slanted his eyes briefly toward mine. "The last time you were this quiet, Kendrick, you were plotting the downfall of Jeremy Bancroft's father."

I'd promised Bodie I wouldn't say a word to anyone about Walker Nolan. It wouldn't be the first time I'd kept something from Henry.

It probably wouldn't be the last.

"I'm not plotting anything," I told the boy next to me. "Promise."

"I feel so very comforted," Henry said. He came to a stop at a red light and turned to look at me head-on. "This is my comforted face."

"You sound like Asher," I retorted. "He has a face for every occasion."

"Whereas *you*," Henry said, "just have a poker face, the appearance of which is typically a cause for concern."

"I'm not the only one who's been quiet," I pointed out. Henry had passed the first half of this drive just as caught up in his thoughts as I was in mine. *And I'm not the only one with a poker face*, I added silently.

I'd been thinking about Walker Nolan. What had Henry been thinking about?

"John Thomas Wilcox." Henry had a gift for changing the subject and making it sound like he wasn't changing it at all. "Today in fifth period. Whatever he said about you, about Ivy, he is not worth even a moment of your thoughts."

"Doesn't it strike you as a little hypocritical to tell me not to pay attention to anything *John Thomas* says about Ivy?" I asked lightly. "It's not like you've ever been a member of the Ivy Kendrick fan club."

I expected Henry to come back with a quick retort, but instead, he fell silent again.

A year before I'd arrived at Hardwicke, Henry's father had died in a car accident—or at least that was the story most people believed. Henry had told me the truth: his father had committed

suicide, and Ivy had covered it up. No one but Henry and Ivy—
and now me—knew what had really happened.

She made me complicit. I could still see the anguished expression on Henry's face when he'd said those words.

I hadn't meant, even for a second, to make him feel like that
again.

"You're nothing like John Thomas," I told Henry. "I know
that. I'm sorry. I just—"

"Dislike being advised on how to deal with him when you're
quite capable of handling the John Thomas Wilcoxes of the world
on your own?" Henry suggested.

"That," I agreed. "But also—I wasn't even thinking about him.
I was thinking about what happened today, about the bombing."
That was as close to the truth as I could come without breaking
my promise to Bodie.

I was thinking about Walker Nolan and Daniela Nicolae.

"It's different," Henry said softly, "for those of us who've lost
people."

Hardwicke was a world apart from my previous school in
Montana. Anna Hayden's Secret Service detail was a constant
presence in the hallways. Closed-circuit cameras monitored the
entire campus. All visitors were pre-screened. Although discreet,
the school's security officers were also armed.

Going to a school that was more secure than most government facilities had a strange effect: at Hardwicke, students were
more aware of the potential for wide-scale attacks, but they'd
fostered in us a deep-seated belief that it couldn't happen *here*.

Some of our classmates had been shaken by today's attack.
Others, like John Thomas, had been more able to shrug it off.

But Henry was right—it would always be different for people like us.

The closer you'd been to death, the easier it was to feel him breathing down your neck—and the necks of those you loved.

"I can still see Ivy with that bomb strapped to her chest." I hadn't told that to anyone. I turned to look out the window to keep Henry from seeing the expression on my face. "Sometimes," I continued softly, "I wake up in the middle of the night, and for a second, I'm back in that basement with a rogue Secret Service agent."

There was a moment of silence, and then Henry gave me tit for tat. "I'm the one who found my father."

I didn't turn to look at Henry. If I'd been looking at him, he wouldn't have said the words.

"That's what I thought about when I heard about the attack," Henry said. "That's what I saw. My father was just . . . lying there, on the floor. His eyes were open, but . . . empty. I wasn't supposed to be home that weekend. None of us were. And when I found him . . ."

My eyes found their way to his, drawn by magnetic force.

"I left," Henry said. "I just . . . I left. And I got the call a few hours later about the crash."

The crash that Ivy staged.

Grief was like a set of stacking dolls, each subsequent trauma encompassing all of those that had come before. At four, I hadn't known how to mourn my parents—*Ivy's* parents, really. But I'd mourned them at thirteen, when Ivy had walked out of my life, and at fifteen, when Gramps had started to slide. I'd felt it again and again and again these past months.

No one had died today in the bombing. But we hadn't known that, not at first.

Henry swallowed. I could see him locking down his emotions, hiding them, even from himself. "Tess. What I just told you—"

"Stays between us," I said. Henry Marquette didn't trust easily. We had that much in common. "I can keep a secret," I said.

I was already keeping so many. What was one more?

CHAPTER 11

When we got to Ivy's house, there was a car parked across the street. Unlike Walker's, this vehicle fit the profile I'd come to associate with many of Ivy's clients—dark-colored, tinted windows, driver standing just outside. I scanned the front lawn, and my eyes came to rest on the car's owner.

William Keyes.

Henry caught my gaze and cocked his head to the side, a silent *Everything okay?*

I had no idea who Keyes was waiting for—Ivy or me. Either way, I gave a brisk nod. "His bark's worse than his bite."

Henry gave me a look. "I severely doubt that is true."

"Either way," I said, "William Keyes won't do more than gnash his teeth at me."

I was a Keyes.

"Is this the point where you ask me to steal his car as a distraction?" Henry asked, arching an eyebrow at me. "Or did you have another felony in mind?"

"Very funny," I told him, reaching for the door.

"I could walk you in," Henry offered, his voice softer this time.

I opened the car door. "Relax, Sir Galahad," I told him with an eyebrow arch of my own. "I can take care of myself."

I slammed the door and went to face the music—whatever that music might be.

"Theresa." Keyes stood with his back to the front door. My first name had also been his late wife's. Growing up, Ivy and Gramps had only called me by my given name when I was skating on thin ice. I didn't know what to read into the fact that William Keyes was using it now. "Where is she?"

That was less of a question than a demand. The *she* in question could only be Ivy.

"Nice to see you, too," I muttered.

"Were the circumstances different, I would happily spar with you, my dear, but this is not a game, and I am not playing. Where is Ivy?"

"I don't know," I said, glad, for once, that Ivy had kept me in the dark.

"You have a cell phone." That was a statement, not a question. "Call her." Keyes gave the order like he was God, setting down an eleventh commandment.

I folded my arms over my chest and leveled a narrow-eyed stare at him, all too similar to the look he was aiming at me. "Why?"

"Because," he snapped back, "she'll pick up *your* call."

I wanted to refuse out of principle, but Ivy would want to know that Keyes had come to our home. And *I* wanted to know what exactly he was so dead set on saying to her.

I took out my phone and dialed. Ivy picked up on the third ring.

"Are you okay?"

"I'm fine," I told her. "But I'm not alone. A certain someone was waiting for me when I got home for school. Tall. Cranky. Overly fond of the Earl of Warwick."

Keyes snatched the phone from my hand. "You will tell me what you are playing at here, Ivy."

Those words confirmed for me that there was more going on here than I knew—and Ivy was in the thick of it all.

She won't tell you anything, I thought in his direction.

On the other end of the phone line, Ivy must have said something to similar effect.

"I've heard things," William Keyes told her, the edge in his voice making the words sound less like a statement and more like a threat.

What kind of things? I wondered.

"There are questions about the way this is being handled, and I don't need to tell you what those questions could do to the party in the midterms." Keyes didn't wait for a response before he went straight for the jugular. "The youngest Nolan boy came to visit you last night. Why?"

Listening to this conversation was like watching the old man play chess. Each move was calculated for maximum effect, part of a larger plan.

Unfortunately for William Keyes, when he'd taught Ivy to play his game, he'd taught her a little too well. She wouldn't tell him anything she didn't want him to know. Keyes turned his back on me as he replied to whatever she'd said. I couldn't make out his words.

Less than a minute later, he cursed and hung up the phone. When he turned back to me, his expression was perfectly controlled. He held the phone out to me. I closed my fingers around it and then made a move of my own.

"Daniela Nicolae," I said. A split second of surprise crossed his face before he banished it in favor of a scowl. "You said there were questions about the way *this* was being handled," I continued. "I'm assuming the *this* in question is the bombing."

The kingmaker's eyes raked over me, the way they did when we played chess, assessing the extent to which I'd taken his lessons to heart.

"There is one thing on which that godforsaken mother of yours and I agree," he said finally. "And that is that whatever is or is not happening, it's no concern of yours."

I expected that from Ivy and Adam. I hadn't expected it from him.

Keyes assessed me dispassionately. "You dislike being kept out of the loop," he said. "That, you get from me." He strode past me. "Come along."

I stayed glued to the spot.

William Keyes turned back toward me. "I am many things, Theresa, but I am not a man who would leave his only grandchild alone in a house like this one at a time like this. Ivy is playing with fire. I'll not have you burned. If she cannot provide adequate security for you, I most assuredly will."

This was why Ivy hadn't ever wanted Keyes to know about me. He was a man who gave orders and exerted absolute control over everyone in his domain. The moment he'd found out I had his son's blood, that domain included me.

"If you would prefer," Keyes said, his voice silky, "I can arrange for Hayes to stay here with you until Ivy returns." He nodded toward his driver.

Strategy. Resources. Influence. Family mattered to Keyes—but putting his man inside Ivy's house? Having eyes on her base of operations?

That had value, too.

I decided on the lesser of two evils. "Where are we going?"

We went to the Mall. In any other city in the world, that might have involved shopping, but the National Mall wasn't the kind with shops. Keyes and I stood, side by side, next to the Reflecting Pool. Behind us, the Lincoln Memorial loomed over the tourists below. On the far side of the Reflecting Pool, the Washington Monument cut a striking figure against a graying sky.

"The Marquette boy drove you home." Keyes seemed to direct that observation more to the water than to me. "His mother is an Abellard, is she not?"

I decided that was a rhetorical question.

"It is important," Keyes said contemplatively, "to make friends with the right kind of people."

In his eyes, Henry was the right kind of people.

"Did you meet Walker Nolan when he came to visit Ivy?" Keyes queried, and my gut told me this was what he'd wanted to ask all along.

I was comfortable with silence, comfortable with letting questions go unanswered. Sometimes it was my best tool for making a person say more.

"There are times," Keyes sighed, "when you remind me very much of my wife."

I wasn't going to give him any information about Ivy's case, and he wasn't going to share what he knew with me. But I felt like I should give him something in exchange for what he'd just said about the grandmother I'd never met.

"The minority whip's son is running for student council." That was as close to a peace offering as I could come. "I intend for him to lose."

That got a small snort out of the old man. "Funny," he said, "isn't it, that sometimes the loser matters more than the person who wins?" He glanced up from the pool. His gaze settled on something and then he turned back to me. "Give us a moment, would you, Tess?"

Us? I turned to look at a woman standing nearby, a scarf hiding her hair, sunglasses obscuring her face. Even with the camouflage, I recognized her immediately.

Georgia Nolan. The First Lady.

I tried to reconcile the fact that she was here with the reality that we were in the middle of a media blitz about the hospital bombing. This wasn't the time for the First Lady to be taking a stroll through the National Mall.

She's here to see Keyes. Why?

I turned and walked toward the Lincoln Memorial, coming to stand at the base of the steps, looking out at my paternal grandfather and the First Lady. Her Secret Service detail was standing a discreet distance away. She and Keyes stood several feet apart, neither looking at the other as they spoke.

What could have possessed her to come here to talk to him? And if he'd planned to meet her, why bring me along?

I didn't get answers to those questions. Three minutes after Georgia had arrived, she was gone.

CHAPTER 12

I arrived back at Ivy's house to see flashing lights. I was out of the car before Keyes could order me to stay put. I pushed past the police cruiser in the driveway.

"Ivy?" I called out her name a second before I laid eyes on her. She was wearing a navy blazer, her light brown hair clipped neatly back from her face.

"I assure you," Ivy was telling an officer, the very picture of composure, "everything is fine." She saw me approach. "Now, if you'll excuse me, I have to see to my daughter."

Having dispatched the police officer, she ushered me into the house.

"What happened?" I asked her, my voice low.

"As far as the police are concerned," Ivy said, "nothing. The alarm went off quite by accident."

"What really happened?" I countered.

I could see Ivy weighing her choices. Ultimately, she must have decided I could handle the truth. "There was a break-in.

They tossed my office but didn't find what they were looking for."

I didn't question why Ivy had sent the police away. If someone had broken through her security, she wouldn't want that to get out.

"What were they looking for?" I asked.

Ivy glanced toward the door, as if she could see through it. "Leverage."

William Keyes waited for the police to leave before he approached the house.

"Wait upstairs," Ivy told me.

She didn't ask where I'd been when she'd arrived home. I wondered if the kingmaker would point out that if I hadn't gone with him, I might have been here when someone broke in. And then I wondered if she would counter that it seemed awfully coincidental that he'd gotten me out of the house right before someone had broken in and torn her office apart.

Looking for something. Something to do with Walker Nolan. My mind was jumbled as I ascended the spiral staircase. I paused at the top but heard nothing.

Keyes met with Georgia Nolan. The president's son knew this terrorist attack was going to happen. People are asking questions.

The thoughts came rapid fire, one on the heel of another, until Ivy appeared upstairs. Her gaze faltered for a moment when it landed on me.

"Is this the part where you get mad at me for the things I can't tell you, or the part where I remind you that you can't trust

William Keyes?" There was no edge in Ivy's voice, no hint of anger or exasperation.

She sounded tired.

There were so many things I wanted to say to her. I wanted to tell her that she could trust me, that all keeping me in the dark accomplished was pushing me further away. I wanted to say that it wasn't fair that she got to protect me, but I was expected to just sit back and let her, as Keyes had put it, *play with fire*.

I wanted to tell her that she wasn't allowed to do this to me again. But she was tired, and she was here, and she was in one piece.

"This is the part where I do my homework," I said softly, "and you order takeout, and we both pretend that everything is fine."

CHAPTER 13

The next morning, things at Hardwicke were back to normal—more or less.

"Don't look now," Asher whispered. "But I believe you're being paged."

Vivvie immediately turned to look. Stealth wasn't her strong suit. "I'd say that's more of a beckoning," she told Asher after a moment's deliberation.

"A summoning, perhaps?" Asher countered, wiggling his eyebrows.

On the other side of the Hut, Emilia Rhodes narrowed her eyes at me and crooked her finger. Asher was right. I had been summoned. With one last glance at Asher and Vivvie, I gritted my teeth and went to see what Emilia wanted.

"We're polling strong with the robotics club and the jazz band." Maya Rojas ran her fingers along the tip of her straw as I took a seat at their table. "I can deliver the girls' basketball team, and Tess having nominated you seems to be carrying some weight with freshman females."

"But," Emilia prompted.

"*However*," Maya said, hedging slightly, "Henry is also polling well with freshman girls. And sophomore girls. And most of the junior class."

"And John Thomas?" Emilia was undeterred.

"He's got strong support from some of the party crowd, as well as a large contingent of freshman and sophomore boys." Maya's mother was a pollster who crunched numbers for the president. Apparently, Maya had picked up a thing or two about the art of polling along the way.

"We need the underclassmen," Maya said. "They don't know any of the candidates that well, so their votes are the most up for grabs."

Emilia turned her attention from Maya to me. "You're the freshman whisperer," she said bluntly. "Any suggestions?"

First period didn't start for another ten minutes. That was ten minutes too many.

"I'll get back to you on that one," I said. It was too early for this.

Emilia opened her mouth to object, but before she could push out the words, her phone buzzed on the table.

So did Maya's.

So did mine.

There was a moment of silence and stillness at our table as we processed the fact that all over the Hut and out in the hallway, other phones were going off, too.

Maya—a three-sport athlete—was quicker on the draw than either Emilia or me. She hit a button on her phone, then sucked in a breath, and reached out to stop Emilia before she could look at hers.

"Must have been quite a night!" someone called out.

I looked down at my own phone. *A picture text.* I hit the screen to enlarge the picture. In it, Emilia was slumped against a bathroom wall. Her hair was plastered to her face. She was fully clothed but also fairly clearly trashed.

Shaking off Maya's hold, Emilia picked up her own phone. She stared at the picture. Her fair skin went paler. Her lips pressed themselves together, but I could see her chin trembling.

"No one cares," Maya told her. "So you had a good time one night. It's not like half the school hasn't done the same."

Emilia was still staring at the picture. I reached over and took the phone from her hand, banishing the picture from her screen. Emilia kept staring at her hand, even once I had her phone.

"Why have I not heard this story?" Emilia's friend Di joined our table. "You have heard all my stories, naughty girl."

Considering that *Di* was short for *diplomatic immunity* and that she had a fondness for dares, her "stories" probably put Emilia's to shame.

"Who got this text?" Emilia found her voice. It was low, almost guttural. "Who's seen the picture?"

Based on the murmurs and curious glances from the other students in the Hut and this hallway, I had a pretty good guess regarding the answer to that question—just like I had a pretty good idea of who might have sent it.

"No one cares," Maya told Emilia again. "We all get a little crazy sometimes."

Emilia stood up and grabbed her phone back from me. "I don't."

Emilia wasn't in my physics class, but she was the topic of conversation nonetheless.

"I didn't think she had it in her."

"When was that taken?"

"I always thought she was so perfect."

"Wait, wait—who am I?" At the lab table next to mine, a boy adopted a glazed look and let his mouth go slack.

Several tables away, Henry stood up. He crossed the room, then laid his palms flat on the boy's lab table and just stood there.

Slowly, the boy's friends stopped laughing.

"I give up," Henry said, his voice measured and calm. "Who are you?"

The boy developed a sudden interest in his lab notebook.

"Is Emilia okay?" Vivvie's question drew me back to the lab table we were sharing. Vivvie lowered her voice. "I mean, I know she's probably not thrilled, but on a scale of the *complete opposite of okay* to *okay* . . ." Vivvie caught her lower lip between her teeth, her eyes round. "Is she okay?"

I glanced back at Henry, then answered. "She'd want us to think she is."

"Hypothetically speaking," Asher said, coming up next to me in the cafeteria, "if one were planning to execute an act of derring-do to draw any and all disapproving murmurs away from one's twin, would it be better if said act involved a hand-made hang glider or—"

"No." Henry cut Asher off before he could list the second option.

"It's really sweet that you want to do something for Emilia," Vivvie told Asher, "in a completely inadvisable kind of way."

"Exactly," Asher declared. "I am the very soul of altruism, which is why I'm trying to decide between hang gliding off the chapel roof and—"

"No." Henry gave Asher a look.

"Perhaps you don't get a vote," Asher told Henry.

"Perhaps you gave me veto power when were seven," Henry countered. "And perhaps you jumping off a building is the last thing Emilia would actually want."

"Darn you and your infernal logic, Marquette!" Asher, his expression the very picture of woe, reached across Henry and snagged a cookie.

"This whole thing will blow over," I told Asher.

The murmurs had already died down considerably. Like Maya had said that morning, the picture really wasn't *that* scandalous. The only reason it had gotten any traction at all was because it was Emilia Rhodes—picture-perfect, angling-for-valedictorian, eyes-on-the-prize Emilia. She managed her reputation with the same fierceness with which she attacked SAT prep. She'd culti-vated an image, and this wasn't it.

"Consider it my opening salvo." John Thomas Wilcox slid behind me in the lunch line. He kept his voice low—clearly, those words were meant only for my ears.

Henry was at the cashier now. Asher and Vivvie were talking to each other.

John Thomas leaned into my personal space. I helped him out of it. Forcibly.

"Careful," John Thomas sneered. "You wouldn't want to get sent to the office for fighting."

Whatever. I noticed that he didn't attempt to leer at me again.

"If you ask me," he announced, his voice louder this time—and designed to carry, "someone did Miss Priss a favor. No one should be wound *that* tight."

I reached the front of the line and gave the cashier my student ID to pay for my food.

"The picture makes her seem more human," John Thomas continued behind me. "Like she really knows how to have a good time."

Once the cashier handed my card back, I turned to leave. The expression on my face never changed. Eventually, John Thomas would realize he hadn't gotten a single verbal reply out of me.

Some people weren't worth the breath it took to shoot them down.

I'd made it halfway to our normal table when I noticed that Emilia had a visitor at hers. *Mr. Collins.* He was the photography teacher. Even from a distance, I could see the disapproval on his face and the flash of panic that crossed Emilia's as he led her out of the room.

"Pity," John Thomas said, coming up behind me once more. "The Hardwicke administration has never been known for their approval of good times. Especially," he added, "when someone is careless enough for that good time to be caught on camera."

CHAPTER 14

I skipped lunch.

The Hardwicke administrative building had once been a residence. Now it was a historical landmark. The headmaster's secretary looked up from her desk when I entered.

"Tess," she said warmly. "What can I do for you?"

I wasn't sure that twinset-wearing, cookie-baking Mrs. Perkins *had* any setting other than warm.

"I'm looking for Emilia Rhodes," I said. There was a chance that John Thomas had misled me, a chance that Mr. Collins had merely pulled Emilia aside to speak to her himself.

Mrs. Perkins cured me of that notion. "She's in with the headmaster. You can wait if you'd like." She tilted her head to the side. "But isn't it your lunchtime? You really shouldn't get in the habit of skipping meals, Tess."

A phone on her desk rang. She answered it, and when she turned to consult her computer, I ducked past her desk and made a beeline for the headmaster's office.

Adam had said my father had always had a tendency to act with no mind to the consequences. I took that to mean I came by it honestly.

I twisted the knob and pushed the door in just as Headmaster Raleigh was gaining momentum on a very pointed lecture. "You are, I can only assume, well aware of the Hardwicke policy on alcohol and other such substances," he told Emilia. "While we cannot police your behavior outside these halls, the distribution of this picture reflects poorly on both you as an individual and on this institution—"

"I didn't distribute it." Emilia's voice was steady enough, but I could tell her composure was hard-won.

"Be that as it may," the headmaster continued, "this is hardly behavior befitting a would-be student-body president. I believe it would be best, for all involved, if you withdrew your name from the race."

The Emilia I knew would have refused on the spot. The girl sitting in front of the headmaster's desk did not.

"I understand you intend to apply to Yale next year." Raleigh hit Emilia exactly where it hurt. "Hardwicke has enough students apply each year that the admissions committee relies heavily on the recommendations of our teachers and staff. You want to put your best foot forward. *This*"—the headmaster nodded toward a phone he'd placed in front of Emilia—"is hardly your best foot."

I stepped forward, drawing Raleigh's attention to me. Emilia didn't even turn to look, her eyes locked on the front of the head-master's desk, her head bowed.

"Ms.—" the headmaster's voice boomed with disapproval, but he still hesitated when it came to my name.

"Kendrick Keyes," I supplied. Headmaster Raleigh flinched slightly at each of the names. *Ivy Kendrick. William Keyes.* Like it or not—and most days I didn't—those names meant something at this school and in this town.

"This is a private conversation," the headmaster informed me. "Unless you want to face disciplinary action yourself, I strongly suggest you leave the way you came. Immediately."

"Just like you're strongly suggesting Emilia drop out of the student council race?" I asked. "Remind me: Was there alcohol or any kind of illegal substance in that picture? Was Emilia holding a drink?"

"I will not warn you again, young lady."

"There's really no way of telling what's going on in that picture, is there?" I continued. I'd never done well with warnings. "She could have the flu. She could have just pulled an all-nighter. Someone could have slipped something into her nonalcoholic beverage of choice."

"Stop, Tess." Emilia's voice was hoarse. "Please. Just stop."

The phone on the table buzzed. An instant later, mine did, too. Emilia didn't move, but the headmaster did. He picked up the phone. A few seconds later, I heard a video start to play.

"Look at her. She's so wasted! Say 'wasted,' Emilia!"

Whatever Emilia said in response was incomprehensible. Her speech was slurred past all recognition.

In the present, Emilia lifted her head. Her shoulders shook. I crossed the room and went for the phone, hitting stop as several boys were snickering offscreen and one nudged her with his foot.

"I'll step down." Emilia forced herself to look at Headmaster Raleigh.

"I think that would be wise," he said quietly.

"And what about the boys in that video?" I asked. "The ones taping a girl without her consent? What about the person who's sending these texts?"

Now that he'd gotten what he wanted out of Emilia, Headmaster Raleigh seemed less concerned with my presence in the office. "Every effort will be made to find the origin of these texts," the headmaster promised.

"And if I told you that John Thomas Wilcox told me that he'd sent the picture?" I asked.

Emilia was the one who answered. "It would be your word against his." She shook her head. "He said, she said." Robotically, she turned back to the headmaster. "If that's all, I'd like to do some studying before my next class."

CHAPTER 15

I didn't see Emilia again until World Issues. The moment Dr. Clark told us to break into groups, Emilia asked to go to the bathroom. I had two choices: stay and be interrogated by both Henry and Asher about what had happened in the headmaster's office, or follow Emilia and risk having my head bitten off.

I chose the latter.

When I asked for permission, Dr. Clark assessed me silently. "Off the record," she said, "if what I'm hearing about how this situation with Emilia was handled is true, I disagree with it on every level." She nodded to the door. "Go."

I went.

When I got to the bathroom, Emilia was standing in front of the mirror, applying lip gloss. "Don't worry," she told me, an edge in her voice. "I'll still count your favor paid in full."

I stepped forward. "That's not why I'm worried."

Emilia put the cap on her lip gloss and turned to look at me. "You don't get to be worried about me," she said vehemently. "You don't even like me."

She'd told me once that Asher was the likable twin. He was the one people trusted. She was the one who had focus. The one who did everything right.

"You weren't drunk in that picture," I said softly. "Were you?"

"You saw the video." She clamored to hide the naked emotion in her eyes.

"Yeah," I said. "I did."

In Raleigh's office, when I'd thrown out the possibility that someone had slipped something into Emilia's drink that night, she'd told me to stop. *Begged* me to stop.

It would be your word against his, she'd said later. *He said, she said.*

No matter how hard I tried, I couldn't keep from replaying John Thomas's leering words from earlier that day: *If you ask me, someone did Miss Priss a favor. No one should be wound that tight.*

From the beginning, that picture had hit Emilia with crippling, devastating force.

"I'm not talking about this," Emilia said, her voice taut. "You're not talking about it. *No one* is talking about it." She turned on the faucet and began washing her hands. "There's nothing to talk about."

Yes. There is. I didn't say that. I didn't get a vote about whether we talked about this or not. No one got a vote but Emilia.

"I still owe you a favor," I said.

Emilia reached for a paper towel. "Do I look like I want a pity favor?" she asked.

"Do I look like I feel even an ounce of pity for you?" I shot back.

For the first time, Emilia allowed herself to look at me. Really look at me. I met her stare unflinchingly.

"Fine," she said after a moment. "You still owe me a favor. I'll let you know when I want to collect."

"You do that," I told her. "And if you decide you want to collect now—I can get you back in that race."

"The headmaster—" Emilia started to say.

"I can take care of the headmaster."

"That picture—"

"By the time I'm done," I said, "that picture will win you this election."

John Thomas. She didn't make the last objection out loud.

"Him," I said, "I'll take care of for fun."

There was a long moment of silence, and then Emilia tossed her ponytail over her shoulder. "There's no way you're that good."

I smiled. "Try me."

CHAPTER 16

Emilia and I went back to World Issues. It took me less than a minute to get Vivvie on board. I texted Ivy that I was going to Vivvie's place after school and bided my time until the bell rang. On the way to Vivvie's, I made four phone calls.

The first was to Anna Hayden.

"How would you like to stick it to John Thomas Wilcox?" I asked her.

There was a brief pause. "I'm listening."

"He took that picture of Emilia." I couldn't tell Anna more than that—not what I suspected about the circumstances in which that picture had been taken, not the devastating effect that even looking at it had on Emilia. But I could give Anna a moment to think about the fact that in another world, John Thomas might have been sending around pictures of her.

"The headmaster pressured Emilia into dropping out of the race because of that picture," I continued. "I plan to convince him that was a very bad idea."

I told Anna what I had in mind.

"I know you probably can't participate yourself," I said. Anna wasn't in the limelight as much as she would have been if her father had been president, but she was the only one of the presidential or vice presidential children who wasn't already of age. That attracted a certain amount of attention. "But if you could pass the word on—"

"Oh, I'll participate," Anna cut in, an edge in her voice. "And so will my friends. Just send me the link and tell me when."

The next two calls went to Lindsay Li—she of the blackmailing ex-boyfriend—and Meredith Sutton.

Right as we reached Vivvie's place, I made one final call.

The apartment Vivvie shared with her aunt had round-the-clock security downstairs.

"How are things going?" I asked Vivvie as we reached the elevator. "With your aunt?"

"Good," Vivvie replied with a little half smile. "She got a job at a local gallery." Vivvie paused. "We don't talk about my dad much," she said quietly.

Vivvie's father had been part of the conspiracy to murder Justice Marquette. Once things had started to unravel, Major Bharani had "committed suicide."

Vivvie and I both knew that he had been murdered.

"Sometimes . . ." Vivvie said, and then she trailed off.

"Sometimes," I prompted.

Vivvie stared at our reflection in the elevator's metal door. "Sometimes, I wake up in the middle of the night, and my aunt's just sitting in the living room, staring at nothing and cleaning her gun."

Given the sequence of events that had brought Priya Bharani into Vivvie's life, I supposed a certain amount of late-night paranoia was understandable.

"On the bright side," Vivvie commented, determined to end the conversation on a high note, "she's got great taste, and she lets me borrow her clothes."

The elevator came to a stop. The doors opened. Vivvie's apartment was the only one on the floor. She unlocked the front door, and then we got to work.

"I think the picture of Emilia was taken in a bathroom?" Vivvie caught her bottom lip between her teeth and rocked from her heels to her toes. "I'll get some pens and paper," she declared. "My bathroom is through there."

While Vivvie went in search of writing supplies, I went to check out the lighting in the bathroom. Setting my bag to one side, I lowered myself to the floor. I slumped back against the wall next to the bathtub, letting my head loll to one side.

"How's this?" I asked Vivvie when she came in.

She stared at me for a second. "Go like this," she told me, bending her head down and flipping her hair over in front of her face. I did as she instructed and watched through my hair as she went over to the sink and got a handful of water. She dripped it on me.

"Now lean back," she said.

I did.

"Eyes mostly closed," Vivvie said. "Head a little farther to the side. Legs a little farther apart."

Once I'd perfected the pose, Vivvie handed me a sheet of paper and a red marker. Two minutes later, she took my picture. Then we switched places, and I took hers.

"Not bad," Vivvie said, looking at the pictures on my phone. Each of us was slumped against the wall, our positions mimicking Emilia's in the picture almost exactly. The sign propped up against my chest read, *DOUBLE STANDARD*.

I scrolled from my picture to Vivvie's. Her sign said simply, *I STAND WITH EMILIA*.

"You're sure you want to do this?" I asked Vivvie. She looked nearly unconscious in her picture—and just as wasted as Emilia.

Vivvie thrust out her chin. "I'm sure."

So was I. Five minutes later, the pictures were uploaded. Ten minutes after that, the others started trickling in.

"Vivvie?" an accented voice called out.

"In here," Vivvie called back. She tried to look like she wasn't up to anything and failed miserably.

Her aunt appeared in the doorway. The woman did not ask what her niece and I were doing in Vivvie's bathroom. "I see we have a guest," she said instead. Her accent sounded British—and very posh. Like Vivvie, she had brown skin and black hair, though hers had a bit more natural curl. "Hello, Tess."

"Hey, Ms. Bharani," I said.

"Priya," she corrected. "Please."

"Priya."

"I am assuming that Ivy and Bodie know you are here?" Priya asked me.

I nodded. Priya's gaze lingered on my face for a moment. She wasn't the type of woman who missed much.

"I hope you'll stay for dinner," she said finally.

I got the sense that wasn't a request.

By the time takeout arrived a few hours later, my picture and
Vivvie's had been joined by more than thirty others. It had started
with Anna, Lindsay, and Meredith and spread from there. Their
friends. Their friends' friends.

All Hardwicke students. All girls.

I STAND WITH EMILIA.

"What did you girls do today?" Vivvie's aunt asked.

Vivvie and I looked at each other. "Nothing," we chimed in
unison.

Priya arched an eyebrow. "I find I doubt that very much." She
tilted her head to the side. "Vivvie, I noticed that Jacques is on
duty downstairs. Since it appears we will have leftovers, perhaps
you could bring him a plate?"

Vivvie's eyes sparkled. She whispered something to me about
her aunt and the night guard having a surplus of sexual tension
before bounding off to deliver the food. Once the front door
clicked behind her, Vivvie's aunt turned her attention to me.

"Ivy has been trying to get in touch with me."

That wasn't what I'd been expecting her to say, but the second
the words left her mouth, I realized that she'd sent Vivvie out of
the room for a reason.

"I cannot give Ivy the information she seeks," Priya continued. "You may tell her that it would not behoove either of us for
certain parties to realize that she'd been making inquiries. I certainly cannot be seen answering them."

When I'd asked Vivvie what her aunt did for a living, all Vivvie had been able to tell me was that her aunt had worked overseas. Taking in the measured tone in Priya Bharani's voice and the pleasant smile on her face, I doubted suddenly that she'd been working in an art gallery over there.

Priya put her hand over mine and lowered her voice. "I am grateful," she said, "for what Ivy has done for my niece. But I cannot tell her that the group she is looking for is known by Interpol as Senza Nome. The Nameless," Priya translated. "I cannot," she continued quietly, "tell her that they've been on various watch lists since the 1980s, or that they seem to operate primarily through infiltration—of other terrorist organizations, as well as world governments.

"I cannot speak of this—not to your sister, not to her friends at the Pentagon, not to anyone."

Except for me. I was a teenager. Even a cursory check would show that Vivvie and I were friends. Vivvie's aunt couldn't take Ivy's call. She couldn't be seen talking to her, or to Adam.

But she could whisper in my ear, and I could whisper in Ivy's.

The front door slammed, and Priya began clearing away the plates, like nothing had happened.

"So," Vivvie said, popping back into the kitchen and grinning, "what did I miss?"

CHAPTER 17

I delivered the message. To say that Ivy and Adam weren't pleased that Priya had made me her messenger would have been an understatement.

Bodie just rolled his eyes. "Intelligence types," he scoffed. "When things go cloak and dagger, you can't trust them farther than you can throw them."

Adam gave Bodie a disgruntled look that reminded me that *Adam* was in military intelligence.

"So Vivvie's aunt is—" I started to say.

"Vivvie's aunt is an appraiser," Ivy cut me off, "specializing in non-Western antiquities."

"Retired," Bodie clarified. "A retired *appraiser*."

In other words: whatever Vivvie's aunt had done overseas and whoever she'd done it for—it was classified. And that meant that there was a good chance that what she'd told me was classified, too.

"Would I be right in assuming you have homework?" Ivy asked me.

"Really?" I said incredulously. After what I'd just told her, she expected me to trot upstairs and do my homework?

"Please, Tess." Ivy caught my gaze and held it. "I'm sorry Priya put you in the middle of this. It won't happen again."

It was on the tip of my tongue to tell her that it would happen again. For as long as she was *Ivy Kendrick*, there would always be people who saw me as a path to her. No matter how hard Ivy tried to keep me out, there would always be times when I knew things I shouldn't.

Daniela Nicolae works for a terrorist group that specializes in infiltrating governments and other terrorist groups. My brain didn't stop there. *It's not a coincidence that her time in Doctors Without Borders overlapped Walker Nolan's. It can't be.*

I didn't say any of that out loud. "Were they involved?" I asked instead. "Walker Nolan and that woman they have in custody."

That was a stab in the dark, but Ivy's lack of response told me it had been a good one. I turned that over in my head. The fact that Walker had come to Ivy in the first place suggested that he wasn't part of this group. But for all we knew, Nicolae's assignment could have been trying to convert him.

"Walker found out what his girlfriend was doing," I said, putting the pieces together. "He found the plans for the bombing, and he came to you. Why didn't he go straight to his father?"

There was another silence, but this time Ivy was the one who broke it. "The goal was to keep the president's hands as clean as possible, given the circumstances."

The circumstances being that the president's son was involved—quite possibly *intimately* involved—with a member of a terrorist organization.

"Your job is to keep this quiet." I looked from Ivy to Adam to Bodie.

"Once the terrorist was in custody, I briefed the president." Ivy measured her words. "This is coming out," she said bluntly. "The ball is rolling. People are talking. It's only a matter of time before someone obtains proof. My job," she said emphatically, "is to make sure it doesn't come out until after the polls close next Tuesday."

Until after midterm elections.

Presidential approval rating. Transparency. Corruption. I imagined what the redheaded pundit I'd seen on the news would have to say if she knew there was a connection between this terrorist group and Walker Nolan. Any hint of a scandal could sway the results of midterm elections. But something like this? The president would lose his majority in the House *and* the Senate. He'd lose any chance at a second term himself.

"I should get to work," Ivy said. I heard the words buried underneath: *I've told you everything I can tell you. I've told you more than I should.*

I understood where she was coming from. Logically.

Ivy walked me to the bottom of the stairs. I could see her, wanting to say something, not knowing what to say. I could also feel her wanting to get rid of me, *needing* to pursue the lead that Priya had given her.

I mattered to Ivy. But there were times when her job had to matter more.

"Just for the record," I said as I started climbing the stairs, "there's a decent chance you might get a call from the Hardwicke headmaster sometime in the next couple of days."

There was a beat of silence. "I don't want to know," Ivy decided.

It was probably better that way. She had her job—and I had mine.

CHAPTER 18

It took thirty-six hours for our little social media experiment to come to the headmaster's attention. On Friday morning, I was called into his office.

Mrs. Perkins gave me a sympathetic look. "Tess, dear, there are times when it's best not to poke a hornet's nest," she advised.

I didn't reply.

Mrs. Perkins sighed. "Go on in."

The headmaster was standing at his window. "Sit," he said without turning around.

I sat and leaned back in my chair, balancing it on two legs. The headmaster's silence was probably aimed at making me sweat, but thus far, things were going exactly according to plan. While I waited for Headmaster Raleigh to tell me that my behavior was unfitting of a Hardwicke student, my eyes found their way to the wall behind his desk. It was bare.

The front legs of my chair thudded against the floor.

Weeks ago, there had been a framed photograph on that wall—of Headmaster Raleigh and five other men, taken at a Camp David retreat. All three of the known conspirators in the murder of Justice Marquette had been there that weekend. It was entirely possible that the fourth co-conspirator—the one whose identity we didn't know—had been there as well.

The headmaster took the photo down. I tried not to read too much into that.

Headmaster Raleigh turned away from the window. He took a seat at his desk and turned his desktop computer screen to face me. "What is the meaning of this?"

This was a series of pictures—representing more than 80 percent of the female students in grades nine through twelve—like the ones Vivvie and I had taken in her bathroom. *Slumped. Unfocused. Seemingly drunk—and holding a sign.*

"You—all of you—will take these pictures down, or I will have the lot of you up on misconduct charges."

That was an empty threat. I doubted the headmaster wanted to deal with the parents of *all* those girls—or to explain to those parents that the Hardwicke administration still hadn't managed to track down the person who was texting around pictures of borderline unconscious teenage girls.

"Remind me again," I said. "Is it performance art or organized protest that's against the Hardwicke code of conduct?"

The headmaster's eyes narrowed.

I took advantage of his stormy silence. "In the past decade, Hardwicke has had exactly one female student-body president. For a school that claims to value diversity, tolerance, and equality, that's shockingly disproportioned, wouldn't you say? And now our only female candidate has been strong-armed into dropping out of the race, despite the fact that she has broken no actual Hardwicke rules."

On my phone, I pulled up the picture Vivvie had taken of me and then slid the phone across the table.

DOUBLE STANDARD.

Raleigh looked at the photo like it was a snake. "There is no double standard at play here," he said tersely. "I assure you that had Ms. Rhodes been male, the outcome would have been the same."

"You can tell the press that when they call for a quote," I suggested in the most helpful of tones. "I wasn't sure they'd be interested in our little protest, but given that one of the girls participating in this protest is the vice president's daughter . . . it's seeming like we might be able to find some takers."

"Is that a threat?"

"That's a statement of probability," I told the headmaster.

The headmaster looked as if he might actually leap over the desk to throttle me. "I did not require Ms. Rhodes to step down. I suggested she might find it a wise course of action."

"Strongly suggested," I said.

"Fine," he returned. "Strongly suggested."

I reached into my bag and pulled out a stack of pictures. My final phone call had paid off.

"I'm going to *strongly suggest*," I told the headmaster, "that you take a look at these, and then tell me again that there's no double standard at Hardwicke."

I slid the pictures across to him. Luckily for me, some of the freshman boys on the lacrosse team were still holding a grudge about the extreme hazing. And as it turned out, they'd taken some very interesting pictures of upperclassmen at a couple of team parties.

"I especially like the one of John Thomas Wilcox doing a keg stand," I said, a sarcastic edge creeping into my tone. "It's so much less incriminating than a picture of a girl leaning against a wall, with nary an ounce of alcohol in sight."

The headmaster thumbed through the pictures. "Where did you get these?"

"Does it matter?" I asked.

"I suppose you want me to suggest to Mr. Wilcox that he step down from this race as well?"

"You could," I said. "Of course, then you would probably have to open nominations back up so that Henry Marquette wasn't running unopposed." My lips curved up in a subtle smile. "I'm sure the student body wouldn't have any trouble finding another female nominee."

"Yes, yes," the headmaster said, seeing a way out of this. "Of course." Then he seemed to realize that I was *still* smiling.

"It's the funniest thing," I said. "People keep telling me that *I* should run."

I could see Raleigh playing the scenario out before his eyes with no small amount of horror. The last thing he wanted was *me* in a position of power.

"Perhaps," he allowed through gritted teeth, "I could have another discussion with Ms. Rhodes. Convince her that I might have been . . . hasty. That she *should* run."

"If you think that's best."

"This little social experiment of yours comes down," he said flatly.

"The pictures come down," I agreed. I stood and turned toward the door. Halfway out of the office, I stopped. I could feel the headmaster seething behind me.

He wasn't the only one who was angry. "My first week at this school," I said without turning back to face him, "an upperclassman boy was showing off photos he'd taken of a freshman girl, sans clothing."

I didn't say who the girl was. I didn't say who the boy was. That wasn't my truth to tell him—and he didn't need to know. He did need to know that Emilia's situation hadn't happened in a vacuum. He needed to know that the Hardwicke administration was culpable, that the way he'd mishandled Emilia's situation *mattered*.

"I'm the only reason *those* photos weren't distributed," I continued, steel in my voice. "You might think I'm a troublemaker, Headmaster, but believe me when I say that I solve more problems for you than I cause."

CHAPTER 19

When Bodie picked me up after school, there was a garment bag hanging in the backseat.

"Ivy making an appearance at some kind of event tonight?" I asked him.

"Nope." Bodie took his time with elaborating as he pulled past the Hardwicke gate, nodding to the guard on duty. "You are."

I eyed the garment bag with significantly more suspicion. "What kind of event?"

"The kind at which your attendance was imperiously demanded."

I didn't have to ask who had demanded my presence. "Since when does Ivy acquiesce to William Keyes's demands?" I asked.

"Since Monsignor Straight-and-Narrow backed up his father's request."

I raised an eyebrow at Bodie. "Monsignor Straight-and-Narrow?" I said dryly. He had to be referring to Adam, but as far as nicknames went . . .

"Not my best," Bodie acknowledged. "It's been a long week."

It had been four days since Walker Nolan had come to Ivy. Three since the bombing. Two since I'd delivered the message about the group Daniela Nicolae worked for.

"I know Ivy wants me kept in the dark on this whole thing, but can you at least tell me that she's not being stupid?" I asked. "That she's just managing the press and plugging leaks and has no intention of investigating this terrorist group herself?"

There was a pause.

"Ivy doesn't do stupid," Bodie told me.

He didn't say that she wasn't looking into this terrorist group.

"Of course she does stupid," I replied, thinking of the way she'd come for me when I'd been kidnapped, trading her life away for mine. "She's a Kendrick. Self-sacrificing heroics are kind of our thing."

The dress in the bag was white and floor-length, with just enough fabric in the skirt to swish. Silver beading formed a wide band around the waist and accented the neckline, which cut across my collarbone. A single white strap crossed my back, leaving the rest bare.

"You look beautiful."

I turned to scowl at Ivy.

She held up her hands. "I come in peace."

"Tell me again why I have to go to this thing?"

Ivy came to stand behind me in the mirror. Wordlessly, she zipped the dress up just past the small of my back. I couldn't help looking for similarities in our reflections. Ivy's hair was light brown and dancing on the border of blond. Mine was darker, but just as thick. Her hair was straight; mine had a natural wave. Our faces had the same general shape to them, the same cheekbones, the same lips, but I had my father's eyes.

"The event you're going to is a fund-raiser." Ivy stepped back from the mirror and answered my question. "For an organization that provides emotional and financial support to veterans and the families of those killed in combat."

Abruptly, she turned and busied herself with my dresser, picking up stray ponytail holders and pins. *Killed in combat.* I knew who Ivy was thinking of when she said those words.

"Bodie said that Adam asked you to let me go," I commented, trying not to think too hard or too long about Tommy Keyes.

Ivy turned back to me. "Adam doesn't ask me for much." She turned me back toward the mirror and began working her fingers through my hair.

Don't. A voice inside me objected—an unwanted reflex. *Don't touch me. Don't pretend like this is something we do.*

That was a knee-jerk reaction. No matter how far Ivy and I had come, I could never quiet the part of me that had wanted her in my life so badly for so long, without even knowing that she was my mother. I couldn't shut myself off from the Tess who'd grown up on the ranch with Gramps, the one who would have given anything to hear from Ivy more than three times a year.

That part of me had been disappointed again and again.

Ivy pulled two chunks of hair out of my face and into a twist at the nape of my neck and then stepped back. She'd noticed the way I'd stiffened at her touch.

I didn't enjoy hurting Ivy, any more than she enjoyed hurting me.

"You're not going tonight?" I asked, trying to pretend that neither one of us had the power to hurt the other.

"No," Ivy replied, clipping the word. "I have work to do."

Work. I spent three seconds wishing that Bodie had been able to promise me that Ivy wasn't looking into Senza Nome and another three wondering what she'd already found.

"I hope I'm not interrupting."

Ivy and I turned in unison. Adam stood in the door to my room, dressed in his most formal uniform. Silver buttons gleamed against his dark blue jacket. His bowtie was Air Force blue; an assortment of medals and insignia decorated his lapel.

"You're right on time," Ivy told him.

"May I?" Adam asked, tearing his eyes from Ivy and approaching me. My gaze went to a box in his hand. *Jewelry.* He withdrew a pair of pearls.

"Knock yourself out," I told him, unsure why the words felt so heavy in my throat.

He fastened the pearls around my neck. "They were my mother's."

My grandmother's.

"Ivy!" Bodie's voice broke into my thoughts. "You're going to want to get down here!"

Adam and Ivy shared a split-second gaze before making a break for the stairs. I followed, cursing the dress for slowing me down. By the time I made it downstairs, Adam and Ivy were staring at an electronic tablet. I approached with caution, ready to be rebuffed.

Neither one of them pushed me away.

Craning my head, I took in the website that held their attention. My brain couldn't process the words on the page, because it was focused wholly and entirely on the picture.

Daniela Nicolae.

She was wearing a gray jumpsuit. Her hands were cuffed in front of her body. There were dark circles under her eyes. Her head was held high. Her stomach bulged against the fabric of the jumpsuit.

My mouth fell open as I processed that bulge.

The terrorist—the woman Walker Nolan had approached Ivy about, the one I suspected he might be involved with—was pregnant.

CHAPTER 20

This is coming out. As I stepped out of Adam's car, Ivy's words from earlier that week came back to me. *My job is to make sure it doesn't come out until after the polls close next Tuesday.*

The terrorist responsible for the hospital attack was pregnant. And there was a possibility—maybe a good one, based on Ivy's reaction to that picture—that she was pregnant with Walker Nolan's child.

That wasn't just a bombshell. That was nuclear.

Adam murmured something to the valet and then came around to my side of the car. He offered me his arm.

We're really doing this, I thought as I took his arm. *Coming here, pretending everything is fine.*

Neither Adam nor Ivy had said anything to confirm what I suspected. That Daniela Nicolae was pregnant—and that someone had leaked a photo geared at publicizing that fact—was undeniable. But the idea that the baby might be Walker Nolan's?

That was nothing but conjecture on my part. A worst-case scenario.

Anything bad that can happen will. That was Murphy's Law. I was beginning to suspect that in Ivy's line of business, it was fact.

"Deep breath," Adam advised me. A moment later, we walked up a marble staircase and through a set of double doors.

Rows of circular tables stretched the length of the ballroom. Marble columns lined the walls. Massive red velvet curtains were gathered and tied back at each corner. Adam said something about the building being a renovated opera house.

I barely heard a word.

Anything bad that can happen will.

"Tess, my dear, you look lovely." William Keyes zeroed in on Adam and me with military precision. He pressed a kiss to my cheek, then turned to Adam. "It's good to see you, son."

"I'm not here for you." My uncle's voice was as terse as I'd ever heard it. When Ivy had been held hostage, Adam had asked his father for help. William Keyes had refused. If I hadn't revealed myself as his granddaughter, if I hadn't made the kingmaker a deal, Ivy might have died—and William Keyes wouldn't have lifted a hand to stop it.

Adam would never forgive him for that.

"You're here for your brother," Keyes acknowledged, putting a hand on Adam's shoulder, then one on mine. "We all are."

Adam remained stiff under his father's touch.

And I thought Ivy and I had issues.

Keyes let his hand drop from Adam's shoulder but kept his grip on mine. "Come, Tess," he said. "There are some people I'd like to introduce you to."

Adam stepped closer to Keyes, lowering his voice. "I didn't bring her here for you to parade her around and show off the newest Keyes."

He'd brought me here to honor my father. The last thing Adam wanted for me was a life lived under the kingmaker's thumb.

"It's fine," I told my uncle. I would have rather had my toenails torn out with rusty pliers than have Keyes parade me through this crowd, but I had also noticed a familiar pair of figures embedded in the crowd.

The president and First Lady. Ivy had said that she'd briefed the president on Walker's relationship with Daniela Nicolae. There was no doubt in my mind that President Nolan would have been informed about the leaked photos immediately, but he and Georgia gave no visible sign that their reign was on the verge of ruin.

I allowed Keyes to escort me from one set of DC society players to the next, my eyes on the prize the whole time. Adam never allowed me out of his sight.

"I know what you're doing," he murmured as we got closer to my target.

"Who?" I murmured back. "Me?"

"William." The president of the United States had a powerful voice and a smile you could trust. He shook my grandfather's hand. "Good to see you."

President Nolan was an excellent liar.

William Keyes was a better one. "Always a pleasure," the king-maker replied, a matching smile on his face and a glint in his eyes. "I understand you've met my granddaughter?"

His granddaughter. I couldn't have been the only one who detected the trace of possessiveness in the kingmaker's tone. The president had met me before William Keyes even knew I existed. The president was unquestionably on better terms with Ivy.

But I had the kingmaker's blood.

"Tess." The First Lady stepped forward and pressed a quick kiss to my cheek. "You look wonderful, darling."

You know, I thought. *About your son. About Daniela Nicolae.*

There was no hint of it on her face. She looked so poised, elegant and warm and not the least bit like a queen whose kingdom was on the verge of crumbling around her. Her dress was white, knee-length. The matching blazer had beadwork more intricate than anything on my dress.

Not so much as one blond hair out of place, I thought. But Georgia Nolan knew. I *knew* in my gut that the president had told her.

Maybe I'm wrong. Maybe the baby isn't Walker's. Maybe I'm making something out of nothing.

"Adam." The president shook Adam's hand, then looked just past his shoulder. "I wasn't aware that Ivy was coming tonight."

Ivy?

Adam, Keyes, and I turned to see her making her way through the crowd. She was wearing a black dress—fitted, with a high neck. Between elbow-length black gloves and the way her hair looked pinned up in an elaborate twist, she looked like the second coming of Audrey Hepburn.

Or, I thought, taking in the pace of her steps and the tension around her mouth, *like hell's own fury.*

"Ivy." Georgia greeted her just as she'd greeted me. "You look lovely."

"Is everything all right?" the president asked her, the edges of his smile straining slightly against his face.

"Adam." Ivy's voice was perfectly pleasant. "Why don't you show Tess the sculpture garden?"

In other words: she wanted me out of hearing range. *Now.*

Adam took my arm again. No sooner had we turned away from the group than I heard the president address Adam's father.

"A pleasure as always, William." That was a dismissal. William Keyes was not a man who appreciated being dismissed.

I glanced back over my shoulder. Beside me, Adam spoke. "There's no love lost between my father and President Nolan."

I knew Adam was attempting to divert my attention from Ivy and the Nolans, but there was a chance he'd tell me something that was worth a diversion, so I reluctantly turned back around.

"My father and the First Lady knew each other when they were young," Adam continued. "They grew up in the same town. Georgia left for college and came back engaged." My uncle had my full attention now. "My father is not, nor has he ever been, a graceful loser."

My brain whirred, going back over every interaction I'd seen between the president and William Keyes, between Keyes and the First Lady.

Funny, isn't it, that sometimes the loser matters more than the person who wins?

"Captain Keyes." A voice jostled me from my thoughts. Its owner stepped in front of us and shook Adam's hand. "Thank you for your service."

My gaze went from the man shaking Adam's hand to the teenage boy standing beside him.

John Thomas Wilcox.

Congressman Wilcox bore little resemblance to his son. He was shorter than John Thomas and broader through the shoulders, a side part covering thinning hair.

"Congressman," Adam acknowledged. "Thank you for your support."

"The foundation's work is a cause worth supporting." Congressman Wilcox had the ultimate political smile. "One that resonates with both sides of the aisle."

Those words reminded me that Congressman Wilcox—the *minority* whip—fell squarely on the other side of the political aisle from the president—and the kingmaker.

"And this must be your niece," the congressman turned to me. "Theresa, is it?"

"Actually," John Thomas said, offering me a slick, insidious smile of his own, "it's Tess."

"My son," the congressman told Adam. Then he turned his attention back to me. "I believe you two are in the same grade at Hardwicke."

"Small world," I said, the muscles in my jaw tensing.

"John Thomas, perhaps you could take Tess for a little spin around the room while I talk with her uncle?" Congressman Wilcox suggested.

John Thomas did not seem to find that idea any more appealing than I did. His father's gaze darkened almost imperceptibly.

"I'd love to," John Thomas said tersely. He reached for my arm. I jerked back.

"Don't touch me," I said. My voice was low, but the words cut through the air like a knife.

Adam shifted his weight, shielding my body with his. "Another time," he told the congressman. Smoothly, he extricated us from the congressman's grasp. He didn't speak to me until we'd made it outside to the sculpture garden. A military band played to one side.

"I take it you're not a fan of the congressman's son," Adam said.

John Thomas had sent that picture of Emilia to the entire school. If someone had, as I was beginning to suspect, slipped something into Emilia's drink that night, John Thomas's name would be near the top of my suspect list.

"Not a fan," I confirmed.

Adam was comfortable enough with silence that he didn't ask me to elaborate and didn't press to change the topic of conversation. We came to stand near a statue of a soldier.

"Why do you think Ivy's here?" I asked finally, breaking the silence, my thoughts still back in the ballroom with Ivy and the Nolans.

"If I had to guess," Adam said after a long and considered pause, "I'd guess that she's having some trouble locating her client."

CHAPTER 21

Ivy was gone by the time we went back into the ballroom for dinner. Either she'd gotten what she'd wanted from the Nolans, or she'd concluded that they had nothing to give her.

The evening's speaker was a soldier who'd lost his entire unit to insurgents. He'd been injured and discharged. Within a year, he'd lost his sobriety and his career prospects, and within three years, his children and his wife.

As I listened to this man talk about hitting rock bottom and finding a way to pull through, it was easy to forget about the world around me: about Adam and the kingmaker, about the president and the First Lady, about Walker Nolan and whatever had brought Ivy to this hall.

By the time dessert was served, the speech had concluded, and the foundation was honoring the evening's platinum donor. William Keyes accepted the glass plaque gracefully, and when asked to speak a few words, he did a good imitation of someone who was reluctant to take the spotlight.

"My son Tommy enlisted the day he turned eighteen. To be honest," Keyes said, his eyes on our table—on Adam, on me, "I thought it was a mistake. I thought it was a mistake when he left for basic training. I thought it was a mistake when he shipped off overseas, and when I received word that he'd been killed on his second tour of duty—I thought surely, *surely* that was a mistake." Keyes was a man who knew how to use his silences. "Over the years," he said, "I've come to realize that there is a difference between a *sacrifice* and a *mistake*."

Adam—my always-in-control, never-flinching uncle—stood and stalked out of the room. Keyes continued speaking. I was aware of the eyes on our table, aware of the eyes on me.

The moment the old man finished his speech, under the cover of the applause, I went out the way Adam had gone. The door opened into a hallway. I followed it, looking for Adam.

A hand locked over my elbow.

"Fancy meeting you here." There was an edge in John Thomas's voice and a glint in his eyes. I pulled back from his grasp, but he tightened his hold.

"I need to thank you," he said, "for that lovely display with my father."

He slurred his words slightly. I eyed the door to the ballroom, willing it to open, willing someone to join us, but it was just me and John Thomas and an empty hall.

"You think you're so smart," John Thomas said. "You think you're so special, Tess *Kendrick*. Tess *Keyes*. But you're not. You're nothing." He leaned forward, bringing his lips close to my face. I could smell the alcohol on his breath. "You're just a scared little girl."

I shoved the heel of my hand into his nose. Hard. John Thomas stumbled back, his hand going to his face. When it came away bloody, he stared at me, stunned.

"You . . . you . . . hit me," he said dumbly.

I took advantage of his surprise and headed back to the ballroom. But when I tried the door, I discovered that it had locked behind me.

"I can't believe you hit me, you psychotic little . . ."

I blocked out the sound of his voice and took a right into a hallway lined with doors—including a family bathroom.

I reached for the door as John Thomas rounded the corner after me.

"I told you Emilia was just my opening salvo," John Thomas called. "Wait until you see what I have planned for your little boyfriend."

It took me a second to catch the reference. *Henry*. Henry Marquette was not my boyfriend. But the threat was enough to keep me frozen in place.

"Marquette's had you on your back since you got here," John Thomas sneered. "I wonder if his pillow talk ever included anything about his father."

Those words knocked the breath from my body.

"The congressman is very good at paying attention," John Thomas said. "In that respect," he slurred, dragging the cuff of his sleeve across his nose, bloodying it, "I'm my father's son."

Unwilling to let him see that his words had hit their target, I opened the door, stepped into the bathroom, and locked it behind me, my mind reeling. *John Thomas knows something about Henry's father.* Something that he thought could hurt Henry's campaign. *Something he thinks could hurt Henry.*

I stayed in the bathroom for a full five minutes before I unlocked the door and eased it back open. John Thomas was nowhere to be seen, but the hallway was occupied. *A couple.* The woman had red hair, a blue dress. She was wearing matching heels. The man was her same height, seemingly twice as wide. He pulled the woman tight to his body, his hands roaming over her curves. I couldn't make out either of their faces, but I could see a thick silver ring on the man's right hand as he shuddered and his fingers entangled themselves in her hair.

The sound of incoming footsteps pried the two apart. I stepped back from the door, letting it close and hoping they wouldn't take note of it—or me.

A few seconds later, I heard Adam calling my name. When I opened the door back into the hallway, the couple was gone.

"Are you okay?" Adam asked me.

I stepped toward him. "Are you?"

It wasn't until half an hour later, when we made it to the valet stand, and I saw the thick silver ring on the hand of the man in front of us in line that I realized who he was.

Congressman Wilcox.

And the woman standing between him and John Thomas— the woman who *didn't* have red hair and *wasn't* wearing a blue dress—was the congressman's wife.

CHAPTER 22

Walker Nolan showed up on our doorstep Saturday morning, looking hungover and on the verge of collapse.

Ivy rounded on me. "Upstairs," she ordered. "Now."

"It's okay." Walker's voice was hoarse. "She's going to see it anyway. Everyone is."

There was a beat of silence.

"See what?" Ivy asked.

Walker stared at her for several seconds, nonresponsive.

"Walker," Ivy said sharply.

He swallowed, his eyes regaining some of their focus. "Can I come in?"

"My name is Daniela Nicolae."

Walker's *it* was a video—one that had arrived in his inbox that morning.

"I live next door. You pass me in the coffee shop. I'm a nice girl, the kind you smile at when you walk by." The terrorist's eyes were dark, a stark contrast to her fair skin. "I am a doctor. I am your neighbor. I am your friend. And everything you know about me is a lie."

Daniela spoke with a faint accent, one I couldn't quite pinpoint.

"I have been raised for one purpose and one purpose alone. Mine is a glorious calling. And by the time you know me for who and what I am, it will be too late."

She taped this before the bombing, I realized. *Before she knew it would fail.*

"I am one of many. You work with us, side by side. You lift a hand to wave as we are out watering our lawns. We are everywhere. We are in your government, your law enforcement, your military. We see everything. We know all of your secrets." Even with a screen between us, her gaze was eerie in its intensity. "And we wait."

The camera panned out and the terrorist's hand rested on her stomach—her very pregnant stomach. Her expression flickered, and for a moment, I saw a quieter, raw emotion underneath. "I wish that it could be different. I wish that my child could know her father. I wish that there was no part of me that loved him. I wish that he did not love me. I wish . . ." She swallowed. "I wish that I were not so good at my job. I do, Walker. But I am what I am, and you are the president's son."

Her hand fell away from her stomach. "My name is Daniela Nicolae. And the time for waiting is over."

The clip ended abruptly, the screen going to black.

"She made it," Walker said. "For me. For after."

"Walker." Ivy's voice was calm but every bit as intense as the terrorist's had been. "What did you mean when you said everyone was going to see this?"

Walker looked like he hadn't slept in days. He looked like he might never sleep again. "I'm not the only one that video was sent to."

There were some secrets that not even the great Ivy Kendrick could bury. Pandora's box had been opened. There was no closing it now. By noon, the video had gone viral. By twelve ten, it was playing on every major news channel.

"The president's son invited a terrorist not just into his home but into his bed! We have to ask: What exactly did Walker Nolan tell this woman? Why was he such an easy target? And how long has the president known the truth?"

The female pundit who'd flamed the Nolan administration after the bombing wasn't debating anyone this time. She was sitting behind a desk, speaking directly into the camera.

"We know that these groups specialize in turning people. They recruit American citizens. Has the president's son been interrogated? Are we sure they didn't get to him, too?"

On and on it went. Walker was either an accomplice or a patsy. He'd *chosen* to turn down Secret Service protection. He'd made himself a target. And if the president couldn't safeguard his own family, how could we expect him to safeguard this country?

As far as blows went, this one was lethal.

Less than an hour later, the president issued a statement. He said that he was grieved that his own son had been made a victim and thankful that Walker had uncovered the duplicity in time to save hundreds of lives.

"Let me be clear," President Nolan finished. "The United States does not negotiate with terrorists. We do not fear them. We will not allow them to divide us. This country is strong. We are proud. We are united. And the war on terror is one we *will* win."

CHAPTER 23

On Monday morning, Maya was somewhat muted as she told Emilia that her approval ratings were at an all-time high among freshman and sophomore girls. Given that *muted* wasn't typically an adjective that described Maya Rojas, I didn't need the pollster's daughter to tell me that, like Ivy, her mother had worked through the weekend, or that President Nolan's approval rating was at an all-time low.

Opposite Maya, Di flipped her white-blond hair over one shoulder. "Hands," she said, her Icelandic accent making the word sound sharper. When none of us moved, she rolled her light blue eyes. "I do not bite," she said. "Much. Give me your hands."

Maya offered hers, and Di whipped out a pen and wrote something on the back of Maya's right hand. Then she turned her light blue eyes to me.

"Hand."

"Pass," I said.

"You cannot pass," the ambassador's daughter said, waving my words away. "You are the one who started this."

I glanced over at Maya's hand. Di had written four letters on the back. *ISWE.*

As in: *I STAND WITH EMILIA.*

"The freshman girls are writing it on their hands." Di gave me a steely-eyed look. "Now we write it on ours."

Emilia remained strangely silent. A week ago, she would have ordered me to play along.

I held my hand out to Di, appraising Emilia the whole time. The words *thank you* hadn't left Asher's sister's lips once since I'd gotten her back in the race. I understood that she *couldn't* thank me—not without acknowledging, even if just in her own head, that this wasn't just about the election.

I watched as Di wrote the letters on my hand. *ISWE.*

"I come bearing donuts." Asher appeared next to our table. "And the bearer of donuts," he intoned, "was greeted with trumpets and pomp." He waited patiently—presumably for both trumpets and pomp.

Instead, he got Emilia giving him the look of a sibling who knew her brother all too well. "What did you do?" she asked him flatly.

"Nothing," Asher answered with a charming smile.

Emilia's eyes narrowed slightly. "What are you going to do?"

"Can a boy not just bring his dearest, darling twin a sugary confection in celebration of the beauteousness that is Monday?"

"No," all four of us answered at the same time.

"Perhaps I am overwrought with filial guilt," Asher suggested. "For I have betrayed my family by standing in this election with that rogue Henry Marquette."

"Perhaps," Emilia countered, "you blew something up and want me to be the one to break it to Mom and Dad?"

Asher winked at her. "That is possibly not entirely false."

"Do I want to know what you blew up?" Emilia asked him with a long-suffering sigh.

"That would depend on how attached you were to the stone gargoyle that used to sit on our front porch."

I snorted and snagged a donut.

Asher took that as an invitation to plop down beside me. "How goes the campaign?"

We didn't get the chance to answer.

"Better than some people's, I'd wager." John Thomas strolled over but didn't sit down. He probably enjoyed towering over us, looking down. "I just heard the most unsettling rumor," he said, relishing the words.

Until that moment, I'd forgotten about John Thomas's promise that Henry was going to be his next target. With everything that had happened, I'd forgotten to ask Ivy if it was possible that Congressman Wilcox might know what she'd covered up for the Marquette family.

I'd forgotten to ask her if there was any way that the congressman's son might know the truth about Henry's father, too.

"Now would be a good time for you to leave," Asher said. His voice was cheerful enough, but I could hear a thread of warning underneath.

"I just wouldn't feel right walking away," John Thomas countered. "The least I can do is warn you about what I heard." He gave every appearance of sincerity, except for the slight uptick of his lips. "Addiction is a disease. I had no idea Henry's father had gone through such a *rough* time prior to his death. In and out of rehab—"

Asher stood up. "Don't," he gritted out. "Talk. About. Henry's. Father."

Asher was a person who was constantly in motion—always laughing, always smiling.

He wasn't smiling now.

"I'm not talking about Henry's father." John Thomas stared Asher down. "I'm just telling you what other people are saying."

Addiction. Rehab.

John Thomas doesn't know that Henry's father killed himself. That should have come as a relief. *He doesn't know that Ivy covered it up.*

But apparently, that wasn't the Marquette family's only secret.

"Asher." Emilia's voice cut into my thoughts. "Don't."

Don't waste your breath. Don't let him get a rise out of you.

Emilia's warning drew John Thomas's attention. The congressman's son leaned down and brushed a strand of hair out of her face. Emilia stiffened under his touch. Her breath went shallow.

"Don't touch her," Asher said, his voice razor sharp. He had seriously considered jumping off a building to save his twin even an ounce of scrutiny. The desire to protect her ran deep.

"Didn't your sister ever tell you?" John Thomas met Asher's eyes as he rubbed Emilia's hair back and forth between his fingers. "I was her first."

Emilia shuddered. One moment Asher was beside me and the next John Thomas was on the ground and Asher was on top of him.

"If she told you she didn't want it," John Thomas whispered, "she lied."

Asher snapped. There was no other word for it. He moved with manic fury, his fist plowing into John Thomas's face again and again.

John Thomas smiled the whole time.

"Asher," Emilia said. He didn't hear her, didn't hear me, didn't hear anything, lost to a haze of fury.

There was a blur of movement to my right as someone pulled Asher off of John Thomas. It took me a moment to process the fact that it was Henry. Asher struggled against his hold, lunging forward. Henry jerked him back. His arms tightened around Asher's torso.

"Enough, Ash," Henry said.

When teachers descended on us a moment later, John Thomas was still lying on the ground bleeding. He was still *smiling*. He caught my eyes, and I could practically hear him gloating, *You're not the only one who can execute a plan.*

CHAPTER 24

Asher was suspended for two weeks. He was lucky he wasn't expelled. Enough people had seen the fight to paint a consistent picture: Asher had thrown the first punch. John Thomas hadn't even fought back. Fewer of us had heard John Thomas goading Asher into the fight.

When the headmaster had asked Emilia if John Thomas had been bothering her, she'd shaken her head. She didn't meet Asher's eyes. She didn't say a word.

No amount of explaining could compensate for that.

Asher caught her on the way out of the headmaster's office. "Em—"

"Don't," Emilia told him forcefully. I translated: *Don't ask her what John Thomas had been talking about. Don't ask her why she hadn't answered the headmaster's question with a yes.* "You finally got yourself suspended," she snapped at Asher. "Are you happy now?"

"I was just . . ." Asher started to say, but Emilia didn't let him finish. She put a hand on his chest and pushed him back.

"I didn't ask you to."

A very bruised John Thomas declared himself my partner in Speaking of Words.

Henry came to stand between us. "A real man never just assumes someone wants to be his partner," Henry said, staring at John Thomas with an expression that sent chills down my spine. "A real man asks."

Henry's voice was low and rife with the implication that he wasn't really talking about group projects.

"A real man does not coerce. He does not pressure," Henry continued. "He does not just take what he wants. He *asks*." Henry kept his eyes fixed on John Thomas for a moment longer, then turned to me and demonstrated. "Would you like to work together on this assignment, Kendrick?"

If looks could kill, the one I leveled at John Thomas Wilcox in that moment would have put him six feet under.

"I'd love to," I told Henry, turning my back on the minority whip's son.

Unfortunately, there was an odd number of students in the class, leaving John Thomas free to tack himself onto our group. Clearly, he hadn't taken even one of Henry's words to heart.

He'd taken them as an invitation to spar.

"Shame about Asher," John Thomas said offhandedly. "Guy's always been a little unhinged."

For an instant, I wondered if taking a swing at John Thomas myself might be worth a two-week suspension.

"In a couple of weeks, Asher's suspension will be over." Henry's voice was mild, perfectly controlled. "But you," he continued, looking at John Thomas like he could see into and through him and there was nothing to see, "will continue to be an utter disappointment to anyone who has ever given you the benefit of the doubt."

Disappointment was a word that hit John Thomas where it hurt.

"What about you, Tess?" John Thomas asked, once he'd recovered. "Are you *disappointed*?"

"No," I said. "I don't give the benefit of the doubt to people like you."

There was another brief, tense moment of silence.

"Did you know Hardwicke keeps records?" John Thomas asked, breaking it. "About medications, diagnoses, mental health risks . . ." he trailed off. "You'd be surprised how many girls at this school say they're going to summer camp but actually check in to eating disorder clinics. And your little friend Vivvie?" John Thomas continued. "*She's* an interesting one."

Vivvie had told me once that her freshman year had been a dark time. She hadn't gone into specifics, but I knew antidepressants had been involved.

After everything Vivvie had been through this semester, the idea of John Thomas breathing a *word* about her to anyone was enough to make me wish that Asher had hit him harder.

Henry laid a hand lightly on my shoulder—a reminder that John Thomas was trying to do to me exactly what he'd done to Asher: bait me into a fight, push me to the edge.

Two can play that game. My better self fought briefly against the urge and lost.

"It's funny," I said, meeting John Thomas's gaze. "I saw your father Friday night. He was looking pretty cozy with a woman who wasn't your mother."

"Tess." Henry could fit a world of censure into a single word. *Don't sink to his level. Don't play his game.*

"Red hair," I continued. "Blue dress. Enjoys breathing heavily into your father's hair while he strokes the back of her neck."

John Thomas's face went very still. "You don't know what you're talking about," he said, his voice taut.

"Why don't I ask your father about her?" I leaned forward. "I can tell him you let something slip about their relationship one day in class."

My words hit their target. The look on John Thomas's face told me two things: he knew about his father's relationship with this woman, and Congressman Wilcox knew that he knew.

"He won't believe you," John Thomas said.

"I think we both know that he would, especially once I mention the way you've been shooting your mouth off about Henry's family." I leaned back on the heels of my hands. "*The congressman is very good at paying attention.*" I repeated the words that John Thomas had said to me at the charity event. "You got your information about Henry's family from your father, and something tells me he wouldn't be too happy to find out you're flapping your lips. Knowledge is power," I said lightly, "and here you are, just giving the congressman's away. And for what? Some high school election you're not even going to win?"

I'd only seen John Thomas and his father interact briefly, but that was enough for me to guess that the congressman wouldn't choose to expend even an ounce of political capital on his son's petty high school concerns.

"You'll keep your *mouth shut*," John Thomas gritted.

I smiled. "How hard do you think it would be for me to set up a little chat with the congressman?" I asked rhetorically. John Thomas had struck at Henry and Asher. He'd terrorized Emilia. He'd threatened Vivvie. I wasn't above issuing a threat of my own in return.

"Because the next time you come after one of my friends," I said, leaning forward, placing my face within an inch of his, "I will bury you. And your own father will be the one to throw the dirt on top, because Henry was right." I pitched my voice low, barely more than a whisper and all the more cutting for it. "You are a disappointment."

CHAPTER 25

Henry didn't say a word about the way I'd used Congressman Wilcox as leverage against his son. In exchange, I didn't tell Henry that sometimes people like John Thomas just saw *taking the high road* as *weakness*.

If I had to dirty my hands to convince John Thomas that attacking my friends was a bad idea, then so be it. If I could have punished him for what he'd done to Emilia, what he was *still* doing to Emilia—if I could have made him pay without forcing her into something that she had very clearly communicated that she did not want—I would have, tenfold.

Lunchtime came, but I wasn't hungry. I bypassed eating and ducked into the courtyard. I'd planned on grabbing a table, but my feet kept walking—past the chapel, past the Maxwell Art Center, out to the playing fields. The air was cold in DC in November, but I had Montana in my blood.

The chill didn't bother me any more than the insults of boys like John Thomas Wilcox.

Letting the wind nip at my face, I thought over what I'd said to John Thomas—and his reaction. Ivy had told me once that being a fixer came with a cost. Given what John Thomas had done to Emilia, given what he'd said to Asher and the way he'd smugly announced that Henry's father was an alcoholic, pretending like it *grieved* him to impart the news—

I wasn't going to feel bad about pushing back.

I wasn't going to wonder what kind of person that made me.

Eventually, my face went numb from the wind. I walked back toward the main building, sure of one thing. If John Thomas said a *word* about Vivvie, if he so much as breathed in her direction, if I had to follow through on my threat—

I would.

I headed back to the cafeteria but took the long way. Past the computer labs, past the library—I paused. There was a sound, a high-pitched gurgling, like muddy water through a whistling pipe.

The hallway was empty except for me, the door to the library slightly ajar.

What is that sound?

That was when I saw the liquid oozing out from underneath the door. At first I thought it was water, but then I realized. *It's red.* My heart thudded in my chest. I took a step toward the door. *Red—it's red—thick—*

The door creaked, and *something* spilled into the hallway. It took me a moment to recognize the shape as human and another to recognize it as John Thomas Wilcox. *Hands. Feet. Eyes. Mouth.* All the parts were there, but the whole . . .

Red. Red on his chest. Red on his hands.

The horrible gurgling sound was coming from him.

I leapt forward, jarred out of my horror by the realization that if he was gurgling, if he was wheezing—he was still alive. My brain flipped into hyper gear. His white shirt was soaked in blood beneath his Hardwicke blue blazer. I ripped the blazer open, looking for a wound.

"Help!" The word ripped its way out of my throat, savage and raw. "Somebody, help!"

John Thomas's mouth opened and closed as he gasped for air, that horrible gurgling sound punctuating each gasp.

I tore off my own blazer and pressed it to his chest. *Stop the bleeding. Have to stop the bleeding.* I yelled for help again. I *screamed* for it.

"Shot." John Thomas choked out the word.

He's been shot.

"It's okay," I told him, lying through my teeth. "You're going to be okay."

I could feel his blood on my hands. I could smell it.

"Tell." He managed another word. The gasping increased.

I kept applying pressure with one hand and grabbed my phone out of my pocket with the other. My hand shaking, I dialed 911.

"Didn't." John Thomas gargled the word. He surged upward. He grabbed hold of my shirt. His eyes met mine. "Tell."

A second later, he was sprawled back on the ground, his head lilting to one side, the floor below him soaked in blood.

"What is your emergency?"

On some level, I was aware that the 911 operator was talking on the other end of the phone line. On some level, I remembered making the call. But on another, baser level, all I could think about was the body.

The body that used to be John Thomas Wilcox but wasn't anymore.

No more gasping. No more gurgling. His eyes were vacant.

"What is your emergency?"

"He's dead."

I didn't even realize I'd spoken until the operator responded. "Who's dead?"

"A boy at my school." The words burned my throat. Tears burned my eyes. I couldn't think. I couldn't *breathe.* "Someone shot him. I . . . I tried to help . . . I yelled for help, but no one—"

"Miss, I need you to stay calm. I've got police en route. Do you see any indication that the shooter is still in the area?"

The hall was empty except for me and the body that wasn't John Thomas anymore.

"Has anyone else at your school been shot?" the operator asked. "Is this a spree?"

I don't know.

I wasn't sure whether I just thought the words, or if I actually managed to say them, too. My hand dropped to my side, the phone with it.

Why hadn't anyone come when I'd screamed?

What if John Thomas isn't the only one? I thought. That was enough to spur me into motion. One second I was standing there, my limbs dead weight, and the next, my phone was on the floor, and I was running for the cafeteria.

For Henry and Vivvie.

I broke through the door into a room filled with unnatural stillness. People were huddled in groups. I could hear someone crying.

Multiple someones.

"Tess."

I turned toward Henry's voice. He was here. He was whole. I took a step toward him.

Henry's fine. My brain struggled to process. *They all are.* No one was hurt. No one was screaming.

Henry made it to my side, his stride long and the expression on his face as intense as I'd ever seen it. Something gave inside me.

"Shot." The first word I managed to form was the same one John Thomas had said to me. "Someone shot him."

Henry reached for my shoulder. He squeezed it. "I know."

Someone shot John Thomas Wilcox.

Henry knows.

"You know?" The words came out in a whisper.

"Everyone knows," Henry told me, his voice taut. "I am so sorry. I know your families are close."

Close? My brain struggled to parse what he was saying. *Sorry?*

Sorry that I had been the one to discover the body? Sorry that I yelled and yelled and no one came?

"Dead." I meant to ask questions, but that was all that came out. "He's dead, and—"

"You don't know that," Henry cut in.

Yes. I do.

"Tess." An added layer of strain entered Henry's voice. I followed his gaze down to my hands.

Blood. John Thomas's blood on my hands. Dead. He's dead—

"Tess," Henry repeated, his voice soft, "what happened? Are you hurt?"

"No," I said, and somehow, staring down at my bloody hands, Henry's touch warm through my clothes, the dam broke, and words came rushing out at warp speed. "Someone shot him. I found the body. I yelled for help. I tried—"

Henry ducked to capture my gaze. His mint-green eyes held mine. "Someone shot *who*?" he asked.

"John Thomas Wilcox." I stared at him, my brain processing the fact that Henry *hadn't* known about John Thomas, that he'd been talking about something else.

Someone else.

I heard the sound of sirens in the distance. I stared past Henry to a flat-screen television on a nearby wall.

A reporter was talking into a camera. I couldn't hear her— couldn't hear anything, couldn't feel anything, not my arms or legs, not my tongue in my mouth. But as shock set in and darkness bit at the corners of my vision, I could make out the words on the ticker tape going across the bottom of the screen.

Someone shot him, I'd told Henry.

His reply had been hoarse. *I know.*

I stumbled backward, my hands looking for purchase against the wall as I absorbed the message on the ticker tape. When I'd said *Someone shot him*, I'd been talking about John Thomas Wilcox.

Henry had been talking about President Nolan.

CHAPTER 26

President Nolan has been shot. Someone shot the president. The words played on a loop in my head. They didn't make any more sense sitting on the floor with my back to the wall than they had in the cafeteria.

We were in lockdown. Less than a minute after I'd heard the first siren, all of us were shuffled into classrooms. The lights were turned out. The doors were barred. Guards were posted in the halls.

The Secret Service had removed Anna Hayden from the premises.

I'd ended up in a science classroom. Henry was there. Vivvie, too. Two dozen of our classmates were crammed in with us. Some were crying. Some were frantically texting their families.

Some were looking at me.

The blood was dry on my hands now, but my clothes were still soaked with it. *My pant legs. The cuffs of my shirt. The lapels, where John Thomas had grabbed me.*

John Thomas had been shot, and someone had tried to assassinate the president, and there was blood on my hands.

"What did you see, Tess?"

The whispered question broke through the whir of my thoughts. In the dark, hushed room, I wasn't even sure who'd asked it.

"What happened?"

"Whose blood is that?"

More voices, more questions. I didn't realize I was shaking until Henry laid a hand on the back of my neck.

The questions were just going to keep coming. They would come and come and come, and the answers would always be the same.

Someone shot John Thomas. Someone shot him, and I found him, and—

The guard at the door received a call. "We're clear," he said a moment later. "There's no evidence of a gunman on campus."

The lights came on. The room exploded into conversation, a dull roar that pressed in against my ears. If there wasn't a gunman, if this wasn't the start of some kind of shooting spree— then John Thomas had been the only target.

Someone had wanted him dead.

I will bury you. I remembered saying those words to John Thomas. I remembered meaning them. John Thomas had been making threats—and my gut said that my friends hadn't been the only targets.

Nauseous, I began scrubbing at the dried blood on my hands. The door to the room opened. On some level, I was aware of a police officer stepping into the room. I heard him say my name, but I barely recognized the sound of it. All I could think about was getting rid of the blood.

"Hey," Vivvie said softly, reaching out to grab my wrists. "It's okay. You're okay."

I jerked back from her grasp. She turned to look at Henry, and he stepped forward.

"Tess, these gentlemen need to speak with you," the teacher called from the front of the room.

I would talk to the police. I would tell them everything, just as soon as I got the blood off my hands.

Henry caught one of my wrists in each of his hands. His touch was gentle, but when I tried to break his hold, I couldn't.

"Water," Henry told me. He had an uncanny knack for sounding calm and reasonable no matter the circumstances. "You need water." He guided me over to the emergency shower. He pulled the cord. Water rained down. Slowly, Henry guided my arms into the spray. He ran his hands over mine, gently scrubbing at the blood crusted to my palms, my fingernails.

For a moment, I watched as if from a great distance, his fingers working their way between mine, his skin brown and smooth, mine paler than usual beneath John Thomas's blood.

"I'm okay." If I said the words, I could believe them. I came back to myself, felt Henry's touch on my skin, felt his body next to mine. He seemed to realize, the same second I did, that this was the closest the two of us had ever been.

We both froze. Henry stepped back. I stared down at the pools of red washing into the drain.

"Miss," I heard someone say behind me. "If you'll just come with me, we need to ask you some questions."

Vivvie handed me a stack of paper towels. As I dried my hands—mostly, though not entirely, clean now—Henry eyed the police officer.

"Perhaps you could give her a moment?" he said. That wasn't really a suggestion. Staring down the police officer, Henry slipped off his Hardwicke blazer and began unbuttoning the white collared shirt underneath. It wasn't until he stripped the shirt off that I realized his intent.

"You don't have to," I started to say.

"Kendrick," Henry replied firmly. "Do shut up." He was down to his undershirt now, but he spoke with the polish of someone wearing black tie. Moving efficiently, he handed me his shirt. All too aware that every set of eyes in the class was on the two of us, I turned to the police officers.

"Can I change?" Like Henry, I aimed for a tone that invalidated the question mark at the end of that sentence. The officer gave a curt nod.

"We'll need to bag your shirt."

Bag it. For evidence. That sent another wave of whispered conjectures through the room. With one last glance at Henry and Vivvie, I made my exit. In the bathroom, I took off my own shirt and looked at the unblemished skin underneath. *Clean.* My body was clean. My hands were mostly clean, but I could still *feel* the blood.

I could still smell it.

I slipped on Henry's shirt. It was too big for me. As my fingers struggled with the first button, I breathed in. This time, instead of blood, I smelled the barest hint of Henry.

My fingers made quick work of the rest of the buttons. I didn't even stop at the sink on my way out of the bathroom. I handed my shirt to the police officer.

And then came the questions.

CHAPTER 27

"I was coming back from the playing fields. I entered through the south entrance. I was walking past the library when I heard something. I turned around and saw blood coming out from under the library door. Then the—"

The body. It's just a body now.

"Then John Thomas fell out into the hallway."

I'd been through this a half-dozen times. The detectives kept saying that any information, even the tiniest detail, might help, so we kept walking through it again and again. The officers and I were sequestered in the headmaster's office. Headmaster Raleigh stood in the doorway, presiding over the interview.

"Mr. Wilcox was still alive at this point?" the detective prompted.

I nodded. "He was bleeding. I didn't know at first that he'd been shot, but there was so much blood." I swallowed. I'd been in shock. I wasn't going back down that road. "I knelt next to him and tried to stop the bleeding. He—John Thomas—he said he'd been shot."

"He actually said the words *I've been shot*?"

"No," I said through gritted teeth. "He just said *shot*."

And then he'd said *tell* and then *didn't* and then *tell* again. We'd been over this. And over it. And over it.

"I yelled for help, but no one came."

"As I've mentioned," the headmaster interjected, "news of the assassination attempt on the president had commanded the staff's attention, not to mention that of the other students. There was quite a bit of chaos. Under normal circumstances, I assure you our campus security would have been alerted within seconds."

The police had already sent someone to talk to campus security. There were closed-circuit cameras everywhere at this school. The hope was that the cameras might be able to tell the police what I couldn't—who had shot John Thomas Wilcox.

How did someone even get a gun into the school? That was one of a half-dozen questions echoing through my mind each time I walked through what had happened.

"What were you doing out at the playing fields?" This was the first time one of the detectives had steered the questioning toward what I'd been doing *before* I'd discovered the body.

"Thinking." One word was all I needed to answer the question, so one word was all I used.

The two detectives exchanged a look.

"You said you headed back at about ten to," the one on the left said, looking through his notes. "You discovered John Thomas's body. The 911 call came in at three after the hour."

Thirteen minutes from the time I'd started walking toward the building until I'd dialed 911. Ten minutes of walking, three of yelling for help—and yelling and yelling, and no response.

"Tess, dear." Mrs. Perkins stuck her head into the office. "I talked to Ivy. She's on her way."

The headmaster paled slightly and stepped forward. "Gentlemen, I believe this interview has gone on long enough. The girl has told you what she remembers. I can attest to the fact that the playing fields are a good jaunt from the main building, and Hardwicke has no policy against students walking the campus to think during lunch."

The headmaster came to stand behind me, placing a hand on the back of my chair. "If you have any additional questions," he told my interrogators, "I'm afraid they will have to be asked in the presence of a parent and whatever legal counsel they may choose to employ."

I was a minor. The police hadn't had any qualms about taking my statement about finding John Thomas—but the headmaster's words served as a reminder that they couldn't really question me without Ivy present.

Not about my own whereabouts prior to the murder.

Not about my relationship with John Thomas Wilcox.

Ivy arrived fifteen minutes later. "Are you all right?" she asked, her voice quiet.

I nodded. She recognized that nod as a lie.

I wasn't okay. Standing there, in Henry's oversized shirt, the bottoms of my pants still stained with John Thomas's blood, I wanted nothing more than to hand the reins over to Ivy, to let her *fix* this.

Fix me.

"Ms. Kendrick." One of the officers stood and introduced himself to Ivy. "If you and Tess could bear with us for just a bit longer, we have a few more questions we'd like to ask."

"Tomorrow." Ivy also had a fondness for one-word answers.

That wasn't what the officers wanted to hear.

"With all due respect, Ms. Kendrick, we really need to—"

"You really need to think about the fact that, according to my sources, you've had my minor daughter in questioning for almost an hour—without my permission or a child advocate present. Whatever questions you haven't asked in that time can wait." Ivy looked from one officer to the other, her expression deadly. "She's a child. She's traumatized, she's exhausted, and she's still wearing a dead boy's blood."

Ivy's words had their intended impact: the officers looked distinctly wary *and* they remembered that there was blood on my clothing.

"We'll need those pants," one of the officers said. From the expression on his face, he half expected Ivy to bite his head off for even asking. Instead, Ivy turned to me and nodded. "Bodie's in the hallway. He'll have a change of clothes."

I didn't spend even a second wondering how Bodie had known to bring a change of clothes, or how it was that Ivy's read on the situation was so precise. She'd gotten me out of the room.

After I surrendered the bloodied pants, she took me home.

CHAPTER 28

"Drink this." Ivy handed me a mug filled with warm liquid. My fingers encircled the mug, but I didn't lift it to my lips.

Ivy hadn't asked me to tell her about finding John Thomas. She hadn't cross-examined me. She hadn't called a lawyer or started acting like one herself. She'd sat in the backseat next to me on the car ride home. She'd put an arm around me when we'd arrived at the house and climbed out. She'd made this drink and slid it across the kitchen counter to me.

"Hot chocolate with a splash of coffee." Ivy met my eyes over the mug. "Nora Kendrick's cure for all ills."

I'd spent most of my life thinking that Nora Kendrick was my mother. Swallowing back the rush of emotion that accompanied that thought, I lifted the mug to my lips and let the drink warm me from the inside out.

"Have you heard anything?" I asked Ivy once I'd found my voice. "About President Nolan?"

Ivy turned and began making herself a mug of hot chocolate, too. "I spoke to Georgia." A slight hitch in her voice contradicted her outward calm. "The president is still in surgery. We won't know how extensive the damage is until he gets out."

People died in surgery. They died in surgery all the time.

I could see awareness of that fact in Ivy's eyes. She'd worked on President Nolan's campaign. Whenever he or the First Lady had problems, Ivy was their first call. Georgia treated her like a daughter.

"You haven't asked me," I said, offering her an out from thinking about it, from talking about it, "what I saw."

Ivy turned back to face me, her own coffee mug held between two hands. "Do you want to talk about it?"

Did I want to talk about John Thomas's last gasping moments? About pressing my hands to his chest, trying to staunch the flow of blood? About the moment when his eyes went empty, and his head lolled to the side?

"I hated him." I stared down at my hot chocolate. "The boy who got killed, John Thomas Wilcox—I hated him."

Ivy knew when to keep quiet. I filled the silence, unable to stop talking now that I'd started.

"He was a horrible person. The day I arrived at Hardwicke, he was showing off pictures of the vice president's daughter." I paused and let that pause do the talking about the *type* of photos John Thomas had taken. "She's fourteen. He told her he liked her. He told her she was special, and then he *laughed* at her while he flashed those pictures around.

"This morning, he baited Asher into a fight. He told the entire school that Henry's father was in and out of rehab before he died." The more I talked, the faster the words came. "He texted these pictures of Emilia where she's totally out of it to the whole school. A video, too." I swallowed, remembering the words John Thomas had used to taunt Asher. "He said things about that night. I don't know how much Emilia remembers. I don't know if John Thomas assaulted her, but he enjoyed making her think that he did."

Ivy held her expression carefully constant, but I caught a surge of anger in her eyes.

I closed mine. "An hour before he died, John Thomas told me that he'd accessed Hardwicke's confidential medical files, that he knew who'd been treated for eating disorders and depression and—" I swallowed back the fury that still wanted to come, thinking about the way he'd singled out Vivvie. "He threatened to tell everyone the details."

"What you're saying," Bodie commented from behind me, "is that the kid had enemies."

I wondered how long he'd been standing there, how much he'd heard. I twisted in my seat.

"I'm saying that I'm one of them." I turned back to Ivy. "I threatened him in class this morning. I told him that I would bury him."

And now he was dead. I knew that didn't look good. I couldn't quit thinking about the blood, the empty look in his—

"Hey." Ivy reached across the counter and took my hand in hers. "No amount of hating him caused this."

I nodded, as if I could will myself into believing what she'd said. "Right before you showed up, the police started asking more pointed questions." I met her eyes. "They're not going to have to talk to many people to figure out that John Thomas and I didn't get along."

"Don't worry," Ivy told me. "I'll take care of it."

When Ivy Kendrick said she'd take care of something, she meant it.

"I tried." My voice broke on that word. "When I saw him, I tried to save him. I screamed for help, and no one came. I called 911—"

Ivy came around to my side of the counter. She wrapped her arms around me. For once, I didn't stiffen in her grasp. "If I could take this away," she said, "if I could snap my fingers and go through this for you, feel it for you, I would."

"I'm fine." I managed to form the words, but we both knew that was a lie.

Bodie crossed in front of us, pulled a large glass out of the cabinet, and started rummaging around in the fridge. After a few minutes—and some rather questionable blender use—he put the glass in front of me. "Drink this," he told me.

The liquid in the glass was murky brown.

I eyed Bodie warily.

"Drink," he told me.

"Is that your hangover cure?" Ivy asked him.

Bodie ignored her. He nudged me with his foot. "Drink," he ordered.

I took a gulp of the liquid and almost choked on it. "And the purpose of me drinking this is what exactly?" I asked, grimacing.

"Distraction," Bodie replied. "You're welcome."

Before I could formulate a suitable reply, Ivy's phone rang. She moved to answer it, then let her hand fall back to her side. I could see her thinking, *Tess needs me right now.*

I could also see her wanting to answer.

"Answer it," I told her. "Take the call."

The president was in surgery. There was no way of knowing if he'd make it out alive. Whoever was calling Ivy right now, she needed to pick up.

After a split second of hesitation, Ivy did as I said.

"Georgia. How is he?" Ivy turned and walked out of the room before I could get a sense of Georgia's reply. After a long moment, I turned back to Bodie.

"Take another drink," he advised.

"Very funny." I took a gulp of my hot chocolate instead. "Do they have any idea who shot the president?" I hadn't wanted to ask Ivy, but now that it was just Bodie and me, I couldn't keep the question back.

Bodie didn't respond, but his eyes betrayed the answer. *Ivy* had an idea, one that—if it weren't for me—she'd be following up on right now.

"Does she think this has something to do with Senza Nome?" I asked. "The group that targeted Walker Nolan, the group Daniela Nicolae works for—does Ivy think they're involved?"

Before Bodie could answer—or tell me to stop asking questions—Ivy walked back into the room.

"The president is out of surgery," she said, her voice strangled. "There was a lot of damage. They don't know if . . ." She shook her head, shaking off an unwanted rush of emotion the way a dog shakes water off its fur.

"Go," I said, meeting Ivy's eyes and nodding toward the door. "Whatever Georgia needs, whatever she called to ask you to do— just go."

Ivy hesitated. She didn't want to leave, but we both knew she couldn't stay here, holding my hand, when the stakes were this high.

"Bodie can keep you company," Ivy said after a moment. "I'll drive myself."

Ivy wasn't known for her driving prowess—and given that we were talking about an *assassination attempt*, I didn't want her out there alone.

"Don't be stupid, Ivy. Take Bodie with you."

She bristled. "Tessie, I'm not leaving you alone after what you've been through today."

I didn't tell Ivy my name was *Tess*, not *Tessie*. I didn't tell her I could take care of myself.

"I'll call Vivvie," I countered instead. "She was born to slumber party. We'll be fine."

Ivy was quiet for a second, maybe two, as she turned that possibility over in her head. "I love you," she said. "More than anything. You know that, right?"

"Sure." I didn't want those words to affect me the way they did. I didn't want them to mean that much. I didn't want them to hurt.

"I mean it, Tessie. If it came down to the rest of the world or you, I would pick you every single time."

Tears I'd kept at bay all day stung my eyes. "Be careful," I told her, my voice fierce.

She ran her hand over my hair one last time, then turned and walked to the door, her heels clicking a steady beat against the marble floor. "I always am."

CHAPTER 29

"I would ask if you're okay, but at this point, that seems a little passé." Vivvie gave me a very small smile. Seconds ticked by, and she just couldn't help herself. "Are you okay?" she blurted out.

"Yeah," I said. "I'm okay."

Vivvie peered at me. "Does that mean that you're actually okay, or that you're stoically projecting that you will be okay at some undefined point in the future?"

I bit back a smile. Vivvie was Vivvie, no matter the circumstances. "Probably the second one," I admitted.

"You do stoic well," Vivvie told me. "Does Stoic Tess want to talk about it or not want to talk about it?" After a second or two, she answered her own question. "Not talk about it," she said, translating the expression on my face. "I can do that." She paused. "Just to clarify, does *it* include the attack on the president? Or just . . ."

She didn't say John Thomas's name.

"Ivy's out there right now, doing who knows what," I said. Not thinking—and not talking—about the attack on the president wasn't an option. I could only suppress so much. "She got a call from the First Lady," I continued.

Vivvie's eyes widened. "Did she say—"

"Ivy didn't say what Georgia wanted. She didn't say anything about who they think is responsible for shooting the president."

Senza Nome. The name Priya had given the terrorist group echoed in my head, followed on its heels by Daniela Nicolae's ominous words. *The time for waiting is over.*

We'd thought the video Daniela Nicolae had made was about the hospital bombing. We thought that she had failed in her mission.

Maybe we'd thought wrong.

"You've got that look on your face," Vivvie told me. "The one you get when you're thinking about something you probably shouldn't be thinking about."

Vivvie's aunt had sent her out of the room before she'd passed on the message about Senza Nome. Whether I liked it or not, the less Vivvie knew, the safer she was.

On some level, I recognized that my reasoning sounded exactly like Ivy's.

"Henry and I were talking the other day." I felt like I needed to tell Vivvie something true, even if it wasn't the truth I most wanted to share. "About the way that things like this hit us harder than they hit other people because of what we've already lost." I paused, searching Vivvie's dark brown eyes the way she'd searched mine earlier. "Are *you* okay?"

"I should be," Vivvie offered with an uneven smile that wavered as she spoke. "I didn't like John Thomas. I didn't see it happen, like you did. And it's not like I actually *knew* the president, but . . ." She caught her bottom lip between her teeth. "My dad was President Nolan's doctor. He saw him every day, and I just keep thinking . . ." Vivvie's voice got softer the more she spoke. "I just keep thinking that if my dad were alive, if he'd never gotten involved with the conspiracy, never done what he did to Justice Marquette—my dad would be there, with the president, working to save his life."

Vivvie looked down at her hands, folded in her lap. "And then," she continued, "I think about how if my dad were here, I'd make dinner and put it in the refrigerator so he'd have something to eat when he got home. And I think about the fact that if my dad were here, he'd be worried about me. He'd be in doctor mode one minute and dad mode the next, and he'd call me when he could and tell me that it was normal to feel grief when someone you know is killed, even if you didn't like the person. He'd tell me that it was okay to be scared that something like that could happen at my school, and he'd tell me not to worry." Vivvie pressed her eyes closed, and I knew that she was counting on her eyelids to hold back tears. "He'd tell me that he would never let anything bad happen to me."

My heart twisted as she whispered those words. Vivvie was the one who'd discovered her father's involvement in Justice Marquette's death. When he'd found out that she knew his secret, he'd hit her.

"You miss him," I said softly.

"I shouldn't." Vivvie was vehement. "I know what he was. I know what he did. I shouldn't miss him."

I tried to catch her gaze but failed. "He was your dad."

Vivvie wrapped her arms around me in a strangling-tight hug. We stayed like that until she pulled back.

"So," Vivvie said, wiping a tear roughly off her face with the back of her hand. "We've established that you're not okay and that I'm not okay. Would it be weird to suggest we could be not-okay while baking cookies?"

I pushed back against the memories and buried the secrets as far in my psyche as they would go. "Cookies it is."

CHAPTER 30

I woke up in the middle of the night. On the other side of my queen-size bed, Vivvie was out like a light. Restless and unable to even think about going back to sleep, I slipped out of bed and made my way to the door. I kept thinking about John Thomas. About his blood on my hands. About his final words.

Tell, he'd wheezed. *Didn't.* And then: *Tell.*

What had John Thomas been trying to say?

Was he asking me to tell someone that he *didn't* do something? Or was he saying that *he* hadn't told?

Told what? I paced as I thought. The light wasn't on in the living room, so it took me a moment to realize that Ivy was sitting on the sofa.

"Tess." Ivy's voice was hoarse. "What are you doing up?"

"I could ask you the same thing," I said. When she didn't reply, it occurred to me that she might have gotten news.

Bad news.

"The president—" I started to say.

"No change in his condition." Ivy's voice was emotionless. "They're not sure when he'll wake up."

Or if he'll wake up. My brain supplied the words that Ivy wouldn't say.

"Vice President Hayden was sworn in as acting president." Ivy's tone never changed. "Senza Nome has claimed responsibility for the attack."

I crossed the room and sat down next to her. "You're going to see the terrorist they arrested, aren't you?" I asked quietly. "Daniela Nicolae. You're going to find out what she knows about the attack."

I knew Ivy. She couldn't *make* the president wake up. But she could hunt down every single person involved in this assassination attempt. Whatever she had to do to get in a room with Nicolae, to interrogate her about Senza Nome—Ivy would do it.

"Tessie—" Ivy broke off, unable to say more than my name.

I wanted to tell her that it was okay. I wanted to tell her that I understood that there were some things she couldn't tell me. I wanted it not to matter.

But it did.

It always would, with Ivy and me.

"Do you think Walker told Daniela something without realizing it?" I asked, throwing the question out into the void. "Do you think the president's son is the reason Senza Nome was able to pull off this attack?"

There was another long silence, just like I knew there would be. *Stop it,* I told myself. *Stop asking. Stop pushing. Just stop—*

"I don't think Walker knew enough about his father's security detail or Secret Service protocol to give Senza Nome the information they would have needed to make this happen." Ivy gave me one sentence—just one.

She gave me what she could.

"Walker didn't have that information." I repeated what Ivy had told me, then read between the lines. "But Senza Nome would have had to get it from somewhere."

CHAPTER 31

The next day was midterm elections. Hardwicke canceled school. Vivvie went home. There was still no official update on the president's condition. My mind awash in what Ivy had told me, I went in for questioning in John Thomas's murder.

"How would you describe your relationship with John Thomas Wilcox?"

Given everything that had happened in the past twenty-four hours, even being here, answering the detectives' questions about John Thomas, felt surreal.

"John Thomas and I were in the same grade. We had one class together," I said. Ivy had told me to stick to the truth but keep my answers brief. "He struck me as cruel."

Ivy probably wasn't pleased that I'd volunteered that information, but I didn't see the point in pretending that I hadn't found John Thomas reprehensible. If the police hadn't already heard that I didn't like the guy, they undoubtedly would soon.

"Cruel how?" the detective on the left asked.

Before I could answer, the door to the interrogation room opened and a man in an expensive suit strode in. He had the air of a person who was used to making an entrance.

"Tyson." Ivy greeted him, a slight narrowing of her eyes my only clue that she wasn't pleased to see him.

"Ivy," he returned smoothly before turning to the detectives. "Brewer Tyson," he said, introducing himself like his name held the strength of an argument in and of itself. "I'm representing Ms. Keyes."

Without waiting for an invitation, Tyson took a seat next to Ivy.

"I was under the impression that you had not hired counsel," one of the detectives told Ivy.

She'd discussed this with me. She had a law degree. She could serve as my guardian *and* my attorney—and use the fact that we hadn't hired someone to send the message that I had nothing whatsoever to hide.

"I didn't," Ivy said, eyes on Tyson, "hire an attorney."

"I work for Ms. Keyes's grandfather," the lawyer volunteered. "I'm merely here to ensure that things go smoothly for everyone involved." Brewer Tyson folded his hands on the table. "Shall we proceed?"

There was a second or two of silence, during which I thought Ivy might actually kick the kingmaker's lawyer out of the room, but instead she turned, closemouthed, back to the detectives.

"You were getting ready to tell us why you considered John Thomas Wilcox to be a cruel person," one of the detectives said.

"Was she?" Tyson asked. "I'll advise my client," he said, his gaze going briefly to me before returning to my interrogators, "that she is under no obligation to answer that question."

"It's okay," I said. "I'll answer. John Thomas liked to hurt people." I stuck to simple, declarative sentences. "He picked on younger kids, anyone he saw as weak. He especially liked playing games with girls."

"What kind of games?" the detective on the right asked.

I measured my reply. "He liked pictures. Taking them. Sharing them. He made a lot of innuendos. He'd get in your personal space, touch you when you didn't want to be touched."

"Did he ever lay hands on you?" the officer on the left asked. "Did he *play games* with you?"

Maybe they were just trying to establish the facts—or maybe they were trying to establish motive. Either way, I stayed calm as I replied. "He grabbed my arm a few times when I wasn't appropriately cowed by who he was and what his father did. But that was it."

The detective laid a picture on the table. *Emilia, slumped against the bathroom wall.* "We were able to trace this picture to a disposable cell phone in John Thomas Wilcox's possession."

That wasn't a question, so I didn't reply.

"Would you consider this girl to be one of John Thomas's targets?"

This girl. Emilia didn't even get a name.

"I understand that this picture was distributed to the whole school," the detective continued. "Was that why Asher Rhodes attacked John Thomas?"

For the first time, I had to work to stay calm. "You'd have to ask Asher," I said.

The detective who'd asked the question leaned forward. "I understand that you witnessed the attack."

The attack. The way he referred to it set my teeth on edge.

"John Thomas incited that fight on purpose," I said. "He baited Asher."

"And why would John Thomas Wilcox do that?" the detective pressed.

"To prove that he could."

There was a beat of silence. "If that's all you have to ask my client," Tyson put in, "let's wrap this up."

The last thing the detectives wanted was to "wrap this up" so soon.

"Would you say that Asher Rhodes has a temper?" the one who'd asked me about the fight said. "Is he easy to provoke into violence?"

"No." The response came out sharper than I'd meant it to, so I forced myself to tone it back a notch before continuing. "Asher is very easygoing. A little goofy." I searched for a better way to describe Asher. "Kind."

"Then why rise to the bait?" the officer asked. "What could our victim have possibly said that could justify—"

I snapped. "John Thomas told Asher that he'd slept with his sister. He said that if Emilia claimed she didn't want it, that was a lie." Those words hung in the air. My tone was low and deadly. "Like I said, John Thomas liked to hurt people." I paused. "I despised him. He was a bully and a coward and I didn't think he was worth the breath it took to say his name. But—" I held fast against the memories that wanted to come. "I tried to save him. I tried to stop the bleeding. I yelled for help. I called 911." I never broke eye contact, never slowed or sped up my speech. "I didn't have anything to do with John Thomas's murder. And neither did

Asher. He was suspended yesterday. He wasn't even on campus when John Thomas was shot."

There was a beat of silence.

"We're done here," the lawyer said, gathering his things. I glanced at Ivy. She gave a slight nod. I stood.

"To be clear," one of the detectives said, standing as he spoke, "Ms. Kendrick Keyes is not a suspect in John Thomas Wilcox's murder. Surveillance footage taken just outside the Hardwicke library confirms her statement about how and when she discovered the body."

It was not lost on me that they had waited to point out that I wasn't a suspect until now. They'd probably hoped that I would point the finger at someone else if I thought that they suspected me.

They'd probably hoped that I would jump at the opportunity to tell them Asher was a violent, violent boy.

"What about security footage from inside the library?" I asked. If security had caught the shooter on camera, the police wouldn't have been sitting here cross-examining me. And that meant either that John Thomas's killer hadn't been caught on camera, or the footage had been erased.

"I'm afraid we're not at liberty to discuss the details of this case."

I hadn't been holding my breath that they would.

"One last thing, Tess," the quieter of the two detectives said, using my name in what I suspected was an attempt to put me at ease. "Can you identify this young man?"

Another photograph was placed on the table. It was a bit grainier than the photo of Emilia, like it had been obtained by freezing a frame of video surveillance footage. It had been taken in the courtyard. I could see the Hardwicke chapel in the background.

Even from a distance, I recognized Asher's red hair, the set of his features.

My eyes were drawn to the time stamp on the video.

"Asher Rhodes may have been sent home yesterday morning, but he came back to campus." The detective confirmed what I was seeing. "This footage puts him at Hardwicke just prior to the murder."

I tried not to let the question—or the sickened feeling in the pit of my stomach—show on my face. *What were you thinking, Asher? What were you doing at Hardwicke?*

The detective leaned forward. "Is it your testimony that Asher Rhodes believed that John Thomas Wilcox had assaulted his sister?"

Opportunity.

Motive.

If I'd realized Asher had been on campus that afternoon, I wouldn't have given them the latter—not if I could have helped it.

"I don't know," I said, my mind racing as I stared at the time stamp on that picture. "You'd have to ask Asher."

CHAPTER 32

As I stepped out into the sunshine, Ivy on one side and the lawyer on my other, I went for my phone. Brewer Tyson cleared his throat.

"Calling your friend at this juncture would not be wise," the lawyer said.

I understood that it might not look good if phone records showed that I'd contacted Asher as soon as the police finished with me. But I needed to talk to Asher. I needed to ask what he'd been doing on campus.

I needed to warn him.

"Visiting your friend," the lawyer continued, "would also not be wise. You should plan on giving Mr. Rhodes a wide berth for the time being."

It wasn't in me to give any friend a "wide berth"—especially one who might be in trouble.

"Shockingly," I told Brewer Tyson, "you don't get a vote about who I talk to or who I see."

The lawyer glanced at Ivy. "She sounds just like you."

Ivy narrowed her eyes at him. "Your presence is no longer required," she said tersely. "And tell Keyes that the next time he blindsides me like this, he won't like the outcome."

Ivy didn't wait for a response before guiding me to the car.

"He's right," she said quietly once the lawyer was out of ear-shot. "I know that Asher is a friend, Tess, and I know it goes against everything in you to stay away from a friend at a time like this, but I don't trust the police. The surveillance footage might have convinced them that you didn't shoot John Thomas, but I don't want them wondering if you helped plan it."

"Asher had *nothing* to do with this," I said. "I have no idea what he was doing back on campus, but Asher didn't shoot John Thomas."

"I'm not saying that he did," Ivy replied. "But we both know that Hardwicke is more secure than most of the Hill. There's no way a visitor could have gotten a weapon into the school, and that means the police will be looking at students."

Ivy pinned me with a look. "There will be pressure to close this case and close it fast. I won't let you get caught in the crosshairs." Ivy walked around to the passenger side of the car. "I'll do what I can for Asher, Tess, but I need you to steer clear."

Before I could reply, Ivy had climbed into the front seat of the car and closed the door behind her, taking it for granted that she'd been heard and understood and that her dictate would be obeyed.

I climbed into the backseat and shut the door—a little harder than necessary.

"Georgia called." Bodie directed those words to Ivy, not me. "She's holding a press conference at the hospital."

And just like that, helping Asher was on the back burner. Within an instant, Ivy was dialing and on the phone. "Jason. Put Georgia on. I don't care if she's busy. She is not addressing the American public until I can verify that she is in a place, mentally, where she can handle the questions they are going to throw at her."

Fifteen minutes later, Bodie pulled up to the hospital where the president was being treated. From what I'd gathered based on Ivy's side of her conversation with the First Lady, this press conference *was* happening, whether Ivy liked it or not.

"Tessie?" Ivy was already halfway out the door when she remembered I was in the car. "I meant what I said about Asher. You can't call him, you can't go over to his house, you can't e-mail—not until things die down."

I tried to imagine someone telling *Ivy* that she had to stay away from a friend at a time like this.

"You need to trust me on this one, Tess. I told you I would take care of this situation—take care of you—but you have to let me."

"*Trust,*" I repeated sharply, unable to keep a wealth of emotion from marking that word.

"Fine. You don't have to trust me," Ivy corrected, her voice tight. "You just have to listen to me." She turned around in her seat, pinning me with an intense stare. "This is a high-profile murder investigation. I will do whatever I have to do to protect you, even if I have to protect you from yourself."

The last time Ivy had decided I needed to be protected from myself, she'd thrown me on a private jet and shipped me off to Boston. The great Ivy Kendrick didn't mess around, and she didn't bluff.

"I need your word that you won't try to get in touch with Asher," she told me. "And if you won't give me your word, I need your phone."

Give me your word or give me your phone. That was an ultimatum.

"You don't get to tell me what to do," I snapped back. "You don't get to make this kind of decision for me." I meant to stop there. "You don't get to make *any* decisions for me, not ever."

There was a moment of stark silence. Ivy didn't flinch, didn't argue, didn't so much as raise an eyebrow. "Your word or your phone," she repeated.

Bodie caught my eyes in the rearview mirror. If there was understanding in his eyes, there was a warning, too.

I was treading on thin ice.

"Fine," I said tersely, my fingers closing around my phone. "You have my word. I won't call Asher. I won't e-mail him. I won't go see him."

A second later, Ivy was gone.

As Bodie pulled away from the curb, I gritted my teeth. When I'd given William Keyes my word that I'd let him into my life if he saved Ivy's, I'd kept it. When I'd told Emilia I owed her a favor, I'd paid it back in full. I kept my promises.

Ivy was the one who broke hers.

"Some people would tell you that you can't keep punishing her forever," Bodie said. "But they'd be underestimating your dedication to the cause."

"I'm not punishing her," I insisted. I just couldn't make myself forget. I could never predict when the wound would break back open.

She promised me I could come live with her, and then she left me. She was my mother, and she left—

"If Asher were *her* friend," I said, cutting that thought off as wholly as I could, "if *she* knew a friend was in trouble—Ivy wouldn't stay away."

"Can't argue with that logic," Bodie admitted. "Pretty sure I've *been* that friend. But them's the breaks, kitten. She's the adult. You're the kid." Bodie pulled into a parking space and scanned the growing crowd in front of the hospital.

Georgia's press conference was starting soon. As angry as I was with Ivy, I couldn't keep from thinking about the way that Daniela Nicolae had promised that the time for waiting was over. *First the bombing, then the president.*

And now Ivy was up there at the First Lady's side.

Forcing myself to stay calm, I made a call and lifted my phone to my ear.

"Breaking that promise of yours already, kitten?" Bodie asked.

"No," I said. "You're going to watch Ivy's back, and I'm getting a ride home."

CHAPTER 33

As I climbed into the passenger seat of Henry Marquette's car, his eyes met mine. The last time he'd seen me, I'd been covered in John Thomas's blood.

The last time I'd seen him, he'd been stripping off his own shirt for me to wear.

Henry didn't ask me if I was okay. Instead, he gave me a sardonic look. "Had I realized the position of getaway driver was a permanent one, I would have brushed up on my defensive-driving technique."

I shrugged. "At least this time the car is yours."

"Let that be a lesson to me," Henry said as he pulled into traffic. "Never steal a car for a terrifying girl."

In my memory, I could see Henry's hands covering mine, washing the blood from them in the spray.

"Care to share what, precisely, we are *getting away* from?" Henry asked.

"Sorry," I retorted. "That information is classified."

Henry snorted. "If you were any other girl, I would think you were joking."

"If I were any other girl," I replied, "I would be."

An expression I couldn't quite read crossed Henry's face. "Based on where I picked you up, I take it that Ivy is assisting the First Lady with something?"

"A press conference," I said. "I'm guessing Georgia wants to send a message."

Georgia Nolan was honey-sweet, Southern, and formidable in the extreme. I could imagine the kind of message she would want to send to her husband's attackers. *The United States does not negotiate with terrorists. We do not fear them.* Two days ago, the president's words had fallen flat, but now my eyes stung just thinking about them. *The war on terror is one we* will *win.*

Georgia wasn't the type to back down from a fight.

Neither am I, I thought, and I focused on *my* fight. "I went down to the police station this morning," I told Henry. "The detectives asked a lot of questions about Asher."

Henry didn't need me to spell it out for him. "Asher fought with John Thomas that morning."

"And apparently, something brought Asher back to campus that afternoon."

Henry processed that information in a heartbeat. "There are a lot of people at Hardwicke who might have had reason to want John Thomas dead."

That was Henry's way of saying that Asher didn't do this— but *someone* did.

"Say you had motive," I told Henry, thinking out loud. "Say that John Thomas had hurt you, say that he was threatening you or blackmailing you or that he knew something that you didn't want other people to know . . ." I thought of John Thomas, claiming that he'd accessed Hardwicke's medical records. I thought of the way he'd taken pictures of Emilia and Anna Hayden and who knew how many other girls. "If you *knew* that Asher had punched John Thomas, you'd know that the police would consider Asher a major suspect."

"Especially," Henry added, "if you could lure him back to the school. I take it you've spoken with Asher?"

"No," I said, steeling myself for his reaction. "Ivy made me promise I wouldn't."

I expected Henry to snap, the way he had the last time Ivy had told me to stay out of something. Instead, he just raised an eyebrow. "Did she make you promise that *I* wouldn't?" he asked.

"No," I replied, catching on quickly. "As a matter of fact, she did not."

I might have been a person who kept her word—but I was also the type to look for loopholes.

Henry waited until he got to another red light and then he picked up his phone, set it to speaker, and called Asher.

No answer. Instead, we got Asher's voice mail. *"You've reached Asher Rhodes. I'm off being interrogated for crimes I didn't commit, but if you leave your name and number, I will get back to you as soon as possible."*

"At least he hasn't lost his sense of humor," I said.

Henry wasn't amused. "Asher would have a sense of humor on the way to the gallows." Henry dialed another number. This one went to voice mail, too.

"Hello! You have reached the magnificent sister of Asher. She is unavailable at the moment, quite possibly because she has realized I reprogrammed her voice mail and is off planning my imminent—"

A call came in, and Henry answered, cutting off the voice mail. "Emilia. Is Asher—"

"In way, way over his head?" Emilia filled in. "Yes. He's down at the police station." Emilia swallowed audibly on the other end of the line, but when she spoke again, her voice was steady. "I accidentally left my phone in the courtyard yesterday. Someone texted Asher, pretending to be me. They said that I needed him, and because my brother is an idiot who specializes in idiocy that could get him expelled, he came running back."

Whoever had shot John Thomas had wanted Asher on campus. They'd wanted Asher to take the fall. And they'd known that Asher would literally jump off a cliff for his twin.

"We will find out who did this," I told Emilia. That was a promise—to Henry, to Emilia, to myself.

There was a long silence on the other end of the line. When Emilia spoke again, all trace of emotion had been banished from her voice. "You'll try."

CHAPTER 34

Hardwicke resumed classes the next day.

"My aunt thought they'd cancel for the rest of the week, at least," Vivvie told me as the two of us filed into the Hardwicke chapel for an all-school assembly.

I'd thought the same, but apparently the powers that be at Hardwicke had other plans.

"How was the police station?" Vivvie asked, lowering her voice.

"The good news is that they don't suspect me." I'd never been the type to mince words. "The bad news is that they suspect Asher."

"Asher wouldn't hurt anyone," Vivvie said fiercely. "I mean, he repeatedly face-punched John Thomas, obviously—but other than that, he would *never* hurt someone."

"I know," I said. And I did. I knew that Asher hadn't gone home and gotten a gun. I knew that he hadn't put a bullet in John Thomas's chest.

"Settle, please. Everyone, settle down." Headmaster Raleigh's voice was strong, but his face was morose. For once, the room quieted almost instantaneously. "Here at Hardwicke, we've had a difficult couple of days," the headmaster said. "Many of us are just now coming to understand the enormity of our loss."

In the pew behind me, I heard a couple of girls take jagged breaths. On the opposite side of the room, one or two of John Thomas's friends were bent over, hollow-eyed and ready to punch something.

"John Thomas Wilcox was a bright young man with his whole future in front of him," the headmaster continued. "When he transferred here as a freshman, he immediately began leaving his mark on this school and on each of us. He was a model student, a natural leader, and a wonderful friend."

Already, I could feel the collective memory shifting, as people remembered the good times and forgot everything else. This was the John Thomas most of our classmates would remember: a well-liked guy who knew how to take a joke and how to deliver one. An athlete. An honors student. A life full of potential, cut down too soon.

Across the room, Emilia sat between Maya and Di. As the headmaster spoke, she stared straight ahead, never blinking, her hands gripping each other tightly in her lap.

"In the coming days," Headmaster Raleigh continued, "there will be some changes at Hardwicke. We will be doubling our on-campus security and reviewing all protocols to ensure student safety. Until further notice, students are asked to remain in the main building at all times. If you have information that might be of help to the police, I urge you to speak with your parents and come forward as soon as possible."

• • •

I caught up with Emilia in the girls' bathroom. Her hands were wrapped around the edge of the sink. Her head was bowed, her knuckles white.

"Sitting through that couldn't have been easy," I told her. I leaned back against the bathroom door, making sure no one else could come in and catch Emilia with her armor off.

"Sitting through what?" Emilia shot back. "The beatification of John Thomas Wilcox, or the stares from people I've gone to school with my whole life who think that my brother might have done this?"

I sensed that was a rhetorical question.

Emilia turned to look at me. "If I told you to go away, is there even the least chance you'd listen?"

I let my arms dangle next to my side. "Unlikely."

Emilia forced herself to stand up straight. She turned to face me head-on. "I tried to figure out who took my phone," she said, banishing all hint of vulnerability. "I left it in the courtyard Monday morning." Clearly, Emilia didn't want to talk about her *feelings*. "Someone turned it into the office that afternoon, but no one in the office could remember who."

I couldn't force Emilia to let me in, so I followed her lead and focused on the facts. "John Thomas told me he'd gotten ahold of Hardwicke student files," I said. "The kind of files that contained confidential medical information."

"And this is the boy people are mourning," Emilia said, her voice going hollow. "A model student. A natural leader. A wonderful friend."

The look in Emilia's eyes when she repeated the headmaster's words from that morning reminded me that John Thomas hadn't just enjoyed power. He'd enjoyed making other people feel powerless.

"We need to figure out who at this school had reason to want John Thomas dead," I said quietly.

"Besides me, you mean?"

"Emilia—"

"Don't handle me with kid gloves, Tess." Emilia's fingers curled, driving her nails into her palms. "Say what you mean." Emilia stared at me so hard I could feel the weight of her stare on the surface of my skin.

"You weren't the only one he took pictures of." That much I could say without betraying any confidences—or forcing anything out of her that she wasn't ready to give.

Emilia was silent for four or five seconds before she spoke. "If I were going to guess where one might look for people who knew John Thomas Wilcox for who and what he was," she said quietly, "that social media experiment of yours wouldn't be a bad place to start."

I Stand With Emilia.

Emilia stared at me for a second longer, then turned back to the sink. "This case is going to get national attention. My parents hired a lawyer, but the kind of lawyer we can afford isn't going to be enough." She pressed her lips together. "He was the whip's son, Tess, and Asher is nobody."

I knew, in that moment, that Emilia wasn't just talking about Asher.

"I'll get Asher a lawyer," I promised her. "I'll do whatever it takes." Emilia rinsed her hands methodically and then lifted her gaze to the mirror. At first I thought she was checking her makeup, but then I realized that she was studying her own expression—removing all hints of weakness.

"You don't have to be okay right now," I told her. "Whatever you're feeling—it's okay to feel that way."

Emilia pushed past me. She reached for the door, then paused. "What is it you even think that I'm feeling?" she said, her voice quiet but cutting. "Am I supposed to be sad? Or maybe in shock? Maybe I'm supposed to be spiraling downward. But I'm not. I'm not sad, and I'm not in shock, and I'm not spiraling." She glanced back at me. "You worry about my brother and finding out who wanted John Thomas dead," she ordered. "Because I'm *fine*."

In between second and third period, I called Ivy. *No answer.*

In between third and fourth period, I called Ivy. *No answer.*

At lunch, I called William Keyes. He answered. I asked him what it would take to get someone from Tyson Brewer's firm to represent Asher. There was a pause on the other end of the line as my grandfather processed the fact that I was asking for a favor.

"Just say the word, Tess," Keyes told me. "All you have to do is ask, and I can get your friend an entire team of defense lawyers, the best in the country, free of charge."

Free of charge to Asher, maybe, I thought. Accepting this favor would undoubtedly cost me.

"Do it."

CHAPTER 35

As it turned out, pinpointing which of my fellow students might have wanted John Thomas dead was significantly harder than putting the best defense lawyers in the country on retainer. Even my reputation as a fixer couldn't loosen lips, not when it came to speaking ill of the dead.

"There's a term that psychologists use to describe our memory of moments that surprise and shock us, the ones where we hear news that rocks us to our core." Dr. Clark stood at the front of my last-period class, looking at us one by one.

"*Flashbulb memories*," Dr. Clark said. "That's what they call memories for large-scale, emotionally significant events. Most Americans who were in elementary school or older on November 22, 1963, can tell you exactly where they were when they heard that President Kennedy had been assassinated." Dr. Clark let those words sink in. "The day the space shuttle *Challenger* exploded," she continued, listing off another flashbulb-memory-provoking event. She swallowed. "September 11, 2001."

These were the dates that lived forever in people's memories—bright and detailed, forever memorialized with a kind of visceral horror. I couldn't remember 9/11, let alone the *Challenger* or the day Kennedy was shot.

Monday, November 6, I thought. *President Nolan. John Thomas. November 6.*

"After the events of the past couple of days," Dr. Clark said, "I've been asking myself what people will remember about this week, this tragedy." She took her time with the words, each hard-won—and even harder to listen to. "Will they remember where they were when President Nolan was shot? Will they remember refreshing news pages, desperately waiting for an update on his condition? Will they remember going to the polls in record numbers, because voting was the only thing they could do? Will they remember the First Lady telling them that her husband had been put in a medically induced coma? Will they remember the look on her face as she *swore* on live television that President Nolan would make it through this, that he was a survivor?"

The room was quiet, silent but for our teacher's voice.

"Will people remember the president's sons standing behind the First Lady at that press conference? Will they recall anything at all about the week leading up to the shooting?"

Dr. Clark shook her head. "I don't have any answers for you. I can tell you," she said, looking out at us—and *through* us, "that I was on an airplane on September 11th. It was a transatlantic flight, my senior year in college. I was studying abroad. I remember landing and getting off the plane. I remember people turning on their phones. I remember the news spreading, slowly, from person to person—and the airport . . ." She closed her eyes. "I remember they had the news on. I remember watching. And I remember thinking that I'd almost flown through New York."

I recognized the rawness in her voice and looked down at the edge of my desk, pushing back against the emotion causing my throat to tighten and my eyes to sting.

"I want you all to take a few minutes," Dr. Clark said, "and write—about Monday, about what you remember, about what you think that other people will remember when they look back on that day. Write about the questions you have, what you're feeling. Write about whatever you'd like."

There was a moment of agonized silence.

"Can we write about John Thomas?" a girl from the front row finally asked. Her voice was wobbly. The question sucked the oxygen out of the room.

That was what the students at this school would remember. *That* was their flashbulb memory—hearing the news about the president, and then being shuffled into lockdown, terrified that there was a gunman loose in the school.

"Write about whatever you'd like," Dr. Clark repeated.

I picked up my pen, but no words came. Beside me, Vivvie was already scribbling. My eyes found their way to Emilia. She was sitting very straight, her hands folded in her lap, her head bowed.

I wondered if there was anyone in this class who would admit on paper that John Thomas's death wasn't a tragedy to them.

"If you'd like"—Dr. Clark's voice broke into my thoughts— "you may break into small groups. If you'd prefer to continue writing, rather than discuss any of this with your classmates, simply remain at your desk."

One look in Emilia's direction told me not to even try to approach her. Instead, I found myself sequestered in a corner of the room with Vivvie and Henry.

"We're looking for someone who's a part of the Hardwicke community." I didn't bother beating around the bush. Dr. Clark wanted us to deal with this tragedy. This was my way of dealing. "Someone security wouldn't really screen," I continued, "with a grudge against John Thomas."

Vivvie blinked a couple times. Henry, in contrast, clearly hadn't been harboring any illusions that we would be using this time to share our feelings.

"If Asher were here," Vivvie said, "he would suggest we assign the perpetrator a code name."

"We don't need a code name," Henry said.

"If Dr. Clark comes by," Vivvie insisted, "it would be better if she didn't hear us talking about *the killer*. Let's talk about . . ." She thought for a moment. "The hedgehog."

Henry wisely chose to keep any objections to himself.

"Fine," I said. "We need to figure out who might have had a motive to *hedgehog* John Thomas. The problem is that people aren't exactly in the mood to talk. Not about the real John Thomas."

"Is this the part where you suggest a highly inadvisable way of putting people in the mood to talk, in hopes that someone can shed light on who the"—Henry glanced at Vivvie—"hedgehog might be?"

"It's funny," I told Henry, drumming my fingers one by one on my knee, "but the moment you said *inadvisable*, I had a thought."

Right now, the student body was still in shock. They were mourning. But grief was a multi-layered thing. Eventually, people needed outlets. Eventually, the floodgates broke.

Maybe if I provided the outlet, the floodgates would break a little sooner.

"Do I want to know what you are planning?" Henry asked.

I smiled. "Probably not."

As soon as class let out, I found Di in the hallway. "I have a proposition for you," I told her.

"A proposition?" Miss Diplomatic Immunity countered. "Or a dare?"

"A dare," I said. Di's eyes sparkled. "I dare you," I continued," to host a party Friday night, and I dare you to invite the entire school."

As far as outlets went, I had confidence that any party Di hosted would be a good one.

"That is not much of a dare." Di's Icelandic accent caught on every other word. She folded her arms over her chest and tilted her head to the side, waiting for me to make things interesting.

I thought on my feet. "I dare you to have the party *here*. At Hardwicke."

"You want me to break into the school and convince our class-mates to do the same?" Di asked, her eyes gleaming. "That is illegal," she continued, "and there is a very good chance we will get caught."

"And?" I prompted.

Di ran a hand over her thick, white-blond braid. The edges of her lips curved up into a wicked smile. "Challenge accepted."

CHAPTER 36

Friday night, Ivy made it home just as I was leaving for the Hardwicke party. I had no idea what she'd spent the past forty-eight hours doing, but I did know that the president was still in a coma.

I knew that Ivy was still on the warpath.

"You look nice." Ivy sounded more suspicious than complimentary as she assessed my outfit. I was wearing black jeans and a loose gray top—both items she'd purchased on my behalf.

"I'm going to a party," I said. There was no point in lying to Ivy—not when the truth would cover my goal for this evening just as well.

"What kind of party?" Ivy asked.

The kind where I'm hoping to gather clues about John Thomas's murder.

I grabbed my phone and house keys and shot Ivy a dry look. "Are we really doing this?"

"The thing where I ask a teenager in my custody where and with whom she's spending the evening?" Ivy countered. "Yes, we really are doing this."

"Henry Marquette is picking me up." I stuck to issuing true statements, one after the other. "Vivvie is meeting us at the party. A lot of people from school will be there. It's been a rough week." That was an understatement, and Ivy knew it. "People need a way to forget," I told Ivy, willing her to think that when I said *people*, I meant me. "Even if it's just for one night."

"Will Asher be there?" Ivy knew me well enough to know that I wasn't exactly the party-going type. She wasn't concerned about me letting loose and getting into typical teenage trouble. She was concerned about ulterior motives.

Smart woman.

"Asher was suspended," I told her. "Half the school thinks he might be a murderer. I really don't think he's going to be making an appearance tonight."

Ivy stared at me for several seconds, assessing the truth of those words.

"Are we done here?" I asked.

Ivy held my gaze for another second or two and then nodded. As I turned toward the door, the expression on her face wavered slightly. She looked tired. *Weary*, I thought. *Brittle.*

And then I saw the bruise on her wrist.

I went very still. The bruise snaked out from underneath her sleeve, purplish blue. *Fresh.* I closed the space between us in a heartbeat.

"You're hurt," I said. I'd been focused on the party, on Asher, on keeping Ivy from figuring out what I was up to. I hadn't registered the fact that she had something to hide, too.

"I'm fine," Ivy told me.

I grabbed her hand as gingerly as I could. "You're not fine."

Ivy with a bomb strapped to her chest. Ivy on the verge of dying, because of me. The memories came suddenly and without warning. I felt like a claustrophobic person in a shrinking room, like there was a weight on my chest that wouldn't let up until it had succeeded in crushing my lungs.

Ivy caught my chin in her hand. "Look at me." She repeated the words, again and again, until my eyes focused. "I'm fine, Tessie," she said softly. "I was trying to get a rise out of someone, and I succeeded. She grabbed my wrist, but I'm fine."

She.

"You went to see Daniela Nicolae," I said. I'd known that Ivy had intended to interrogate the terrorist. I'd known she wanted answers. "You went to see a known terrorist and deliberately baited her into hurting you?" My voice went up a notch in volume and pitch.

Ivy tucked a strand of hair behind my ear and then let her hand fall away from my face. "I was trying to bait her into *talking*," Ivy clarified. "The physical attack took me by surprise."

There was enough grit in Ivy's voice to tell me that Daniela Nicolae wouldn't be taking her off guard again.

"Did she tell you anything?" I asked. "About Senza Nome?"

About who shot the president?

Ivy's expression went dangerously neutral, impossible to read.

She told you something, I thought. *Something that upset you. Something you think might be dangerous for me to hear.*

"Enjoy your party, Tessie." Ivy shut the door on that topic of conversation. "Go. Be a normal teenager for once."

I didn't tell her that given what she did—and what I had every intention of doing tonight myself—*normal* was probably a relative term.

CHAPTER 37

"You have barely said a word since I picked you up, Kendrick."
Henry pulled off the highway and arched an eyebrow at me in
challenge. "Meditating on the wisdom of attending a party that
requires both breaking *and* entering?"

I'd been quiet because I'd been thinking about Ivy. About the
bruise on her wrist. About what she'd done to get it.

I was trying to get a rise out of someone, and I succeeded.

"Tess?" Henry used my first name rarely enough that I
couldn't keep my eyes from flickering toward his. In the instant
before I looked away, I got the sense that he saw more in mine
than I meant for him to.

"What's a little B-and-E between friends?" I said lightly.

I waited for Henry to make some kind of comment about my
fondness for felonies. "As your *friend*," he said instead, lingering briefly on the word, "am I allowed to ask where you were a
moment ago? What you were thinking?"

A month ago, Henry wouldn't have asked.

A month ago, I wouldn't have answered.

"Ivy went to see the terrorist behind the hospital bombing."

I could see the gears in Henry's head turning as he processed that information. My heart thudded against my rib cage. I hadn't planned on telling him—on telling anyone—this.

I had always been better at keeping other people's secrets than sharing my own.

"Ivy had a bruise on her wrist." I kept my sentences short. "I saw it. I asked her about it."

Henry read between the lines. "I am going to go out on a limb and wager that Ivy was not in what one would call a *sharing mood* about the bruise—or the terrorist."

I could have snorted. I could have made a wry comment about the fact that the phrases *Ivy Kendrick* and *sharing mood* didn't belong in the same sentence.

Instead, I found myself saying, "Ivy told me that she was trying to get a rise out of the terrorist. I think she was hoping she could bait the woman into saying something about the attack on President Nolan."

There was a beat of silence.

After the hospital bombing, I hadn't told Henry that I suspected Walker Nolan was in some way involved. I hadn't ever told him that Ivy thought there might be a fourth player in his grandfather's death. In the short time we'd known each other, the things I hadn't told Henry Marquette were legion.

But he was there, and he was listening, and all I could think about was Henry playing my partner in crime in the front seat of Bancroft's car, Henry washing the blood from my hands the day John Thomas was killed.

"The group that claimed responsibility for the attack against the president?" I said, letting my eyes linger on his. "The intelligence community calls them Senza Nome. The Nameless. They specialize in government infiltration."

Henry pulled the car to a stop in a residential area about a mile away from the school. His hand hovered over the key for a moment before he turned it, killing the engine.

"I don't suppose Ivy volunteered any additional information," Henry said, his face moonlit through the dash. "About this Senza Nome."

I looked out the window at the darkness enveloping the neighborhood around us. "Ivy doesn't volunteer much."

There was another long silence, and in that silence, Henry's hand made its way to the very edge of mine.

I couldn't make myself pull back.

"Do you have any idea what Ivy was hoping to get out of the terrorist?" Henry asked.

If Henry had said a word—a single word—about my relationship with Ivy, I would have decked him. Better, by far, to talk about government conspiracies than *feelings*.

"Ivy said something the other day," I told Henry. "She said that Walker Nolan didn't have the kind of insider information that Senza Nome would have needed to pull off this attack."

"But someone did," Henry filled in.

"Someone did," I repeated. "I think Ivy suspects they might have someone high up in the government, someone close to the president."

Saying the words out loud solidified the thought in my mind. *Infiltration. Assassination.* It made sense.

"Does Ivy have any suspects?" Henry asked quietly.

"I don't know," I said, my hand easing away from his and his from mine. "I don't know what she suspects or what she's planning."

Or if she'll come home with worse than a bruise the next time around.

Before Henry could reply, I opened the car door. I had two choices: sit around and think about what Ivy was doing, or get out of this car and do something myself.

CHAPTER 38

In the process of breaking into my exclusive private school in the dead of night, I learned three things.

First: there were tunnels that ran underneath the school, a vestige of a train station project that had been abandoned before Hardwicke had acquired the land in the early 1900s.

Second: the Hardwicke administration had sealed all the tunnels but one, which had been cleared by the Secret Service as an additional escape route, should the need to get presidential and vice presidential children off campus arise.

And third: the one functional tunnel wasn't *that* hard to breach after hours if you somehow discovered its existence and had a student ID, a begrudging accomplice in the Icelandic Secret Service, and a lack of basic self-preservation as reflected in a willingness to both scale security walls and risk being caught on camera.

By the time Henry and I arrived at the rendezvous point, there was a freshman directing students to the tunnel's hidden entrance. Henry and I descended in silence. The tunnel was dark and lit only by hundreds of glow sticks that someone—presumably Di—had scattered artistically throughout.

Henry knelt down and picked up a hot-pink glow stick. He held it out to me and gave me a dry look. "There is a high level of probability that we will regret this."

I plucked the proffered glow stick from his hands and smiled. "I don't believe in regrets."

When the tunnel forked, signs posted on the wall instructed us to take a right. We followed the instructions—and the sound of music in the distance.

When we finally reached the end of the line and pushed through a metal grate that had been propped open, it took me a moment to realize where the tunnel had let out.

Is that a swimming pool?

"The Aquatic Complex," Henry told me.

"Yeah," I said, glancing around. "I got that."

Stadium seating surrounded us on all sides. An Olympic-sized training pool was set into the floor. Someone had positioned a trio of kegs along one edge. And farther down, near the diving pool, I could make out what appeared to be a bowl of punch and a veritable castle of red plastic cups.

"This is not going to end well," Henry said, eyeing a couple of seniors climbing up to the diving platform, red cups in hand.

As if summoned by the mere thought of something being a bad idea, Di appeared beside us. She had a bottle of champagne in each hand. With an imperious smile, she set one on the ground and opened the other. Champagne fizzed to the top, and Di held it over her head in victory.

"You asked for a party," she told me, over the sound of the music.

"You might want to turn that down," Henry told her.

"Pshaw!" Di gestured rather liberally with the champagne bottle. "This building has walls so thick that it is practically soundproof!"

Forty yards away, one of the senior boys came barreling off the high dive, fully clothed.

Di frowned. "This is an American custom?" she asked.

"Not exactly," I said.

Di eyed the high dive, then smiled. She took a gulp of champagne, handed the bottle to me, and made a beeline for the ladder.

An instant later, I saw a man wearing a suit and an earpiece walk by, muttering something in Icelandic under his breath.

"How do you think she talked her bodyguard into this?" I asked Henry, tracking Di's security detail as he grimly pulled her down off the ladder.

"By threatening to do something worse?" Vivvie popped up beside us. She was wearing a half-dozen rainbow-colored leis. In contrast, her expression was almost comically serious. "I think you were right, Tess. People are really letting loose. Pretty soon, our classmates are going to be feeling *very* chatty."

Another fully clothed senior came barreling off the diving board.

"Where do we start?" Vivvie asked.

"With anyone John Thomas might have threatened." I paused. "And with the girls from ISWE. All we need is for one person to open up and admit that John Thomas wasn't the guy people want to remember. If we can get one, others will follow."

If the killer was here, I doubted he or she would volunteer their own motive—but someone else might.

"You talk to the girls," Henry said. "I have another target in mind." I followed his gaze to a group of John Thomas's friends standing near the keg.

"You think they might know who else John Thomas had dirt on and what he was planning to do with it?" I asked.

"I think," Henry replied, "that John Thomas liked an audience. Whatever plans he had, he would have shared them with someone."

With that, Henry made his way across the room. I watched as an easy smile crossed his face. My first impression of Henry Marquette had been that he was a little formal, a little stiff. It had taken me longer to realize that he was a master at putting other people at ease—when he wanted to.

As I watched Henry disappear into the crowd of John Thomas's friends, I noticed two of those friends staring at something—or someone.

Emilia Rhodes had arrived at the party.

"Did we know that Emilia was coming?" Vivvie asked me.

"No," I said. "We did not. Come on." By the time I arrived at Emilia's side, there was no doubt in my mind that she'd noticed the whispers and stares. From my place beside Emilia, I stared back at John Thomas's friends, my eyes narrowed. One of them flinched.

"Are they scared of you?" Vivvie asked me over the pounding of the music.

"It is possible," I said, "that I threatened to castrate a couple of John Thomas's friends my first week at Hardwicke."

"Of course you did." Emilia looked from me to Vivvie, then back again. "I don't suppose it will do any good whatsoever to tell you that I don't need you glaring at anyone on my behalf?"

I shrugged.

"Or," Emilia continued, "to suggest that the two of you go on your merry way, and I go on mine?"

"Tess is the patron saint of misfits," Vivvie said brightly. "And I'm a barnacle. Pretty sure you're stuck with us."

"Pretty sure you're here to find a way to help my brother," Emilia countered. "So go. Fix. I don't need a babysitter, let alone two."

Something about the way that Emilia had said that we were here to help Asher told me that she was as well. As she strolled into the fray, I tracked her gaze to a boy sitting up on the bleachers. Unlike most of the guys around him, he didn't look particularly inebriated. Or particularly inclined to chat.

"Who's that?" I asked Vivvie, nodding toward the boy.

"Matt Benning," Vivvie supplied promptly. She had an almost encyclopedic knowledge of everyone at Hardwicke, from the students down to the janitor. "He has a little sister. Lizzie. She's a freshman. Their dad works in Hardwicke security."

Apparently, while I'd been thinking about who had motive to kill John Thomas Wilcox, Emilia had been coming up with some questions of her own.

I caught up to her just as she reached the bottom of the bleachers. "What do you want with Matt Benning?" I asked her.

"What do you think?" Emilia said, her eyes still on her target. "I want to know why anyone suspects my brother of murder when the whole thing—including the real killer—should have been captured on video."

Vivvie popped around to stand directly in front of Emilia. "I know you're not going to want to hear this," she said, "but you should let Tess talk to Matt."

"Why?" Emilia returned. "Because my twin is the one the police are desperate to pin this on, or because people don't like me the way they like Tess?"

"Neither," Vivvie said softly. "Because if John Thomas was threatening someone, if he hurt someone or blackmailed them or made them do something they didn't want to do, they'll talk to you. Not Tess, Emilia. You."

Emilia took a single step back from Vivvie. I could see her wanting to tell Vivvie that wasn't true.

The words dried up on her lips.

"I'll talk to Matt," I told Emilia. *You can do this*, I continued silently. I knew better than to say those words to her out loud.

"Fine." Emilia turned her back on me. She didn't want to do this, but she would—for Asher.

Matt Benning didn't so much as glance my way when I took a seat behind him on the bleachers. He was sitting on the edge of a group of guys, close enough to give the appearance that he was part of their conversation, but making no move to actually join it. He gave off an air of being present but not really a part of things.

I'd been that person, back in Montana.

"Not in the mood for a drink?" I asked him.

He didn't turn around. "Not much of a drinker."

I managed a small smile. "Me neither."

I settled into silence then. I rested my forearms on my legs and waited. Before moving to DC, I'd spent my entire life on my grandpa's ranch. I had a sixth sense for knowing when to approach and when to let a tetchy horse approach me.

Minutes crept by as Matt and I sat on the edge of the crowd, neither one of us saying a word.

"They're going to catch us, you know." Matt's voice was naturally deep and even-keeled. My gut said that he would have been good with horses, too. "There are cameras everywhere on this campus."

I slid down to sit beside him but kept my gaze focused straight ahead. "Not everywhere, apparently," I said.

If there were footage of John Thomas's murder, the police would have already made an arrest. I didn't bother putting that into words. "Were you and John Thomas friends?" I asked Matt instead.

For several seconds, Matt said nothing. "I have a little sister," he said finally. "Freshman. She asked me to take her picture the other day."

It took me a moment to catch the implication—his little sister had been one of the girls to join the ISWE project.

"Did you take the picture?" I asked. If he'd agreed to help his sister with our protest, that told me something about the kind of guy he was.

"I did."

I turned that over in my head for a second or two before I took a risk. "Do you know Asher Rhodes?" I asked. "Because if you know Asher at all, that means that you *know* he didn't kill John Thomas."

Matt neither agreed nor disagreed with that statement.

"If I asked you who on this campus could get around the security feeds," I ventured, "would you tell me?"

Matt turned from me to direct his stare back out at the makeshift pool party going on below us. He picked a stray lei up off the bleachers and held it taut between his hands. "You're assuming I know the answer to that question."

Yes. I am. I let my silence speak for me.

"You're also assuming," Matt continued quietly, "that I'm the kind of guy who likes to talk."

"You're not?" I said.

He rubbed his thumb over one of the flowers on his lei. "I'm the kind of guy who likes to keep his head down."

That was why he was here, sitting on the edge of things, just close enough to blend.

"If you were really the kind of guy who kept his head down," I pointed out, "you wouldn't be here."

At a completely illegal party, where you know we're going to get caught.

Matt responded to my comment by turning to look at a cluster of girls by the punch. It took me a moment to realize that one of them was his little sister, that he was probably here for the sole purpose of keeping an eye on her.

My gut said that Matt was a good guy. But it also said that he wasn't going to make waves. There was a good chance he and his sister attended Hardwicke on scholarship—scholarships they received because their father worked for the school.

He wasn't going to tell me anything his father had said.

He was going to keep his head down and keep watch.

Luckily, I had other options. I leaned back against the row of seats behind me, watching the group of freshman girls Matt had been keeping watch over. They were young—excited to be here and playing it cool.

Something tells me Matt's little sister isn't so into keeping her head down.

I texted Vivvie. And then I waited.

CHAPTER 39

"Here's the deal," Vivvie told me as we walked along the edge of the pool, dodging partygoers as we went. "Lizzie's father is really stressed out right now because there are some major questions about how, exactly, someone managed to black out the library security cameras the day John Thomas was murdered. The police have been all over it. The headmaster has brought in a dozen new security specialists, and long story short—"

Vivvie's version of *short* was somewhat different from mine.

"—the only way it could have been a student is if that student were a *really* good hacker working from the campus's wireless network. Otherwise it would have had to be someone in security or high up in the Hardwicke administration." Vivvie paused. "Very high up," she emphasized.

Before I could reply, a partygoer bopped into view, dancing between Vivvie and me. It took me a second to realize it was Asher.

"Am I the only one who hears 'high up in the Hardwicke administration' and thinks that Headmaster Raleigh definitely has his shadypants moments?" he asked, still bopping around. When neither Vivvie nor I replied, he stopped dancing and lifted his hand in a solemn greeting. "Hello, friends of Asher!"

"Asher!" I said, taking him by the elbow and pulling him toward the side of the room. "What are you doing here?"

I hadn't been lying when I'd told Ivy that I couldn't imagine Asher coming tonight. Given everything that had happened—and the fact that at least one of John Thomas's friends was probably spoiling for a fight—this could go very badly.

"Welllllllll," Asher hedged, dragging out the word. "I may have hitched a ride in the back of Emilia's car. She may not know I'm here."

Nearby, Emilia was talking to a trio of sophomore girls. She glanced at me, then at Asher. Her eyes widened as she registered his presence, then narrowed.

"Emilia may now know I am here," Asher modified.

I sensed the shift in the room the moment John Thomas's friends noticed Asher.

Henry made it to us before they did. "We need to get you out of here," he told Asher.

"I've gone to school with these people my entire life." Asher glanced from Henry to me, bewildered. "If they think I might be capable of murder, I have clearly been doing this lovable-pacifist thing all wrong."

One second Asher was standing beside me, and the next, one of John Thomas's friends had him by the lapels.

"I've very recently sworn off fisticuffs," Asher told him. "Quite undignified, the sign of a lesser man, gets you almost immediately accused of murder . . . *which I did not commit*," he added hastily.

"Let him go," Henry said. Gone was the easy smile he'd used to infiltrate this group earlier. There was nothing even remotely easygoing about this Henry.

All around us, the party fell silent. All conversation died off. The only sound was the constant beat of the bass line.

The boy who had a hold of Asher got in his face. "You're a dead man," he said. "You think the powers that be in this town are going to let some dentist's son get away with doing *anything* to the minority whip's kid?"

I stepped between them. I could see violence in the boy's eyes as I broke his hold on Asher. This was the downside to providing an outlet for secrets and pent-up emotion to come bubbling to the surface.

Any moment, the world could explode.

A flash of light visible out the nearest window took the boy's eyes off me, just for a second.

"Security!" someone yelled.

In the rush of madness that followed, it was every man for himself.

CHAPTER 40

"What could have possibly possessed you to come here?" Emilia gave her twin the single most aggrieved look I'd ever seen my life. "You're grounded," she reminded him. "You're the prime suspect in a murder case. And I specifically told you *not to come*."

We'd made it out of the tunnel and taken refuge in a nearby coffee shop without getting caught by Hardwicke security—probably because security didn't *want* to catch too many Hardwicke students.

"It seemed like a good idea at the time?" Asher offered his sister an eighty-watt smile.

"This is the very definition of a bad idea," Henry told him.

Asher sighed. "I always get those two confused."

I'd promised Ivy I wouldn't call Asher. I'd promised her that I wouldn't e-mail him or go see him. Technically, I hadn't said any-thing about what I would do if he came to see me.

"Are you okay?" I asked him.

"The lapels of this shirt will never be the same," Asher replied mournfully. "But I will persevere."

"No," I said. "Are you okay? After the past few days—"

"Lo, it is a story for the ages," Asher intoned. "Of a boy wrongly accused and a text sent by someone who, it turned out, was not even his sister."

"I might actually kill you," Emilia told him. She turned to Henry. "I might actually kill him."

"I would prefer you did not," Henry told her. "Though I certainly understand the impulse."

"I've missed you guys!" Asher declared. "Except for Emilia. I still see Emilia all the time."

For fear that Emilia might actually do her brother physical harm, I intervened. "What did you find out?" I asked Emilia.

Emilia turned her attention from Asher to me, and as she did, I saw her guard going up, saw the transition from a much aggrieved sister to a person nothing and no one could touch. "Nothing worth repeating," she said.

I recognized, in her voice, that Emilia had heard something tonight. I wondered how much of what she'd heard had sounded familiar to her. I wondered how she was holding up with that, but knew she wouldn't tell me, just like she wouldn't betray anyone else's confidences about John Thomas.

"Anyone who might have had a motive?" I asked.

Emilia shrugged. "Motive? Yes. Opportunity? Ability? Not so much."

"On the subject of ability," Vivvie cut in, "we should add hacking to the list. If the hedgehog was a student, he or she would have had to figure out how to hack the security feeds via the campus wireless network."

"The hedgehog?" Emilia asked, wrinkling her brow.

"I approve!" Asher declared. "Though I am somewhat hurt that the lot of you have been hedgehog hunting in my absence. Just because a person is suspected of premeditated murder doesn't mean they don't have feelings."

"What would it take to hack the security feeds?" Henry asked Emilia, ignoring Asher with the expertise of someone who had been strategically ignoring him for a very long time.

"I don't know," Emilia told Henry. "But I can find out."

To say that Emilia was good with computers would have been an understatement. I had very little doubt that given the time and motivation, she could figure out how to hack the security feeds herself.

"Did you get anything out of John Thomas's friends?" Vivvie asked Henry.

"I discovered how John Thomas found out about my family's personal issues, how he got ahold of Hardwicke medical records."

I'd guessed, the day John Thomas died, that he had obtained the information about Henry's father from his own. I'd overheard enough of Ivy's conversations to recognize just how easily a person could pick up on things they weren't supposed to know.

"Congressman Wilcox kept files," Henry said. "On major and minor players in Washington. Not that uncommon, among a certain set."

My thoughts went to Ivy's files. Her *program*. Ivy's clients could count on her absolute discretion—until and unless something happened to her. If she went off the grid, the program started releasing secrets.

"What *is* uncommon," Henry commented, "is that John Thomas had somehow managed to get access to his father's files. I suspect his father had no idea."

No wonder John Thomas had paled when I'd threatened to tell the congressman what he was up to. It would have been bad enough if John Thomas's father had simply let the information slip in front of his son, but if John Thomas had acquired the information without the congressman knowing . . .

That wouldn't have gone well for John Thomas.

"What other information do you think was in those files?" Vivvie asked, wide-eyed. "I mean . . . are we talking about blackmail material, or BLACKMAIL MATERIAL, all caps?" She punctuated those words with an elaborate gesture.

"If I had to venture a guess," Henry said, "I would go with the latter."

BLACKMAIL MATERIAL, all caps. Silence fell over the table. Emilia was the one to break it. "If John Thomas had access to his father's files," she said, "then we're not just talking about him having dirt on Hardwicke students."

We were talking about Hardwicke *parents*, about politicians and lobbyists and power players of all stripes. If John Thomas had opened his mouth . . .

We're looking for someone with access to Hardwicke, I reminded myself. But I couldn't help thinking that Ivy had said more than once that Hardwicke *was* Washington.

And I knew better than most how dangerous this town could be.

CHAPTER 41

"Ashes to ashes, dust to dust."

John Thomas Wilcox was laid to rest on Saturday morning—less than twelve hours after the party had been busted up. Nearly the entire student body attended the funeral, with their parents in tow. It was a Who's Who of Washington's elite, and all I could think was that if John Thomas had read his father's files, he probably had blackmail material on half the people here.

I wondered if he'd tried to use it.

Beside the open grave, the reverend continued talking, the low hum of his voice assuring us that the Lord worked in unfathomable ways. John Thomas's family stood a few feet away. His mother was shaking, her shoulders rounded, her body on the verge of crumbling in on itself. Beside her, there were two younger boys: one in his early teens and another who couldn't have been older than seven or eight.

The congressman stood on the opposite side of the boys, his hands balled into fists at his side. He looked grief-stricken—there was no other word for the lines of sorrow etched into the corners of his eyes and mouth. His whole face looked heavy, like the only thing keeping his skin on his face was the tense set of his jaw.

The congressman is very good at paying attention. John Thomas's statement—his *threat*—came back to me, and I thought of the way father and son had interacted in the ballroom that night, the look on John Thomas's face when Henry had said the word *disappointment.* Congressman Wilcox might have had a gift for ferreting out the skeletons in other people's closets, but my gut said that he hadn't *paid attention* to his son.

As the service ended, my gaze slid to my left—to Bodie. Adam had told me once that Bodie didn't do funerals, and yet here he was. *With me.*

And here Ivy wasn't.

I hadn't told her I was planning on coming today. I hadn't told her that I needed her here. I hadn't asked her to stay, because she would have. And she would have taken one look at me—the way I was watching the congressman, the way I surveyed the presence of each and every mourner—and she would have known that I had more than one reason for coming.

"You ready?" Bodie asked me.

"Not yet," I said, making my way toward the aisle. A few feet away, I caught a glimpse of a familiar head of strawberry-blond hair. *Emilia Rhodes.* She peeled away from the crowd and made her way to the far side of the grave. She stood, looking down at the casket. Without thinking, I started walking toward her. When I came up behind her, her head was bowed, and her eyes were closed. At first glance, she looked like she was praying, but when

I got closer, I could hear the words her lips formed. They were barely more than a whisper, but her body shook with them.

"*I hope it hurt.*"

That was her prayer. That was her good-bye to John Thomas Wilcox.

After a moment, she looked up from the grave, her face a mask of grief, looking like any other mourner. She saw me standing beside her. "How many times do I have to tell you that I don't need your help?" she asked me quietly.

"At least twice more," I told her.

"I should go," she said. "And so should you."

I didn't take Emilia's advice. Instead, I slipped into the receiving line behind the other mourners. When I reached the front of the line, Congressman Wilcox took my hand. "Theresa," he said. "Thank you for coming."

Did you know that John Thomas was using your files? I curled my fingers around the congressman's. *Did you know that he knew about your affair?*

"I'm sorry for your loss," I said.

"You're the one who found him." Mrs. Wilcox's voice was wispy and rough. "You were with him when he . . ." She couldn't finish the sentence.

"I was with him," I said. I didn't tell her that I'd tried to help. I didn't tell her that I'd pressed my blazer to his chest to staunch the flow of blood. "I'm sorry," I said again, and my eyes went back to the congressman. *I'm sorry that your husband is cheating on you. I'm sorry something in his files might have gotten your son killed.*

I turned to leave, but the congressman reached out to stop me. His hand was heavy on my shoulder. My stomach twisted.

"Did John Thomas say anything to you?" the congressman asked. "At the end, did he . . ." John Thomas's father choked on the words.

Tell. Didn't. Tell.

An hour before John Thomas's death, I'd threatened to tell his father that he was spilling secrets. I'd threatened to tell the congressman that John Thomas had told me about his affair.

Tell him I didn't tell.

"I have to go," I said, pulling away from the congressman's grasp. As I turned to leave, the next mourner in line stepped forward. She was in her early forties, with girl-next-door looks and red hair. She was wearing a black dress and matching heels.

I recognized her immediately.

"Congressman, Mrs. Wilcox," the woman said, her manner professional, more colleague than family friend. "My deepest condolences."

I'd seen the congressman with this woman. I'd seen him burying his hands in her red hair. But as I forced myself to walk past her, it took everything in me not to turn around, because the woman the congressman was having an affair with—the fundraiser wasn't the only place I recognized her from.

Who is this Daniela Nicolae? I could see the red-haired woman asking the camera. *How did she get into the country? And why is an anonymous tip the only thing standing between us and a terrorist attack on American soil?*

Congressman Wilcox was having an affair with the female pundit I'd seen flaming the Nolan administration on the news.

CHAPTER 42

An internet search told me that the pundit's name was Stephanie Royal.

"Pancakes." Bodie set them in front of me.

I gave him a look. We'd gotten home from the funeral ten minutes earlier. He hadn't asked why I'd been so quiet on the drive.

"I can make two things, kid: pancakes and my hangover cure." Bodie arched an eyebrow at me. "Are you telling me you'd rather I haul out the blender?"

I picked up a fork and stabbed it into the pancake in answer.

John Thomas accessed his father's files. I couldn't keep from going back over everything I'd discovered as I chewed. *The congressman has a very* personal *relationship with the Nolan administration's most vocal critic.* I thought about the media leaks. Before Daniela Nicolae had sent Walker—and every major news outlet—that video, there had already been leaks.

The terrorist's name.

The fact that the attack had been averted because of a tip from an anonymous source.

The picture of Daniela Nicolae's very pregnant stomach.

Did Congressman Wilcox have access to information like that? My stomach clenched. *Did John Thomas?*

The front door opened and closed. Bodie's hand went to his side. *To his gun*, I realized a moment later.

"Tess?"

I relaxed the second I heard Adam's voice. Bodie rolled his eyes heavenward but let his hand fall away from the weapon.

"In here, Boy Wonder," Bodie called out.

When Adam came into the kitchen, he and Bodie looked at each other for a few seconds, and then Bodie took a step back from the kitchen island. "I'd offer you a pancake," Bodie told my uncle, "but I figure you're probably watching your girlish figure."

With a wink at me, Bodie strolled out the door.

Adam took a seat next to me at the counter. "For the record, I would have gone with you to the funeral," he said, picking up a fork and stealing a bite of my pancake. "So would Ivy, if she'd known."

I looked down at my plate. I hadn't told them about the funeral, because I hadn't wanted either of them asking questions about why I'd decided to go. I hadn't wanted to tip them off to the fact that while Ivy was off investigating the attack on the president, I was running an investigation of my own.

But if there was even a chance that my case was connected to hers, I couldn't keep that quiet. "Congressman Wilcox is having an affair with a woman named Stephanie Royal."

It was clear from the expression on Adam's face that he knew exactly who Stephanie Royal was.

"Does Congressman Wilcox have high-level security clearance?" I asked. "Could he have been the source of the media leaks about the bombing?"

Adam didn't answer. I took that to mean that a man as powerful and resourceful as John Thomas's father might have all *kinds* of access.

"John Thomas broke into his father's files," I told my uncle. "There's a good chance that something John Thomas saw in those files got him killed."

"Have you mentioned any of this to Ivy?" Adam asked.

I shook my head.

"Why not?" Adam's expression was deadly serious. He expected an answer, and he wouldn't back down until I gave him one.

Because Ivy told me to stay away from Asher. She promised that she would take care of it, but she's done nothing. If she knew I was looking into John Thomas's murder, she would have told me to stay away from that, too.

Instead of putting any of that into words, I took out my cell, called Ivy, and set the phone to speaker.

It went to voice mail.

Considering my point made, I hit *end* and turned back to Adam.

Adam was quiet for several seconds. "The vice president is attempting to move Daniela Nicolae to a classified facility." Adam's words—the fact that he was telling me this—took me completely off guard. "Ivy thinks Nicolae knows something she's not sharing about the attempt on the president's life, and no one trusts the vice president enough to let him remove a piece from the board. That's where Ivy is right now. She's working with Georgia to try to block the transfer."

"Why are you telling me this?" I asked, my brain whirring. "Why are you telling me anything?" Adam didn't exactly have a history of over-sharing—particularly when it came to things like terrorists and Ivy's line of work.

Adam caught my gaze and held it for several seconds. "Because," he said finally, "there's this dance that you and Ivy do, over and over again. The push and pull—it hurts you, and it hurts her, and I would give anything to keep either of you from being hurt ever again." He stood up. "I'll look into the connection between Wilcox and the pundit. I'll look into the leaks."

This was the part where Adam told me to stay out of it. This was the part where he read me the riot act and left me under lock and key.

"Thank you," Adam said instead, looking at me in a way that made me wonder if he was seeing my father. "For trusting me."

I gave a brief nod. I expected Adam to leave then, but he wasn't done yet.

"I heard that my father is bankrolling your friend's defense team."

My gut told me that this was why Adam had come to see me in the first place. This was what he'd wanted to talk to me about, before I'd dropped the bombshell about the congressman.

"If you trust me, Tess," my uncle said quietly, putting a hand on my shoulder, "don't trust him." Adam gave my shoulder a gentle squeeze and then turned toward the door. "Favors from a man like William Keyes always come at a price."

CHAPTER 43

I spent hours wondering what Adam was doing with the information I'd given him. Had he managed to pass it off to Ivy? Did they think there was a connection between John Thomas's death and the information his father had been leaking?

Had Congressman Wilcox really been the source of those leaks?

And if he had been—where had he gotten the information? What other classified information did he have access to?

Does he know anything about the president's Secret Service detail? The question took my breath away. *Could he have acquired that information? Could he have passed it on? Not just to the press—but to the terrorists?*

Whenever I needed to think, I walked. Bodie didn't stop me from leaving the house. I did a loop around the neighborhood, then another. And another. And the entire time, I told myself I was seeing connections where there were none. Even if Congressman Wilcox was the source of the media leaks—and that was still an *if*—that didn't mean he was anything more than a dirty politician trying to get ahead.

Senza Nome specializes in infiltration. They have someone on the Hill. They must.

This time, when I wrapped back around to the house, I saw someone sitting on the front porch. By streetlight, it took me a moment to recognize him.

"Henry?" I called out as I approached the front porch. "What are you doing here?"

He was sitting on the concrete steps. In all the time I'd known him, I had never once seen Henry Marquette sit on the ground. His eyes were shadowed.

"Is everything okay?" I asked him.

Henry looked up at me, his face half in shadow, his eyes catching the streetlight. "The first time I saw you," he said, "was at my grandfather's funeral."

I took a seat beside Henry, unsure where this was going, unsure why he looked like he'd been through a war zone and seen things he couldn't unsee.

"Then afterward," Henry continued, "at my grandfather's wake, I found you with my sister and Asher. The three of you were skipping imaginary rocks." He paused. "Do you remember that?"

"Yes." I remembered Henry looking at us like we were crazy, like he couldn't begin to fathom running barefoot in the grass or playing pretend.

Henry swallowed, then held up one hand. As I watched, he pantomimed tossing a rock. "How was that?" His voice was rough, hoarse.

"Horrible," I told him. "It sank straight to the bottom and didn't skip even once."

Henry let out a bark of laughter.

I showed him how it was done. "It's all in the flick of the wrist."

The edges of Henry's lips curled up slightly. He looked down at his hands, at a "rock" that didn't even exist. "Thalia wakes up screaming sometimes." His Adam's apple bobbed. "First my father. Then my grandfather." Henry's voice hardened with resolve. "I tell her that I will never let anything happen to her, but it's not herself she worries about. She worries about me. About my mom."

I remembered being Henry's sister's age, remembered the cloying fear that someday Gramps or Ivy might go away.

Henry reached into the bag sitting beside him. He held out a white envelope with my name scrawled across the front. I took it from him and opened it. Inside, I found a greeting card. The front was covered in a lacy design, framing what appeared to be an elegant white wedding cake.

"From Asher," Henry said. He rolled his eyes, but the heavy tone in his voice never changed. "Mine had a sparkly pony on it."

I opened the card. On the inside, the words *Congratulations on Your Nuptials* had been scratched out. Above them, Asher had scrawled, *Thank You for Trying to Prove I'm Not a Homicidal Maniac.*

"If John Thomas was killed because of something he saw in his father's files," Henry said, his voice hoarse, "if there's even a chance that there are powerful players involved in this, if someone like that wants Asher to take the fall . . ."

Thalia wasn't the only Marquette afraid of losing someone.

"I made a deal with William Keyes," I told the boy beside me. "The next time the police question Asher, he'll have the best defense attorneys in the country with him. We won't *let* anything happen to him, Henry."

"Kendrick," Henry said, turning to look at me, a sad smile on his face. "There are some things that even you cannot fix. If the right person wants the truth about John Thomas's death to stay buried, how are we supposed to stop them? How are we supposed to stop anything?"

I knew that Henry was thinking about his grandfather's death, covered up as a matter of national security, about his father's suicide, rewritten by Ivy in the blink of an eye. The first time I'd ever seen Henry, he'd stepped in front of his mother at his grandfather's funeral. I'd recognized in him a familiar need to protect the people he loved.

He wanted to protect Asher. And Thalia. And me.

"Ivy has files," Henry said. "The same way Congressman Wilcox does. If we could get a look at them, we might have a better idea of what we're dealing with."

I thought about how desperate Henry must be to want anything from Ivy. And I knew in my gut that there was no world in which Ivy would let us take even the smallest glimpse at those files. So I gave Henry something else.

"John Thomas's father is having an affair with the political pundit who's been leading the crusade against the Nolan administration. Congressman Wilcox might be the source of the leaks on the Senza Nome bombing." I paused. "He certainly benefitted from them."

Wilcox was the *minority* whip. The president's loss was his gain.

"Senza Nome specializes in infiltration," I continued. "If that video of Daniela's is to be believed, they have operatives everywhere, including our own government."

Henry's jaw clenched. I could see him processing everything I'd said. "Leaking incriminating information about the president doesn't make John Thomas's father a terrorist." Leave it to Henry to be the voice of reason, to play devil's advocate. "Congressman Wilcox may be a corrupt politician, but do you know how many corrupt politicians there are in this town? Are the president's hands really that much cleaner?"

President Nolan had covered up Henry's grandfather's murder. He'd been willing to let Ivy die when she'd been held captive by a Secret Service agent on *his* detail.

"If Senza Nome does have an operative in Washington," Henry said, "it could be anyone. And *none* of this helps us protect Asher."

"I told Adam about the congressman's affair. I told him that John Thomas had accessed his father's files. He and Ivy won't let Asher go down for this murder—not when there's a very good chance that this is bigger than any of us imagined."

Henry was quiet for a very long time. "I wish," he said finally, his head bowed, "that I could have the kind of faith in them that you do." His voice was low and rough, and for a moment, I had the sense that there was a depth of meaning to his words that I couldn't begin to understand.

"Do you have faith in me?" I hadn't meant to ask the question.

I never noticed Henry leaning toward me. I wasn't conscious of leaning toward him. But suddenly the space between us was nearly gone.

"I have faith that you will break every rule that you have to break to do whatever you think is right," Henry said. I felt his breath on my face with each word. "I have faith that you won't lie to me. That you won't ever pretend to be something you're not." His eyes caught on mine—caught *in* mine, as if my gaze had swallowed his whole.

My heart beat. My lips parted slightly, my hands bracing against the concrete beneath us.

And then Henry's words hit me. *I have faith that you won't lie to me. That you won't ever pretend to be something you're not.*

I wasn't lying to Henry. But I was pretending. I'd been pretending for weeks, ever since I'd discovered that Ivy believed the conspiracy surrounding Justice Marquette's death wasn't over. I hadn't thought twice about keeping the possibility of a fourth conspirator from Henry.

I have faith that you won't lie to me. I swallowed, my mouth dry. "There's something I have to tell you."

Henry inhaled sharply and leaned back. I felt the moment pass, like air knocked violently from my lungs.

And then I told him.

Henry stood up and began walking—away from what I'd just told him and away from me.

Halfway to the street, he came to a standstill. His fists weren't clenched. He didn't make a single sound. But he might as well have been yelling.

I knew better than to approach. "Henry—" His name stuck in my throat. He didn't give any visible sign that he'd heard me. I could see his shoulders rising and falling with heavy, jagged breaths. I tried to imagine what was going on in his head right now.

And then I wished that I hadn't.

He'd thought that the people responsible for killing his grandfather were dead. He'd thought that even if the world never knew what had really happened, there had been some form of justice. And now he'd found out that he'd thought wrong.

I have faith that you won't lie to me.

"Say something," I told him quietly. He barely moved. He made no sound except for the air making its way into and out of his lungs at an uneven pace, each breath a little sharper than the last.

He was angry.

He was hurt.

He was coming undone—but he wouldn't fall apart. Henry Marquette didn't fall apart. He didn't let himself lose control—

"Henry." I took a step toward him. "Please, just—"

"Yell at you?" Henry suggested quietly. "What is it precisely that you want me to say, Kendrick? That I wish you had done me the decency of telling me the truth weeks ago?"

He hadn't turned to face me. Something in the way he said the word *wish* made my stomach twist. His voice had gone rough when he said it, an audible crack in his hard-won control. "Should I tell you that I had a right to know?" Henry continued, glancing back over his shoulder at me. "That I feel as if I am right back at my father's funeral, staring at infamous fixer Ivy

Kendrick and wondering how she could lie so effortlessly to my mother's face?"

Those words hit me with the force of a blow, and I knew that they were meant to.

"What else does Ivy know?" Henry asked. "Has she even looked into the possibility that someone orchestrated my grandfather's murder?" He stared at me, into me, through me. "Has she questioned whether or not the president was involved? Someone in his administration?"

"I don't know," I told Henry. That admission echoed down the driveway.

"Kendrick, what you don't know," Henry told me, his voice rough and barely more than a whisper, "could fill an ocean." He looked down at the ground, the whites of his eyes standing out in contrast to his dark brown skin. "I told you that Thalia wakes up screaming at night." He'd let me in. He was punishing himself for that now, punishing me. "She crawls into my bed afterward. I let her sleep with me. I let her lay her head on my chest, so that she can hear my heartbeat." His voice shook. "I tell her that we are safe, that nothing is going to happen to us." He paused. "I lie to her. Because this world is not safe. The people who are supposed to protect us, the people we are supposed to trust—*I* know that sometimes they are the ones who do the most harm." He paused, and his already quiet voice got even softer. "How can I protect Thalia, or my mother, or you—from that?"

Henry didn't wait for an answer before he stalked off. It was just as well. I didn't have an answer to give him.

CHAPTER 44

It took me hours to get to sleep that night, and even then, the fight with Henry followed me into my dreams.

"Get up, Tessie." In the middle of the night, a voice jarred me awake. "Theresa." There was a note of urgency in Ivy's voice that hit me like a splash of water to the face.

I sat up in bed. "What happened?"

Ivy ran a hand through my hair, pushing it back from my face. "I need you to pack a bag. Clothes, your school stuff, anything you might need."

"A bag?" I caught Ivy by the arm as she moved to stand. "Ivy, what's going on?" No answer. "Is this about the information I gave Adam?"

Ivy's expression wavered slightly. I could see her locking down her emotions, trying to flip into fixer mode and handle me like any other problem. But she couldn't. Ivy had a way of looking at me, like I held her heart in my hands.

"What's going on, Ivy?"

She pulled back from my grasp and stood, crossing to my closet and pulling out a bag.

"You're sending me away."

No response.

"Is this because my friends and I investigated John Thomas's death?" I asked. "Asher was in danger of being arrested. We had to do something."

Ivy never looked up from her packing. "Stephanie Royal was the one who sent that video of Daniela to Walker Nolan and every major news outlet."

We'd assumed—*Walker* had assumed—that the video of the terrorist naming him as the father of her baby had been sent by Daniela on some kind of time delay, another stage of the same attack meant to destabilize the White House.

"Where did Stephanie Royal get that video?" I asked. Ivy didn't answer, and I thought about what I'd told Adam and amended my question. "Where did Congressman Wilcox get that video?"

From the source. If not Daniela, then the people she worked for. The answer hung in the air between us. But I needed Ivy to say it. I needed her to tell me that she was sending me away because she'd connected Congressman Wilcox to the terrorists, and things were about to get ugly.

My throat tightening, I took a step toward Ivy, and a second later, she'd latched both of her arms around me. I stiffened on reflex, but she held on tightly. After a second or two, I relaxed in her grip, my arms rising of their own volition to hold just as tight to her.

What kind of danger was Ivy in that she was sending me away?

"You have got to stop doing this to me, Tessie," Ivy murmured.

Stop asking for answers she couldn't give.

Stop putting myself at risk.

Stop being so much like her.

I forced myself to pull back. "I should pack." My voice sounded dull, even to my own ears. I crossed the room and began mechanically pulling clothes off hangers.

This was the way it was, with Ivy and me. This was the way it would always be.

"The people Daniela works for ordered her to make that video." Ivy broke the silence. She would regret telling me this. I knew that, and she knew that, but she wasn't any better at watching me walk away than I was at being shut out. "Daniela was supposed to release the video before she was captured. She didn't. It was her job to get close to the president's son, to carry his child. She claims to care for Walker. Our counterterrorism experts believe her, believe that she was unable to stay emotionally uninvolved. There's a theory that says that her own people may have come to see her as a liability."

She couldn't release the video, I thought, translating Ivy's words, *so Senza Nome released it for her.*

That was as close to confirmation of Congressman Wilcox's involvement with the terrorists as I was going to get.

"Where are you sending me?" I asked softly, my throat stinging and tightening around the words. I knew that Ivy loved me. I knew that she would have given her own life to keep me safe. But if she could have snapped her fingers and made me the kind of daughter who didn't ask questions that made her a target, the kind who was less like her and nothing like me—she would have.

I couldn't be that girl for her, any more than she could promise to stay safe for me.

"Somewhere secure," Ivy said, answering the question I'd spoken out loud. "And," she added, "the last place Adam and I would ever want you to be."

CHAPTER 45

I'd been to the Keyes mansion for Sunday night dinners. I'd sat opposite the kingmaker at the antique chessboard in his study. But this was the first time I'd walked up the massive marble staircase to see the second floor.

A long hallway stretched out before us. William Keyes walked me to the end of the hall and opened a door to our left. A massive suite, complete with its own entry, sitting room, and a bedroom large enough to dwarf a king-size bed, lay sprawled out before me. Despite its size, there was something about the suite that contrasted sharply with the looming antiques and surplus of marble downstairs.

"This was your grandmother's favorite room." William Keyes volunteered that information as he came to stand beside me. "She redecorated it, shortly after Tommy died."

"Was this his room?" I hadn't meant to ask the question. The kingmaker wasn't expecting it.

"No," he said abruptly, clipping the word. "It was always a guest room. Theresa just got it in her head to give it a more . . . personal touch." He turned to stare out an arching window set into the far wall. "I believe she was hoping that Adam might bring a girl home someday." Keyes paused, then turned back to me. "I can forgive my son many things, but keeping you from my wife? From me?" The old man shook his head. "We could have given you the life you deserved."

That wasn't a life that Adam—or Ivy—had wanted for me.

The fact that I was here, that Ivy had sent me to a man she despised for protection, told me just how serious the current situation was.

Ivy is going after Congressman Wilcox. She's going to try to prove he's in bed with Senza Nome. The terrorists won't take the loss of an asset lying down.

"Whatever mess Ivy has found herself in," William Keyes said, all too discerning, "I can promise it won't touch you here."

He would protect me. Ivy trusted that, even if she didn't trust him.

"Your friend Asher is now enjoying the benefits of an excellent defense attorney." Keyes said those words casually, but Adam's warning echoed in my head.

Favors from a man like William Keyes always come at a price.

I turned to face the man head-on. "What do you want?"

He assessed the way I was standing, the expression on my face. "You've been talking to Adam," he concluded. "Is it so hard to believe I might want to help you, Tess? That I might want nothing in return?"

I would have liked to believe that. I would have liked to believe that the words he'd just said to me were more than a move in a game of conversational chess.

"In this town, people always want something in return," I said. I met my grandfather's eyes. "You taught me that."

The kingmaker rocked back on his heels, his hazel eyes sharp on mine. "Very well," he said after a moment. "I want you to tell me why you're here. I want you to tell me exactly what Ivy has gotten herself into."

"Why would you care?" I asked, giving myself time to process the question. "Less than two months ago, you were perfectly happy to let Ivy die."

If that barb hit its target, the kingmaker gave no visible indication of it. "I care because what she does affects you. I *care*," he said, "because when Ivy Kendrick's heroics inevitably set the world on fire, I'm going to be the one dousing the flames."

William Keyes. Kingmaker. The one who makes things happen behind the scenes. It didn't surprise me that he kept close tabs on Ivy—or that information about what she was doing was the price he was exacting for the favor I'd asked of him.

"Ivy has connected Congressman Wilcox to the terrorists." I gave him that information in trade for what he'd done for Asher. "I don't know the details, but I'd guess she's out there building a case against Wilcox, preparing to bring him down."

"What about the woman?" Keyes asked, his gaze strangely intense. "Daniela Nicolae. Was Wilcox her contact?" The kingmaker took a step toward me. "What does the vice president intend to do with the terrorist carrying Walker Nolan's child?"

That question sent a chill down my spine. My grandfather keeping tabs on Ivy made sense. His interest in Daniela Nicolae did not.

If you trust me, Tess, Adam's voice whispered in my memory, *don't trust him.*

"Why do you want to know?" The words got caught in my throat.

"Information is power, Theresa. You can never know ahead of time which pieces will be worth the most."

What could my grandfather possibly stand to gain from knowing what the vice president intended to do with a terrorist whose organization had been implicated in the attempt on the president's life?

Did you know that the term kingmaker *was first used to refer to the role the Earl of Warwick played in the struggle between Lancaster and York?* I stared at William Keyes as I remembered his lecture on what happened to weak and strategically impotent rulers. *Warwick deposed not one but two kings.*

"Where are they keeping her?" Keyes pressed again. "The woman carrying Walker Nolan's son."

We are in your government, your law enforcement, your military. William Keyes was a man who believed in building alliances. He despised President Nolan. And now the president was in a coma.

"Daughter," I heard myself say. I never missed a beat in the conversation, though my mind was whirring.

"Excuse me?"

"On the video they released of Daniela naming Walker as the father of her baby, she said that Walker was *her* father. It's a girl."

"What does it matter," Keyes countered, his voice rising in volume, his words snapping out like a whip, "if the child is a boy or a girl? *What has Ivy said about the mother? What is this group's endgame with her? What is their endgame with Walker Nolan?*"

The full intensity of William Keyes's stare was a powerful thing. I felt like he was thumbing through my innermost thoughts like they were nothing more than index cards.

I wondered what would happen if he didn't like what he saw there.

"There's a theory," I said, matching the intensity of the king-maker's stare with my own, "that Daniela has been emotionally compromised, that her own people may have come to see her as a liability." I held his gaze and wondered how much of Tommy— and how much of himself—he saw in me. "And now you're asking me where she's being kept, what the government intends to do with her." My throat was dry, but I didn't back down. "Why do you want to know?"

I waited for him to hear what I was really asking. I waited for him to tell me that he wasn't working with Senza Nome, that he had no interest in *dethroning* kings.

His jaw clamped down, and he said nothing.

"I shouldn't have come here," I said. "Ivy shouldn't have sent me." I grabbed my bag off the floor and went to move past him.

"Not. Another. Step." The kingmaker turned. "Is this what we've come to?" he asked me. "You fleeing my presence?"

A Keyes doesn't flee. A Keyes doesn't back down from a battle. In other circumstances, I could see him telling me those words.

"Ivy sent you here because I have the resources and the man-power to protect you." He took a step forward. "I am also," he said, "not inclined to indulge childish tantrums or impulsive acts the way she might." He walked toward me. I pushed down the urge to step back. "You, my dear, are not leaving this house anytime soon."

"I have school on Monday," I said.

"And to school," the kingmaker countered, "you will go." The hand on my shoulder went to the side of my face. A moment later, he cupped the back of my head, his touch gentle. "I apologize," he said, "if my questions frightened you."

"I'm not frightened," I said. "I'm just wondering what you're capable of. If there are lines you won't cross."

"What must you think of me?" Keyes said, his voice soft and deadly, "to ask that question?" He ran his hand gently over the back of my head, then squeezed my shoulder. For a moment, I didn't think he would let go.

But he did.

He let loose of me, and he turned and walked over to the night-stand. He picked up a picture frame, then returned to my side.

In the picture, I could make out two young boys and their mother. *Theresa Keyes.* The woman I'd been named after, the woman who'd decorated this room.

Keyes stared at the photo, stroking his thumb along the frame. "You're right to be suspicious of me," he said, staring at his dead wife, at the boy my dead father had been. "I have my motives. I always do. But they're not what you think they are, Tess. There *are* lines I would not cross."

"Then why?" I said hoarsely. *Why pump me for information about Daniela Nicolae? If you're not with them, if you're not one of them—why do you need to know?*

I felt something shift in the room, in him.

"Walker Nolan is my son." The kingmaker stared at the photograph a moment longer, then looked up. "My wife didn't know. Adam doesn't know. Walker doesn't know." The kingmaker walked over to the nightstand and set the frame gingerly back down. "No one knows," he said. "Except for Georgia and me, and now you."

Georgia Nolan and William Keyes . . .

Adam had implied that they'd been involved, before either of them were married. When Keyes had found out that Walker had come to Ivy, he'd shown up on our front porch, demanding answers.

Demanding to know what kind of trouble Walker was in.

He and Georgia met that day. . . .

"You see now why I needed to know what Ivy knows about this whole sordid situation," the kingmaker said. "That terrorist girl isn't carrying the president's grandchild." His voice was rougher than I'd ever heard it. "She's carrying mine."

I forced myself to process, forced my mouth to form words. "Why are you telling me this?"

Why would he tell me a secret he'd kept for decades?

The kingmaker's gaze went back to the picture. "I lost Tommy," he said. "Adam thinks me a monster. Walker will never really be mine." His fingers tightened around the edges of the frame. "I treated Ivy like a daughter, and she chose Peter Nolan over me." He forced himself to walk back over to the nightstand and set down the frame. "Come what may, my dear," he said, turning back to me, "I will *not* lose you."

CHAPTER 46

True to his word, the kingmaker didn't allow me out of the house until he personally delivered me to school Monday morning. Headmaster Raleigh called a school-wide assembly for first period. I sat next to Vivvie and tried not to feel anything when Henry walked straight by us both.

I tried not to think about the fact that I hadn't heard from Ivy in twenty-four hours.

"Did something happen that I don't know about?" Vivvie asked. "Because you're making *this face*"—Vivvie adopted a stormy countenance—"and Henry's making *that* face, and—"

Headmaster Raleigh saved me from the rest of Vivvie's inquiry. "Starting today," he announced, signaling the beginning of the assembly, "our new security measures will be going into full effect." He began going through the measures: double the number of security personnel, changes to school policy on search and seizure, strict enforcement of all existing security protocol.

I wondered if I was the only one who noticed how heavily the new security personnel were armed.

The police still hadn't made an arrest in the murder of John Thomas Wilcox. That left the Hardwicke administration on edge.

John Thomas's father is in bed with terrorists, and now John Thomas is dead, I thought. *Someone at this school killed him. The Hardwicke administration should be on edge.*

"Tess." Vivvie nudged me in the side. With a start, I realized the headmaster had stopped speaking. The assembly was over.

As I stood to exit, my phone vibrated in my pocket. I slipped it out, reading the text I'd received. When I looked up, I saw Henry across the room, staring at me.

"Everything okay?" Vivvie asked.

I stuffed my phone back into my pocket. "Everything is fine."

According to the text, Ivy had done what Ivy Kendrick did. There was a problem. She'd solved it. Congressman Wilcox had been taken into federal custody. She'd found evidence—concrete evidence—linking him to Senza Nome.

I pushed my way through the crowd, trying to get to Henry. Cold air hit my face the moment I left the chapel. I called Henry's name, but he kept walking back to the main building. I caught up with him in the hallway, my face numb from even a brief encounter with the wind outside.

"Ivy can connect Congressman Wilcox to Senza Nome."

Henry came to a standstill at his locker. For a moment, he twisted the dial this way and that. When the locker door popped open, he turned his head slightly toward me. I took that as encouragement—however paltry—to continue.

"The congressman is in custody. If John Thomas's death is connected to this somehow, Ivy won't let anyone sweep that under the rug."

Henry shut his locker. He was going to turn his back on me. He was going to walk away.

"Henry," I said. "Look at me. Please."

He met my gaze head-on. Almost immediately, I wished that he hadn't.

Kendrick, what you don't know could fill an ocean.

I'd done to him what Ivy had done to his mother. I'd let him believe a lie. I had decided what he did and did not need to know.

"Not to interrupt an incredibly tense and subtext-filled moment"—Vivvie popped up beside us—"but is *anyone* going to catch me up on our status vis-à-vis Project Free Asher?"

Without another word, Henry walked away. He didn't even say good-bye. Vivvie turned to me, wide-eyed and bewildered. My stomach twisted sharply.

Henry wasn't the only one I'd kept things from.

I told Vivvie then, the way I should have told her weeks ago. I told her that there was a chance that the person who'd orchestrated Justice Marquette's murder—and her own father's—was still out there. Still alive.

Vivvie blinked rapidly, her lips pressed together and forced into a smile that told me she was trying not to cry. "You knew it wasn't over."

"Vivvie." I reached out and took her arm, but she jerked out of my grasp.

"You listened to me talk about my dad," Vivvie said. "And you knew. You knew it wasn't over. You're supposed to be my friend. My *best* friend." She shook her head. "And I know that I might not be yours. I know that you have Asher and Henry, and you probably have tons of friends back in Montana, but you're *my* best friend. Sometimes I think you're my *only* friend. I trusted you when I didn't trust anyone, and—"

The flow of words cut off abruptly.

"I'm sorry," I told Vivvie. "I thought I was protecting you. And it was just a theory."

A theory I'd believed from the moment I'd heard it.

"It's fine," Vivvie said, her voice dull. She forced herself to smile, even as a tear broke free and started carving a path down her face. "I'm not mad."

Henry was angry with me. Vivvie was heartbroken.

"I'm not mad," she repeated. "I just—I need to go."

"Viv—"

I didn't even get her whole name out before she was gone, bolting down the hall before anyone—myself included—could see her cry. As she disappeared around the corner, a member of the security staff walked by and told me to get to class. I waited until he'd passed, then turned and walked away.

I wanted to go after Vivvie, but I wasn't sure I had the right to, so I did what I always did when my brain was too loud and there were no right answers to be found: I walked. I walked down the hall. I looped around and found myself standing in front of the library.

And that was when I heard the first shot.

CHAPTER 47

I thought that I'd imagined it. And then there was a second shot. And a third. *Gunfire.* My brain searched for another explanation, even as my body told me to *run. Run-run-run-run—*

I could feel my heartbeat in my throat, my entire body jarring with each beat. Blood rushed in my ears. I forced myself to move, forced myself to turn, to take a step forward—away.

Away. Away. Run away. Run-run-run—

I caught sight of the library door. I remembered the door opening, John Thomas's bloody body spilling into the hall. I shook. My vision blurred. Shallow breaths burned my lungs.

Blood. Everywhere I look, I see red. John Thomas. His body is on the ground. The walls close in around me.

Shot. Shot. Shot.

He's bleeding. Can't run. Can't move. Can't breathe. The blood—

Hands gripped my shoulders. I lashed out, like a horse with a broken leg.

The person holding me stumbles backward. All I can see is blood. I hear her, calling my name.

I felt like I was watching myself from outside my body. I felt as if something else had control.

"Tess. *Tess.*"

Through the blood, her features come into focus—

"Emilia." I said the name and came back to myself. There was no blood. There was no body. But the gunshots were real. It took hearing another one before I was sure, and by that time, Emilia had locked a hand around my forearm.

"We have to go," she said. "We have to hide."

I let her pull me toward the library door, and then my survival instincts clicked back on. I pushed the door inward. Emilia followed. I considered barricading the door but decided that might just draw attention. If we barricaded ourselves in, the shooter would know we were here.

I pulled Emilia through the stacks. Toward the back of the library, the lights in the stacks were motion activated on an aisle-by-aisle basis. I hunkered down between two shelves, pressing my body as flat to them as I could. Beside me, Emilia did the same. It took a minute for the lights to go off.

Those sixty seconds were the longest in my life.

I could hear Emilia breathing beside me, could feel her breath on my neck.

"What's going on?" I asked her, my voice so quiet I could barely hear the words myself.

"We were supposed to be in class," Emilia said, her voice nearly as low as mine, neither of them anywhere near as deafening as the sound of my own heartbeat. "I forgot something in my locker. I went back, and I saw one of the new security guards pull his gun."

Hardwicke had doubled the number of security personnel on campus. *Heavily armed.* The memory washed back over me. I'd thought—we'd all thought—that the guards were armed for our protection.

"How many?" I said, my voice hushed, my throat tightening around the words. "Just the one guard?"

Emilia shook her head, the motion stilted. We couldn't afford to set off the motion sensors. We couldn't afford the light. We couldn't afford to draw attention to the library.

What do they want?

I didn't waste my breath to risk asking that question out loud. Emilia had no way of knowing the answer—not if she'd seen what she'd seen and then run.

Run. Run-run-run—

Every instinct I had told me to get out of here. I was trapped. And if they looked for us—if they wanted to find us, there was nowhere to hide. And if they weren't looking for us, if this was an attack and they decided to concentrate on the classrooms, then our classmates, the ones who'd made it back to class after the assembly—

Without even realizing I was doing it, I shifted. I was going to get up. I was going to do something. But Emilia's fingernails dug into my arm.

Don't. Like my last question, her plea was silent. *Don't be stupid.*

Don't leave her there alone.

"Henry's out there," I told Emilia, my voice nearly refusing to form the words. "And Vivvie—"

I had no idea where Vivvie was. She'd bolted, minutes before the first shot.

There was a moment of silence out in the hallway, and then a rapid-fire burst of shots, louder than the others. *Closer.*

Emilia squeezed her eyes shut. I eased the phone out of my pocket. *Call. Call for help. Dial—*

No service. I heard footsteps outside the door, heard someone shouting out orders. Why wasn't my phone working?

Had they knocked out the service? *They.*

For the first time, I let myself process the fact that there was a word for the kind of people who infiltrated the security force of an elite private school and then began shooting.

Terrorists.

"Somebody roofied me." Beside me, Emilia's eyes were open now. She was pale and staring straight ahead. "At that party, someone roofied me."

This was the first time she'd ever said the words. I knew that, just like I knew that she didn't want to die without saying them.

We're not going to die. We're not.

"I don't know if John Thomas was the one who slipped it into my drink," she said hoarsely, her lips barely moving, the words barely audible. "I never knew for sure what happened that night, or who was involved. I didn't *want* to know."

Another set of footsteps. Heavy. Running.

A tremor ran down my spine. I forced myself to stop shaking but couldn't stop the horrible questions wending their way through my mind.

How many gunmen were there?

How many people are already dead?

Emilia closed her eyes again, then slipped her hand into the messenger bag she wore over her shoulder.

My breath caught in my throat. *What are you doing, Emilia?*

The lights stayed off as she eased an electronic tablet out of her bag. Her movements tortuously slow, her own breaths shallow, she hit several buttons on the screen.

A second later, the screen was split six ways. *Six video feeds*, I realized.

"I said I'd find out what it would take to hack Hardwicke's security," Emilia whispered. "So I hacked it."

My gaze was locked on the screen. I could see armed guards passing by one camera after another.

There were bodies on the floor.

Grown men. I processed what I was seeing. *Hardwicke security. The first thing they did was shoot the other guards.*

I didn't see any students—not on the ground and not in the halls.

There was a blur of motion in front of one of the cameras, and a second later, the door to the library flew inward. Peering through the shelves, I saw the gun before I saw the man holding it.

I heard the girl with him cry out before I recognized her.

Anna Hayden.

The man with her was Secret Service. His gun drawn, he herded Anna toward the far side of the library. I was on the verge of yelling out to let them know we were here when the door opened again. The agent shoved Anna behind him and started shooting.

Emilia and I sat there, huddled in the dark, unable to move, not even to crawl away from the gunfire, without setting off the light overhead. Anna was screaming. The armed guard shooting at the Secret Service agent was yelling for backup.

Emilia's body pressed itself up against mine. I could feel her shaking beside me. She bit down on her hand to stifle a whimper that tried to make its way out of her mouth.

Don't move. If we move, the lights come on. If we move, we die.

One of the terrorists went down, but another rounded the corner after the Secret Service agent, who switched out guns and kept shooting.

"Anna."

I heard someone say Anna's name—a female someone. At first I thought it was Emilia, or maybe even me, but it wasn't. The stilted, desperate whisper came from the far entrance.

Dr. Clark.

My World Issues teacher looked how I felt—somewhere between gutted and numb. I remembered her lecture on flash-bulb memories. I wouldn't forget a single thing about this day.

I wouldn't ever be able to forget.

Anna edged toward Dr. Clark as two armed guards advanced on the Secret Service agent. I heard, as much as saw, the agent take a bullet to the shoulder.

He kept fighting.

Anna made it to Dr. Clark. Like one of these mothers who suddenly develops super strength to lift a car off her child, Dr. Clark shoved Anna down behind a bookshelf and bolted into the fray. Taking cover where she could, she made her way to one of the fallen gunmen. She grabbed his weapon, then ducked back into the shelves on the opposite side of the room from us.

Don't move, I kept telling myself. *Can't move. Stay frozen. Stay still.*

I watched my World Issues teacher do what I couldn't. The Secret Service agent glanced at her as he took down the terrorist who'd been firing at him.

"How many of them are there?" he asked her.

She stepped out of the shelves, gun still in hand. "I don't know." She swallowed. "Is help coming? Were you able to call out?"

"Communication is down," the agent told her. "The other agent on Starlight's detail is dead. Backup will be here any time, but they won't be able to get in. This place is a fortress. I have to get her out."

The guard turned toward the vice president's daughter. "Anna, are you—"

A shot rang out. An instant later, Anna Hayden's last remaining Secret Service agent slumped to the floor. Emilia's second hand joined her first, pressing over her mouth, holding in a scream as tight as she could.

Secret Service. Shot. I couldn't process what I was seeing, or what it meant. *Someone shot him in the head—*

Not just someone.

As I watched, Dr. Clark stepped dispassionately over the Secret Service agent's body. The gun she'd just fired was still in her hand.

CHAPTER 48

My World Issues teacher just shot a Secret Service agent. She just shot Anna's Secret Service agent.

"Time to come out now, Anna," Dr. Clark said, sounding exactly like the woman who'd stood at the front of our World Issues class and lectured about everything from elections to acts of international aggression. "I don't want to have to hurt you. None of us do." Dr. Clark walked until she was standing directly over Anna. She softened her voice as she looked down at the girl. "None of us want to hurt you," she repeated, "but we will."

"W—why?" Anna choked out the word.

"Believe me," Dr. Clark said, "this was not my first-choice way to spend this morning, but unfortunately, I am not the one calling the shots."

"You . . ." Anna's gaze was locked on the dead Secret Service agent. "You killed Dave."

"He called you Starlight. I take it that was your Secret Service code name?" Dr. Clark's voice was straightforward, no-nonsense.

In other circumstances, it might have been calming. "His job was to protect you. He died protecting you. He would want you to do whatever you have to do to protect yourself now." Dr. Clark waved the gun at her. "Stand up."

Anna was crying. She scrambled backward until she hit a wall.

Dr. Clark simply repeated herself. "Stand up, Anna." She trained her gun on the girl. Anna stood. A moment later, a pair of armed guards came into the room.

"Secure her," Dr. Clark ordered. "Get her in the room with the other high-value targets. If you have to make an example of someone, do try to make it someone disposable."

One of the guards grabbed Anna. She screamed, and before I could blink, the guard had hit her over the head with his gun. The vice president's daughter crumpled to the ground.

"Get her some ice," Dr. Clark ordered. "We want these kids intact."

The guard scooped Anna up and gave a brisk nod. "You're the boss," he said. His tone seemed to tack a disclaimer onto those words: *for now*.

Dr. Clark stared the guard down, her gaze unflinching, her finger steady on the trigger of her gun. "We'll have company any minute. If you're going to mutiny, I suggest you do it now."

The guard looked away before she did. The other guard stepped forward, shoving the man who held Anna toward the door.

"Reinforcements are in place," he reported to Dr. Clark. "We have thirty men. The snipers are on the roof. Campus is secured."

"I want a head count of all students. We need to know who we're missing, and we need to find them. *Now*."

I closed my eyes, unable to keep watching. Every breath I took was deafening in my ears. My heartbeat, the barest shift of position—any second, they'd hear us. Any second, they'd find us.

Blood.

Blood on my hands.

I couldn't let myself get caught up in a flashback, but the present was no better. There was blood seeping into the library carpet.

The Secret Service agent. Two gunmen.

Bodies on the floor, and bodies strewn through the halls— and I was here, trying not to breathe, not to think, not to move. My fingernails dug into the wood of the bookshelf.

Still. So still. Have to stay—

There was a sound. I wasn't sure if it was me or Emilia or the settling of the floor, but Dr. Clark's head whipped toward us. I pressed myself back, willing the dark on our side of the room to swallow me whole.

Don't let her see us.

Don't see us.

Don't—

Dr. Clark strode across the room. *Toward us.* Beside me, Emilia shuddered. Then she shoved her tablet into my hands, threw her head back, and stood up.

There was a two-second delay before the lights switched on. Emilia used those two seconds to stride into the aisle.

"Don't shoot," she said, holding her hands up. "Please, don't shoot."

Asher's twin didn't glance back at me. She didn't give any indication that I was here.

"Emilia." I could hear Dr. Clark's greeting but couldn't see her as I pushed myself back against the bookshelf, quelling the urge to go after Emilia.

I can't help her. And a moment after that: *She did this for me.*

"You're a sensible girl," Dr. Clark was telling Emilia. "Smart. Tougher than you look."

Why? I asked Emilia silently. *Why give yourself up to save me?*

"You killed John Thomas, didn't you?" Emilia said, walking toward Dr. Clark—and away from the motion sensor that controlled the light in my aisle.

Sixty seconds. Sixty seconds until it's dark again. Sixty seconds to hope no one looks through the gaps in the shelves.

"I'm not sure what John Thomas knew, why you wanted him dead." Emilia kept talking, kept Dr. Clark's eyes on her. "Quite frankly, Dr. Clark, I don't care. I don't care why you killed him. I don't care *that* you killed him. But you were also framing my brother to take the fall."

"I assure you," Dr. Clark replied evenly, "killing Mr. Wilcox was not *my* idea, nor was I the one who pulled the trigger. *We infiltrate, we observe, we influence, we recruit.*" Those words had the ring of a mantra, a prayer. "We kill only when we must—to make a point. Some of us take that vow more seriously than others."

I thought of the hospital bombing, the assassination attempt. *What was the* point *of that?*

"Why?" Emilia asked the same question of Dr. Clark that Anna had. She was still walking toward the woman—taking her away from me.

"Ours is a grander purpose," Dr. Clark said. "Everything we do is for the greater good."

"How long have you—"

"Since the year I spent studying abroad," Dr. Clark said. "I wasn't much older than you."

I remembered Dr. Clark describing her own flashbulb moment, getting off a plane right after 9/11.

Everything we do is for the greater good.

Was that what they'd told her? Was that what she believed?

"How many people have died today?" Emilia countered. Her voice didn't waver. It was like the moment she'd come out of hiding, the terror had started draining away. "How is killing people ever for the greater good?"

Dr. Clark didn't answer. Instead, I heard her raise the gun. "Be smart," she told Emilia. "Be sensible. Do what you're told, and you'll walk out of this." She paused. "And so will your brother."

"Asher isn't here."

Dr. Clark's silence spoke volumes. *We can get to him. Anytime, anywhere—we can get to anyone.*

"I'll be smart." Emilia's voice was strong and steady. "What do you want me to do?"

The light above me clicked off with a pop. For a moment, I could feel Dr. Clark looking in this direction.

"Secure her."

It took me a moment to realize that Dr. Clark was talking about Emilia, not me.

"High value or low value?" the guard she'd addressed asked.

"Low."

Low value, because Emilia's parents are dentists, I thought, the realization somehow managing to pierce its way through the constant and overwhelming terror that had claimed my entire body. *Low value, because her family doesn't have anything the terrorists want.*

Anna Hayden's father was the acting president of the United States. *High value.* It wasn't much of a stretch, given my relation to Ivy and William Keyes, to think that they'd consider me high value, too.

I heard the door to the library open.

"Boss wants to talk to you," a new voice informed Dr. Clark. "A couple of kids are missing."

Boss? I thought. *What boss?* Dr. Clark had said that killing John Thomas wasn't her idea. *Then whose idea was it? Who pulled the trigger?*

It had to be someone at Hardwicke. Someone with access to the security cameras. Someone with the authority to bring new people in.

I didn't finish that thought. I didn't move. I didn't breathe. I didn't do anything until I heard Dr. Clark and the others leave.

I heard the door shut behind them. But it wasn't until I looked down at the tablet Emilia had thrust into my hands and saw two guards pass, one escorting Emilia and the other striding next to Dr. Clark, that I let myself suck in a breath of air.

Alone.

CHAPTER 49

I forced myself to move. My leg muscles screamed in objection. My feet were asleep, my muscles in stone-hard knots from holding myself still. My jaw hurt—I'd clamped it down too hard for too long.

I stayed low and moved slowly, trying to avoid the motion sensor. *I have to get out of here.*

Out of this library, and out of Hardwicke. My mind went immediately to the tunnel, the one that let out in the Aquatics Center. If I could get past the guards, get outside, make it to the tunnel—

This place is a fortress. The dead Secret Service agent's words echoed in my mind, followed by a statement issued by one of the guards. *The snipers are in place.*

If I went outside, they'd see me.

If they thought I was making a run for it, they'd shoot me.

No way out. I tried to ignore the low, insistent voice that told me this wouldn't end well, that if the terrorists had used the element of surprise to let more than thirty armed men onto campus, if they had snipers on the roof and were prepared for the onslaught of a SWAT team or worse, I stood no chance of getting out of here.

That voice told me to hide.

It told me to stay here, where it was safe.

There is no safe, I thought. Dr. Clark had ordered the guards to take a head count and figure out who was missing. Once she realized I was unaccounted for, they'd sweep the building.

She'd remember that Emilia had surrendered herself here.

I have to move. I have to go—

"Where?" The word burst out of my mouth, a whisper as raw as an open wound. My chest was tight, each breath hard-won. My throat hurt. My eyes stung

Pull it together, Tess. Think.

I turned my attention back to Emilia's tablet. If she'd managed to tap the security feed, she was on Hardwicke's wireless, and if the wireless was up and running, I might be able to get a message out.

I launched a browser. Every site I tried to go to was blocked. I tried to text, tried my phone again—nothing.

Pulling the security feeds back up, I stared at them, trying to memorize the patterns of movement.

I can't stay here. They'll find me.

I had to move—without being seen.

Experimentally, I tapped the screen. Instead of a split screen, that let me go through the feeds, one by one. There were more than six of them now.

Armed guards at every exit.

There were over thirty cameras in the main building, giving me eyes on most of the rooms.

Including this one.

I couldn't see myself on-screen. That was good, given that whoever was sitting up in the Hardwicke security offices right now was probably seeing the exact same thing.

If Emilia were here, she might be able to tell me how to knock some of these cameras out.

But Emilia had given herself up to save me. Why? I didn't have time to let that question plague me.

You're a fixer, I told myself. *You don't ask why. You take what you're given, and you find a way.*

I went through the security cameras a second time and took stock of where the gaps in the coverage were. *No cameras in the bathrooms. No camera in the security center itself.*

I tried not to dwell on the footage of the classrooms, of the students trapped inside. They lay on their stomachs, hands secured behind their backs.

I tried not to wonder what had happened to the teachers.

By now the Secret Service would have realized there was a problem. People would come for us.

And do what? a voice whispered in the back of my head. There were too many terrorists and too many lives at stake. Too many high-value targets.

Anna Hayden's father is the acting president of one of the most powerful countries on Earth. The moment it had become clear that President Nolan was incapacitated, Anna's father had taken those reins.

They shot the president. They killed John Thomas.

What if taking over Hardwicke had been the goal all along? What if Senza Nome had attacked the president *so that* the vice president would be sworn into office, so that the person in power had a child at this school?

They killed John Thomas. The same day the president was shot, they killed John Thomas. After that, Hardwicke had reason to bring in extra security, and justification for the additional security officers to be heavily armed.

Not just Hardwicke, I thought. Hardwicke *didn't do this.* I swallowed. *The headmaster did.* The headmaster was the one who would have made the call. The headmaster was the one who would have chosen the men to bring in.

A Hardwicke student is killed. I went through it, step by step. *The headmaster has an excuse to hire additional security, to see them heavily armed.*

The president is shot. I forced myself to go further, to take this line of thought to completion. *Once the president is shot, the vice president is imbued with the power of the presidency.*

And the vice president's daughter went to Hardwicke.

They want something. Anna is the leverage. Then again, they'd said high-value targets, plural. *There are other students here who they can use for leverage, too.*

Hardwicke *was* Washington.

I had to do something. Find a way to short out the cameras? Cut the power and the lights?

I forced myself to pull up one of the classroom feeds, forced myself to look at my classmates, lying facedown on the floor.

If I cut the power, one of them is going to try something stupid.

If I cut the power, those guards are going to shoot.

I couldn't risk that happening. I was an unarmed teenager trapped in a building with dozens of armed terrorists. There were snipers on the roof. Soon the terrorists would realize I was missing. Soon they'd be looking for me. The only thing I could do, the only thing I could even *try* to do, was establish a line of communication with the outside world and tell them what I knew about the terrorists' operation—where they were keeping the other students, how heavily the terrorists were armed, how many men they had, the fact that Dr. Clark was involved.

Information is power. My paternal grandfather's words stuck in my mind. *You can never know ahead of time which pieces will be worth the most.*

The more information the police—the FBI—*whoever* was in charge of this operation had, the better our chances of making it out of this alive. I had to find a way of getting a message out. *How?*

My cell phone still wasn't working. *They must be scrambling the signal somehow. But they have a way of calling out. They must.*

The terrorists would want to present their demands. They would want to open up a line of communication with the outside world. I just had to find it—and find a way to co-opt it.

If I were a working phone line, where would I be? I stared down at the security footage in my lap. I thought about the rooms that weren't on there. *The security station.* If I were committing a hostile takeover of Hardwicke, that would be my base of operations. If I could make it up there, if I could distract the person manning it—

This is a bad idea. I knew that, the way you know that people in horror movies shouldn't go traipsing off into the woods.

But it was the only idea I had.

They're going to catch me anyway. Even if I stay here, even if I find somewhere else to hide—they will find me. The question is whether or not I can get a message out before they do.

I might not be Anna Hayden, but I was still a card they'd want in their hands. I'd already been kidnapped so someone could use me as leverage against Ivy once.

If you have to make an example of someone, Dr. Clark had told one of the guards, *do try to make it someone disposable.*

I'd have to take the risk that so long as they had me in their possession, they would want to keep me alive.

For better or worse, I had to try.

CHAPTER 50

I studied the library camera feed long enough to know its blind spots. Crawling along the floor, slowly enough to avoid being caught by the motion sensors, I made it to the door. Next up was the hallway. I listened for footsteps and told myself it wasn't any different from listening to a horse come closer, knowing that if you looked up, it might spook.

Now. Go now.

Avoiding the hallway cameras was harder—impossible if I wanted to get more than a few feet.

I made it as far as the closest bathroom and slipped in.

Automatically, I scanned the room for hiding spots, for shelter. Unfortunately, the urinals offered neither. I tested the window to see if I could work it loose.

No such luck.

Watching the cameras and listening for footsteps again, I waited until it was clear, then slipped back out into the hall.

I wasn't exactly sure where the Hardwicke security offices were, but I knew they were in this building, and I knew they were on the top floor. If there was a way of calling the outside world, I was betting I'd find it there—probably under guard.

Farther down the hall, another bathroom.

Pressing my body back against the tile wall and riding out the rush of adrenaline, I tapped at the screen of the tablet, scrolling through the feed until I got to the staircase. I tried to zoom in, but the maneuver didn't take.

Instead, a message popped up.

ENACT PROGRAM?

Program? What were you doing, Emilia?

The prompt on the screen gave me two options: YES and NO. Before I could think too hard about what I was doing, I hit YES.

SELECT CAMERA TO CLONE.

There were three stairwells in the main building. *If this works, I will worship the ground you walk on,* I told Emilia silently. *I will owe you favors for all time. I will be your friend, the way you were mine.*

I couldn't let myself remember Emilia standing up and stepping out into the aisle. Instead, I concentrated on the tablet. I hit what I hoped were the right commands, and then I cracked the door to the hallway open and made my last dash to the stairs.

The door closed behind me. *Too loud.* This wasn't going to work. It couldn't. But I thought of John Thomas with a hole in his gut and Dr. Clark training a gun on Anna Hayden and the Secret Service agent lying dead on the library floor—

I made it up two flights of stairs before I'd processed the fact that I was running. When I heard the sound of someone entering the stairwell below me, I made a split-second decision.

No time to listen. No time to check the tablet. I stepped into the hall. I was out in the open. I was exposed. And the hallway was . . .

Empty.

There were snipers on the roof and guards patrolling the first two floors and armed gunmen at every exit, but the third floor was quiet.

Right up to the point when it wasn't.

"As of this moment, every child in this school is accounted for and alive."

I recognized the headmaster's voice the moment it broke the silence.

"That can remain true. We can reach a peaceful solution, but that solution will require your cooperation."

It took me two seconds to pinpoint where the voice was coming from and another after that to realize that he wasn't speaking to me.

"Here is what that cooperation will look like. You will release Daniela Nicolae to our custody. As well, you will be provided with a list of others imprisoned by your and other governments without due process or trial. You will use your resources to secure their release worldwide."

It was one thing to realize abstractly that the headmaster was the person in the position to have brought these men into our school. It was one thing to *think* that the man who'd chided you on appropriate behavior could do something like this.

It was another thing altogether to hear him issuing demands.

Drawn like a moth to the flame, I crept toward the voice, hugging the wall.

"A sum of twenty million dollars will be transferred into an account we specify. This money is nothing to us but a gesture of goodwill, from Hardwicke parents understandably concerned about the welfare of their children."

Prisoners. Money. The scope of the demands made my mouth go dry.

"Additionally, private requests will be fulfilled by a small number of Hardwicke parents." The headmaster began reading a list of names, and all I could think was that once upon a time, the picture that had allowed me to tie together three of the players in another conspiracy had hung in his office.

It never ends. I felt hysteria bubbling up inside of me. *Terrorists and politicians and school officials, rogue Secret Service agents, and a White House physician who could be bought.*

Every time I thought it was over, thought it could be over, I was wrong.

"Priya Bharani."

The mention of Vivvie's aunt brought my attention back to the present. She was on the list of Hardwicke parents who would be required to fulfill a "private request." So was Ivy.

"And William Keyes," the headmaster finished.

Ivy and *the kingmaker.* That made me a very high-value target. And the fact that Priya was on the list made Vivvie one as well. *They'll be looking for me. They'll be looking for Vivvie, if they haven't found her already.*

"Details on these requests and instructions for your coopera-tion will follow." Headmaster Raleigh let a single note of tension creep into his voice. I'd made it to the end of the hall. My back pressed against the wall, I leaned out just far enough to catch a fleeting glimpse of what awaited me around the corner.

Headmaster Raleigh was sitting in a chair in the middle of the hallway, facing a camera. There was a piece of paper in his lap.

Behind the camera, there was a woman wearing a twinset and holding a gun.

"We are everywhere," the headmaster read. "We are in your government, your law enforcement, your military. We teach your children."

Mrs. Perkins. I struggled to process what I'd seen—the woman, the gun. *The headmaster's secretary?*

"We know your secrets," Headmaster Raleigh said, and now—only now—I could hear the slight quiver in his voice as he deliv-ered the words that someone else had scripted. "We do this for the common good. The time for waiting—"

A hand closed over my mouth, pulling me roughly back.

"—is over."

CHAPTER 51

I should have fought. I *did* fight, a moment too late. An arm wrapped around my body. I couldn't breathe through the hand over my mouth, couldn't scream. I struggled against my captor's grip, but I was already immobilized.

Too late.

"Be still."

I barely heard the words, but I felt the whisper, directly in my ear. *Henry.* The arm around my waist, the breath on my neck, the body I was trapped against—*Henry's.*

I could feel his heart beating, as hard and fast as my own.

"Nicely done, Headmaster." The sound of Mrs. Perkins's voice served as a stark reminder that nothing—*nothing*—was as it had seemed. "Now it's time we had a chat about our missing students."

As Mrs. Perkins began to prod the headmaster for information, Henry sidestepped to face me, moving with an unearthly silence. His eyes met mine and held them for one second, two—then he removed his hand from my mouth. His index finger went to his lips, and he jerked his head toward the stairwell.

Quiet. This way.

I gave a curt nod to show that I understood. As we made our way back down the hall, he kept one hand on my arm, ready to pull me out of the line of fire at any moment.

Ready to step into the line of fire himself.

I won't let you do that for me, I thought. After Ivy trading her life for mine, after Emilia giving herself up so we didn't both get caught—no one else was taking a metaphorical bullet for me.

No one was taking a *literal* bullet for me, either.

As if he could sense my thoughts, Henry's hand tightened over my arm as we made it to the stairwell. When the door closed behind us, he forced himself to let loose of me.

"Are you certifiably insane?" he asked, his voice hushed but crisp. "What exactly did you think you were doing out there? They could have seen you! They could have *shot* you, Kendrick."

"Mrs. Perkins," I replied, my voice as low as his. "*Mrs. Perkins* could have shot me."

Mrs. Perkins, who could have easily sent a text from Emilia's phone when someone had turned it into the office.

Mrs. Perkins, who might well have—at the headmaster's instruction—put in the call for extra security herself.

Henry took up position between the door and the top of the stairs, tense and unable to know which direction the next threat would come from. "There are cameras," he said. "They'll see us. We should move."

I held up the tablet. "We're in the clear. For now."

I didn't know whether we had minutes or seconds. I didn't know what would happen when someone found us in the stairwell.

"How did you—" Henry started to say, then cut himself off. "Emilia."

I nodded. "Emilia."

I handed the tablet to Henry and let him scroll through the camera feeds. He stopped on one of the classroom cameras. *Men with guns. Students on the floor.*

Wordlessly, Henry handed the tablet back to me.

My heart jumped into my throat. I felt something inside me crumble. *Vivvie.* I lowered the tablet and closed my eyes. *They have Vivvie.* I'd wanted to believe that she'd run. I'd wanted to believe that she'd found a place to hide. I'd wanted her to be safe.

You're supposed to be my friend. My best *friend.* The words she'd said to me before she'd bolted haunted me. *I trusted you when I didn't trust anyone.*

I forced myself to open my eyes. Vivvie was bound and terrified. She was being held at gunpoint—and there was nothing I could do about it.

They're going to find us, I thought, the realization washing over me, coating my body like oil. *They're going to find Henry. They're going to find me.*

"We have to do something." I managed, somehow, to form the words. "They have Vivvie. They have Emilia."

Henry's Adam's apple bobbed in his throat. "There is nothing we can do." His words were as hard-won as mine. "I wish there were. I *wish*," he repeated roughly, "that we could end this, but

I see no way of making that happen and too many ways that we could make things worse."

What are you saying, Henry?

He responded like I'd said the words out loud. "I am saying that the best way of protecting Vivvie—and ourselves—might be to join her."

"*What?*" I said sharply. If I'd been capable of speaking in anything other than a whisper, my voice would have risen.

Henry grabbed my shoulders, turning my body square to his. "We would be safer down in the classroom with Vivvie," he said. "*You* would be safer down there."

In all the time I'd known him, I'd never seen Henry Marquette on the verge of tears, but I could hear them in his voice. I could see the sheen of despair in his gaze. *Always steady. Always in control.*

"You heard their list of demands," Henry told me, running his thumbs along the edges of my collarbone in a motion so gentle I wondered if he was even conscious of it. "They want something from Ivy. *They won't hurt you.*"

Henry wanted me safe. I recognized the impulse. I recognized that whatever anger he'd felt toward me an hour ago dulled in the face of his need to see me taken care of now.

I understood because I wanted him safe, too.

My free hand made its way to his wrist. I held on to him, holding on to me.

"Maybe you're right," I said. "Maybe we would be less likely to get caught in the crossfire if we turned ourselves in." I could feel his pulse. I could feel the heat from his body. "But the chances of getting accidentally shot only matter until they start shooting us on purpose."

Mrs. Perkins had taped the headmaster talking about *cooperation*. The terrorists were making demands. I knew better than most what could—and would—happen when demands like that weren't met.

They'll line us up, one by one. They would start with the low-value targets, the *disposable* ones. They might carve pieces off the rest of us for show.

A sound below sent a jolt of adrenaline straight to my heart. I processed the fact that there were armed men in the stairway below an instant before Henry pressed me back against the wall, his body covering mine. *Shielding* mine.

It happened too fast for me to counter. I stood, frozen. *This is it. No more running. No more maybes.*

A floor below us, the footsteps stopped.

A door opened.

A door closed.

Henry's breath was warm on my face, his lips no more than a millimeter from mine.

The second floor. The guards went to the second floor. On the third, we were safe—for now.

Henry eased back, a millimeter or less between my body and his.

"I won't let anything happen to you," he said roughly.

"Even though I'm a liar?" I hadn't planned on saying those words. I hadn't intended to ask for absolution. I wasn't sure I deserved it.

"We're all liars sometimes, Kendrick," Henry said.

I surged upward, pushing off from the wall and closing the space between my lips and his. For a split second, he stiffened, and then his hands dug into my hair, and he was kissing me back.

I would have pegged Henry Marquette for a gentlemanly kisser—restrained, a little too proper, a little too controlled.

I would have been wrong.

Henry Marquette kissed the way I fought—fiercely. No fears. No hesitations. No regrets. Just Henry and me and a hunger I'd never recognized in either one of us. For this.

For us.

I broke away first, my lips lingering near his for a second or two. Breathing raggedly, I forced myself to get it together. We didn't have time for this.

"We can't turn ourselves in, and we can't stay here." I took a step back and turned my attention back to the tablet in my hand. I didn't look at Henry, *couldn't* look at him. Instead, I scrolled through the video feeds. "I was going to try to get to the security offices, to see if there was a way of getting a message out."

There was a beat of silence.

"You are aware, I assume," Henry said, "that this is the single worst idea in the history of the world?"

Do you have a better suggestion? I let a raised eyebrow do the talking for me.

Henry stared at me. I could see the wheels turning. He was thinking something, *feeling* something, but the exact meaning of the tension in his jaw, the way he was looking at me—that, I couldn't diagnose.

"The tunnel." Henry's voice was—if possible—quieter than it had been up until that moment.

"The one Di had us use to break into the Aquatics Center?" I said. "I thought of that, but there's no way we can make it out of the main building. There are snipers on the roof and armed guards at every exit."

Henry shook his head. "That's not the only entrance to the tunnel."

My mouth went dry. Suddenly, I was back in the library, watching Anna and her Secret Service agent. I hadn't asked myself why the agent had chosen the library for his standoff with the guards.

He told Dr. Clark that he had to get Anna out.

I grabbed Henry's arm, the way he'd grabbed mine in the hall. The part of my brain that was driven by instincts—by an ancient and unmentionable fear of predators, of darkness, of death— kicked into high gear. I ignored the vicious and incessant beating of my own heart. I ignored the lead that lined my stomach when I thought about the fact that I was risking Henry's life, as well as my own.

"I think I know where to look for the entrance to the tunnel in this building," I told Henry. I checked the tablet feeds, then nodded toward the stairs. I forced myself to let go of his arm, forced myself not to touch him, not to think about touching him. "Move."

CHAPTER 52

We made it three-quarters of the way to the library before a man with an assault rifle caught us, head-on.

"Down on the ground!"

I recognized the man as the one who'd hit Anna Hayden over the head, the one who'd implied that he was taking orders from Dr. Clark *for now*.

Mercenary. Unpredictable.

I dropped to the ground. The guard rounded on Henry.

"You!" he said, jabbing the gun in Henry's direction.

Henry held his hands up. He slowly lowered himself to his knees. I saw a flicker in the gunman's eyes. He stepped toward Henry.

"Marquette," I blurted out Henry's last name. "He's Henry Marquette. I'm Tess Kendrick Keyes."

Henry stared down the gun—and the man who held it. When he spoke, each word was deliberate and crisp. "You want us alive."

Don't shoot. Don't shoot him. Please, don't—

After an elongated moment, the guard lowered the gun ten or fifteen degrees—just enough to start my heart beating again in my chest, not enough to stop me from picturing him changing his mind and pulling the trigger.

The guard shifted his gaze from Henry to me. He removed one hand from his gun and lifted it to his ear. I realized that he was talking to someone, sending a message. "I've got eyes on—"

One second, Henry was beside me, and the next, he lunged for the man's gun.

No.

Henry's hands closed around the barrel of the gun and he slammed it back into the gunman's face, throwing his whole body after the blow. The two of them went down. The gun went off.

No.

I leapt forward, nothing in my mind except getting to Henry. If I could get to him, he would be okay. If I could touch him, I could save him. I could *make him* fine.

Please, God, let him be fine.

"Tess." Henry stood up off the guard. I looked for blood, looked for a hole in his shoulder or chest. "Kendrick." Henry's voice was sharper this time. "We need to go. Now."

He's okay. Henry's okay. As we took off running for the library, I fought the urge to glance back over my shoulder. *No blood*, I thought. *There was no blood. Not on Henry. Not on the gunman.*

"He's unconscious," Henry said as we hit the library door. "He won't stay that way."

Maybe one of us should have grabbed the gun—but I didn't know how to shoot it. I doubted Henry did, either.

We have to find a way out of here. We have to find the tunnel before someone comes looking for the man Henry took out.

How long did we have? Seconds? Minutes?

Fueled by adrenaline, I pushed forward. Where had the Secret Service agent been heading?

If I were an entrance to an underground tunnel, where would I be?

"The tunnel's under us," I told Henry. "The entrance probably is, too."

I squatted down, running my hands frantically over the floor. There had to be something. I looked for a flip, a switch, a crack in the floor—

"Here," Henry called. He threw his weight against a book-shelf. It creaked, then started to move. I hurried to help him, not questioning how he'd found it, how we could have possibly gotten so lucky when—

"This way!"

I heard the shout, and then I heard running—toward the library, toward us. The bookshelf gave way. Something clicked, and a second later, I was looking into a dark hole.

The tunnel—if we were lucky.

"You go first," Henry told me. "Give me the tablet, and go."

There was no time to think, no time to waste. I handed him the tablet, then dropped down into the hole and landed hard. I looked up.

"Go," Henry told me again. There was a finality to his tone, and I realized then why he'd asked for the tablet.

He's not coming.

"Henry!" My yell was lost to the sound of the bookshelf mov-ing back into place. A second after the entrance closed, there was silence, and a moment after that, I heard the sound of feet overhead.

Of gunshots.

They won't hurt him. He's a high-value target. He has to be—

There was no way back up.

I have to go.

I had to get help. For Henry—and Vivvie and Emilia and all the others. I stumbled in the dark, feeling my way to the tunnel wall. It was cool and damp to the touch. I kept moving—running, stumbling, falling and getting back up.

I'd *crawl* if I had to.

They have Henry. I didn't let myself consider the possibility that there was no Henry anymore, like there was no John Thomas. I didn't let myself think about Henry's face belonging to a body and not a boy. *They have Henry. They have Vivvie. They have Emilia.*

I pushed myself forward. Finally, *finally*—there was a break in the darkness. The closer I got to the end of the tunnel, the easier it was to make out the slants of light. On the ground, I could make out the outline of two long-dead glow sticks.

Three days. It had been three days since the party, one week since John Thomas had been killed.

It had been less than ten minutes since I'd left Henry, less than an hour since the armed men had fired their first shot.

I put my hands flat on the iron door to the tunnel and pushed. My body protested. So did the hinges on the door, but a second later, it gave. I heard the sound of running water. *It must have rained,* I thought. The drainage ditch had been dry on Friday, but now I slogged through water to get to a single metal rung. I put my foot on it, hoisted myself up. Removing the grate was easy, but getting through was harder wet and alone than it had been on Friday.

I threw my upper body against the ground overhead for purchase. I made it out. I made it to my feet. And then I heard the voice behind me.

"So nice of you to join us, Tess."

I turned slowly. Mrs. Perkins stood behind me. She wasn't visibly armed, but the guards on either side of her were.

Henry stood just behind them.

I could feel my body getting ready to give out beneath me. Henry was alive, I had failed, and the adrenaline that had kept me going for the past hour drained out of me, leaving my body feeling like little more than a shell.

I stumbled. Henry moved past the guards to catch me. The terrorists didn't turn their guns on him. They didn't so much as bat an eye as he steadied my body with his.

Henry held on to me a second longer than he had to. He whispered two words directly into my ear, and then he let me go.

"Take her to the third floor. Put her with Raleigh." Mrs. Perkins offered me a smile, too sharp-edged for her soccer-mom face. "I've heard you fancy yourself an expert problem solver, Tess. I'm interested to see what you make of my current problem."

I barely heard her. I was fixated on two things—the words Henry had whispered in my ear and the fact that the order to take me to the third floor hadn't been issued to the guards.

Mrs. Perkins had issued that order to Henry.

And the words he'd whispered to me as he'd caught me, his body keeping mine vertical?

I'm sorry.

CHAPTER 53

Kendrick, what you don't know could fill an ocean.

Mrs. Perkins reached out and laid a hand on Henry's shoulder. Henry didn't stiffen at the terrorist's touch. He didn't bat an eye.

We're all liars sometimes, he'd told me.

We infiltrate. Dr. Clark's words to Emilia in the library washed back over me. *We observe, we influence, we* recruit.

"Don't fight this," Henry told me. His voice was quiet. I wished he didn't sound like the boy I'd known. I wish I couldn't see *my* Henry in his eyes as he continued. "Don't fight me."

Armed men bound my hands behind my back. They bound me to a chair, and Henry watched.

He knew that when I'd been kidnapped, I'd been bound. He knew that I couldn't even see a roll of duct tape without flashing back, *and he watched.*

"Leave us," Henry told the guards.

I thought of the armed man in the hallway, the way he'd looked at Henry as he said: *You.*

Not *you* as in *now* you *get on the ground. You* as in *I know* you. *You* as in *what are* you *doing with this girl?*

At Henry's request, the guards left us. I stared at the boy I'd kissed less than an hour earlier. I forced myself to look at him, to take in every line of his face, features I'd memorized, features I *knew*—

"Kendrick."

Full lips, wide jaw, piercingly clear eyes.

"Don't call me that," I told Henry. "Don't call me anything."

He lowered his voice. "I tried to get you out."

Anger bubbled up inside me and came out as a strange, dry laugh. "You tried to get *me* out," I repeated. "What about Vivvie? And Emilia?" I didn't give him time to reply. "What about all those freshmen who think you hung the moon?"

Henry's jaw clenched. "I never meant for any of this to happen. If you understood—"

Understood?

"These people killed John Thomas!" The words ripped their way out of my mouth. I hurt, just saying them. "Emilia accused Dr. Clark, and do you know what she said? She said that it wasn't *her* idea. That *she's* not the one who pulled the trigger. But she didn't deny that Senza Nome was behind it."

"I didn't know." Henry's reply was guttural. I barely heard it. "About John Thomas, about his father. Until this weekend, I never even suspected—"

"I had John Thomas's blood on my hands," I choked out. "And you . . ."

He'd washed it off. He'd given me his shirt. He'd taken care of me.

"I didn't know," Henry repeated. "I swear it. No one was supposed to get hurt."

I heard what Henry wasn't saying. *No one was supposed to get hurt* here.

Henry had told me that his grandfather's death had taught him that the people in power couldn't always be trusted. I'd kept the truth about the conspiracy from him for fear of what he might do if he knew. And when he'd heard me mention the possibility of a fourth conspirator, he'd been devastated. He'd told me that he *wished* I'd told him.

Not because he didn't know, I realized, unable to keep from trying to make sense of how a boy who believed in honor—who believed in protecting people who couldn't protect themselves—could have let himself be recruited into a group like this.

He already knew the conspiracy wasn't over. They told him first.

If Senza Nome was trying to manipulate Henry, they might not have told him there were suspects, plural, for the remaining conspirator. They might have led him to believe there was only one.

"The president." I forced myself to say it out loud. "They told you that the president is the one who had your grandfather killed."

Henry stood, staring down at me with the same sick masochism that kept me from looking away from him. He didn't speak—didn't confirm what I'd implied, but didn't deny it, either.

They told you the president killed your grandfather. They made you believe they could make it right.

"They just asked for money at first," Henry said. "Then information."

Information. I thought of all the times Henry had asked me what Ivy was up to. I thought of the two of us, sitting in the dark on the front porch. I thought of Henry asking me about Ivy's files.

He'd used me.

The door to the room opened. Headmaster Raleigh, bound and beaten, was shoved in. Henry tore his gaze away from me, turned, and went to secure the headmaster.

"You don't have to do this, Mr. Marquette," Headmaster Raleigh told him.

"If I want to stay in a position to keep the people in this school safe," Henry told him—told *me*, "yes, I do."

I turned my head down and to the side. I refused to look at him. I refused to even acknowledge that I'd heard the words.

I didn't look back when I heard Henry walking toward the door.

I didn't lift my head until it closed behind him.

I blinked away the tears that blurred my vision. The headmaster came into focus, bound opposite me in this tiny office.

"Whatever they tell you to do," the headmaster told me, blood crusted to his lip, his face swollen, "you do it, Ms. Kendrick."

I was surprised by the fierceness in his tone.

"This is my fault," Raleigh said, as much to himself as to me. "I brought them here. It's my fault."

I thought of Dr. Clark, watching, infiltrating, influencing, *recruiting.* I thought of the headmaster's secretary, with her finger on the pulse of the school. "They were already here."

When Henry's grandfather died, Dr. Clark had tasked the class with choosing a replacement. Because she wanted to challenge us to think critically about the process? Or because she wanted to know what our parents thought? What they knew?

We see everything. We know all of your secrets. And we wait.

I forced my mind away from the memory of Daniela Nicolae's words and back to the man across from me. "Why did you take the picture down?" That question surprised me almost as much as it surprised the headmaster. "The photo of you with the president at Camp David," I continued. *The photo of you with Vivvie's father and one of the other men who conspired to kill Justice Marquette.* "Why did you take it down?"

I'd thought the headmaster was in bed with the terrorists. When he'd read out the words they had written, I'd believed they were his. If it hadn't been for that photograph, for a lingering sense of suspicion cast upon all the men there, would I have questioned that? Would I have realized that the person in the best position to *influence* the headmaster, to *silently observe* everything that went on in these halls, was someone non-threatening?

Someone who goes largely unnoticed.

"What interest could you possibly have in that photograph?" the headmaster asked, sounding more like the aggrieved man who'd sat opposite me in his office more times than I could count. "Really, Ms. Kendrick—"

"Please," I said. "I just want to know."

The headmaster sniffed but deigned to oblige. "I was told displaying that photograph so prominently was a bit gauche."

I heard the doorknob turn a second before the door opened. My wrists tensed against the ties that bound them to no avail. I couldn't move. I couldn't fight back. I was helpless.

Henry had left me helpless.

Dr. Clark shut the door gingerly behind her. She knelt down in front of me. "Look at you, Tess." Her voice was gentle. She murmured the words, like it grieved her to see me like this.

Like she *hadn't* shot a Secret Service agent dead while I watched.

"This isn't how I wanted this meeting to happen," Dr. Clark told me.

"Moira, get away from that young lady or I will—" The headmaster's threat cut off abruptly as he realized there was nothing he could do. Nothing he could say.

Dr. Clark gave no sign that she had heard him. Her warm brown eyes were solely focused on me. "I know how this must look to you, Tess. I know that you cannot begin to fathom what I've done here today, or why. I know that you cannot understand why a boy like Henry would listen to what I have to say—"

"What did you tell him?" I asked, my body tensing against the ties again, causing the chair to jar slightly.

She didn't jump. She didn't blink. "I told him what I am trying to tell you. What's happening here today isn't who we are. This"— she gestured at me, at the headmaster—"is not what we do."

Mine is a glorious calling. The tone I'd heard in Daniela Nicolae's voice in that video was present to the nth degree in my teacher's. This was what zealotry looked like.

This was a true believer.

"I came to this life when I wasn't much older than you," Dr. Clark said softly.

"After 9/11," I said, cutting her off before she could say more. *There's nothing you can say that will make you anything less than a monster to me.* I hoped she could hear that in my voice.

Whether she could or not, she continued, "After the attacks, I wanted to do something. The world wasn't safe. Everything had changed."

"So you became a terrorist," I supplied, my voice razor sharp. "If you can't beat them, join them?"

"No," Dr. Clark said vehemently. "No, Tess. I would never—"

I tuned out whatever it was she would *never* do. She'd killed a man as I'd watched.

"While I was abroad, I was approached by someone. A mentor. He thought that I might be interested in a life of service." Dr. Clark paused. "He was right."

"Service," I repeated dully. "You call this *service*?"

"Our organization was designed to infiltrate terrorist groups. We influence their decisions. We stop them from the inside out. We play their game better than they do."

I was on the verge of asking her how, precisely, the Hardwicke School qualified as a *terrorist group*. But I decided it wasn't worth the words.

"To do what we do," Dr. Clark said, leaning forward and trying to take my hand, "we need eyes and ears everywhere."

"Eyes and ears?" I jerked my hand back. "I'm bound to a chair, I saw you shoot a man dead, and you want me to believe that you just observe?" She believed what she was telling me. She expected me to believe it, too. "You people bombed a hospital!"

"And no one was hurt in that bombing," Dr. Clark said fiercely. "You think that was an accident? A mistake? We don't *make* mistakes."

"Then why—" I cut myself off. "You knew Walker Nolan would tip someone off. That was the point."

"Sometimes the biggest threats come from the inside. Sometimes the system is broken, Tess. Absolute power corrupts absolutely." Dr. Clark glanced at the headmaster, then turned back to me. "You know what it's like to stand up to people in positions of power, Tess. I've always admired the way you defend people who are not in a position to defend themselves." She paused. "Is it so hard to believe that someone like me might want to do the same?"

I knew, just listening to her say the words, that she'd said a variation of them to Henry. She'd told him that the system was broken, corrupt. She'd led him to believe he could fix it.

"You know what President Nolan is capable of," Dr. Clark said. "You know what happened to Justice Marquette, and you know that the Nolan administration covered it up."

"You told Henry that it wasn't over." I forced myself to look Dr. Clark directly in the eyes. "You told him that the president was responsible for his grandfather's death."

"I believe someone in that administration was," Dr. Clark countered. "Marquette was killed by the *president's* doctor and a Secret Service agent on the *president's* detail. That doesn't strike me as a coincidence." She paused. "It shouldn't strike you as one, either."

I imagined Henry, listening to these words. "You told Henry—"

"I told him that we could help him fight back, that we could help him get justice, that *no one* should be above reproach. Four men died. Were we not supposed to notice? Justice Marquette. His doctor. The front-runner to replace him. And a Secret Service agent, shot down by a SWAT team?" She lowered her voice. "The

White House kept a lid on the agent's identity, but we found out. We always find out. There was a reason the Nolan administration wanted this buried, Tess. Who do you think ordered the SWAT team to shoot Damien Kostas? Who do you think ordered that a man be executed, with no due process, no law?"

The fourth conspirator.

"So why not expose the truth?" I asked Dr. Clark. "If you really care about corruption and cover-ups, why not—"

"When someone takes office, we develop a contingency plan. If they're worthy of the office, it need not be activated. If they are not . . ." Dr. Clark executed an elegant shrug.

A contingency plan, I thought. *Like Walker Nolan.* That had to be a plan years in the making. They'd already infiltrated Walker's life before President Nolan was elected. They'd already sent Daniela to him. So when they developed suspicions about the Nolan administration, they didn't have to try to dig up incriminating information.

They already had damaging information of their own.

They'd staged the bombing, revealed the relationship between Walker and the bomber, for the sole purpose of taking the president down.

My brain spun. "So shooting the president, that was what? Another contingency plan?"

"That shooting," a voice said from the doorway, "was the one contingency we hadn't planned for."

I whipped my head in the direction of the voice.

"I need a minute," Dr. Clark told Mrs. Perkins.

"You've had a minute," Mrs. Perkins responded. "And you're wasting your time. This one won't flip."

Dr. Clark stood up. Her lips were pressed into a thin line, the muscles in her face taut. "These things take time."

"Unfortunately, Moira, time is one thing we do not have in any abundance." Mrs. Perkins turned her attention from Dr. Clark to me. The gleam in her eyes was darker and harder than anything I'd seen in Dr. Clark's.

Some people do horrible things because of their beliefs, I thought, a chill settling over my body. *And some people choose beliefs that let them do horrible things.*

"You killed John Thomas," I said, unable to look away from a woman I'd always considered welcoming and warm.

"When the president was shot and it seemed likely the vice president would be taking office, I put a new plan into motion. We needed to kill a student in order to get the headmaster to agree to bring in extra security. *Armed* security." Mrs. Perkins shrugged. "The fact that Mr. Wilcox had been poking around in his father's files made him an obvious choice. We would have had to deal with him eventually. Two birds, one stone. I saw an opportunity." There was a gleam in Mrs. Perkins's eyes when she said those words. "And I took it."

"His father was working with Senza Nome," I said. "He was one of you."

"He was *never* one of us," Mrs. Perkins replied. "Never trusted. He was a viper whose goals aligned temporarily with ours. Why overlook an opportunity like this for someone like that?"

An opportunity to orchestrate a takeover of Hardwicke while the vice president was in charge.

"So that's it?" I said. "You saw an opportunity, and you took it? And you expect me to believe you had nothing to do with the president being shot in the first place? That was just a happy coincidence?" I asked. "Senza Nome claimed responsibility for the attack!"

"Did we?" Mrs. Perkins returned, an edge creeping into her voice. "Did we *really*?" Her eyes bore into me.

Daniela Nicolae had told interrogators that Senza Nome hadn't been behind the attempt on the president's life.

"No matter," Mrs. Perkins said, shrugging. "The attack on President Nolan might have disturbed one plan, but it gave us an opening for another."

One plan. Daniela Nicolae, Walker Nolan, and a PR attack that would have crippled the current administration during midterm elections.

An opening for another. The seizing of Hardwicke.

"Now," Mrs. Perkins declared, "I have a problem, and you, my dear, are going to solve it."

That isn't going to happen.

"Certain parties remain unconvinced that this is a battle they cannot win," Mrs. Perkins continued. "The United States does not negotiate with terrorists, et cetera, et cetera." She gave a roll of her eyes. "And the people who *are* more amenable to negotiating have asked for a show of good faith."

Good faith wasn't a phrase anyone should apply to these people. Ever.

"We need your help," Dr. Clark told me. "*I* need your help to get all of your classmates out of here alive."

All of them? I thought. *Or just the ones who aren't disposable?*

As if to punctuate my thoughts, Mrs. Perkins turned, lifted her gun, and put a bullet between the headmaster's eyes.

My stomach rebelled, nausea slamming into me with the force of a truck. I fought back against it, swallowing and willing my ears to stop ringing.

"Do I have your attention?" Mrs. Perkins asked.

"Yes." I gritted out the word.

Mrs. Perkins knelt next to me, the way Dr. Clark had. The expression on her face was almost motherly. "You and I are going to have a chat, Tess. And then, as a show of good faith, I'm going to let you go."

I stared at the hole in Headmaster Raleigh's forehead, the blood streaming down his lifeless face.

"Let me go?" I repeated.

"Oh, yes," Mrs. Perkins said. "I'm going to let you go, and you're going to tell dear Ivy and the acting president and everyone else who asks everything I'm going to tell you. You will communicate our requests, and you'll encourage the powers that be to respond appropriately."

Respond appropriately. As in, give the terrorists what they want.

"And if they don't?" I asked.

"You're a resourceful girl," Mrs. Perkins said, "related to some very powerful people. I have every confidence that you'll work this out."

My mouth went dry. "And if I don't?"

"I'll give you eight hours. After that, every hour on the hour, I will put a gun to one of your classmates' heads. And, Tess?" Mrs. Perkins reached out and gently pushed a stray hair from my face. "I'll enjoy pulling the trigger."

CHAPTER 54

Less than two hours after I'd heard the first shot, I walked out the front gates of Hardwicke with my hands raised. I was greeted by a SWAT team, the FBI, Homeland Security, and a dozen guns trained at my head.

"Are you armed?" a woman in an FBI jacket asked. "Are you wearing any explosives?"

I shook my head.

"Are you injured?"

I gave another shake of my head.

"We need you to get down on the ground," the woman said. "Face-first."

I did as she asked. A second later, I was being patted down. They found nothing other than the USB drive I wore on a chain around my neck. *Instructions. For the authorities. From Senza Nome.*

They let me sit up. I didn't realize I was bone-cold and shaking until the FBI woman put her own jacket around my shoulders. "You're okay," she told me. "Tess, I need you to listen to me: you're okay."

Maybe those words should have been comforting, but they weren't. I was okay. But if I didn't do exactly as Mrs. Perkins had instructed, if I didn't follow orders, the others wouldn't be. Not Vivvie. Not Emilia. Not even Henry, if they thought they had anything less than his undivided loyalty.

"I need an EMT in here!" the female FBI agent shouted. "She's going into shock!"

People crowded in around me. Agents fired off questions. A medic shined a light in my eyes.

Eight hours, I thought. *I have eight hours.*

"Tess!"

My body responded to Ivy's voice, my shoulders caving inward, my head coming up.

"Oh God, Tessie." Someone tried to stop Ivy from coming to me. She turned on him like nothing I'd ever seen. "That is *my daughter*," she said, fury in her voice and tears streaming down her face. "And the next person who tries to get between me and my daughter is going to rue their existence on this earth." Ivy didn't believe in unspecific threats: "Every secret you've been keeping will find its way out. Every decision you make will be questioned. You will be audited, investigated, and transferred to the most hellish nightmare of a desk job I can find. *Now, get out of my way.*"

Everyone got out of Ivy's way.

She was by my side in a heartbeat. She dropped to her knees, fast enough and hard enough on the concrete that it must have hurt, but she didn't seem to feel it. Her arms encircled my body, pulling me tight against her one second and pushing me away the next as she ran her hands over my shoulders and arms, assuring herself that I was here, that I was in one piece, that I was whole.

Then Ivy was saying my name, over and over again, a low, keening sound. She asked me if I was okay, her hands finding their way to the side of my face. She smoothed down my hair, pressed a kiss to my forehead.

My arms wrapped their way around her. "Ivy."

"I'm here," Ivy murmured into my hair. "You're safe. I've got you, Tessie. I won't let anything happen to you. I won't ever let anything happen to you."

"Ms. Kendrick." The female FBI agent stood a respectable distance away. She'd given Ivy and me our moment but couldn't afford to give us any more. "I understand that Tess has been through a great ordeal, but she's our only source about what's going on in there, and that makes her our best chance at getting the rest of those kids out alive."

Eight hours, I thought. *Less than that now.* I wanted to believe that the FBI could handle this, that if I told them what I knew and what I'd been told, they would find a way to save the day.

But I didn't have that luxury.

Every hour on the hour, I will put a gun to one of your classmates' heads.

"The agent's right," I told Ivy. "I need to talk to them."

I'll enjoy pulling the trigger.

"And after that," I said, my voice low enough that only Ivy could hear me, "I need to talk to you."

Several feet away, behind a law enforcement line, I saw Adam, trying to keep a grip on his emotions as he stared at Ivy and me. And behind Adam, I saw a stone-faced William Keyes. Ivy followed my gaze, and I clarified my previous statement.

"All of you."

CHAPTER 55

It was four hours before the FBI let Ivy and Adam take me home—half of the eight I'd been given gone answering questions and describing the situation on the inside.

The hostage negotiator and profilers had asked me to provide a description of each of the players involved. Homeland Security had then begun running background checks on Mrs. Perkins and Dr. Clark. I'd been able to describe one of the guards—the one who'd knocked Anna unconscious, the one Henry had incapacitated in his quest to get me out—in enough detail for an artist to make a computer rendering.

I told them everything I knew about the terrorists' numbers, the brief dissension I'd sensed in their ranks, the game of good terrorist/bad terrorist Dr. Clark and Mrs. Perkins had played with me. I told them about the tunnel and the security feed and the men I'd seen shot dead.

I told them they had eight hours. I told them what would happen if they didn't give Mrs. Perkins what she'd asked for.

I told them everything except the truth about Henry—and a subset of the demands that Mrs. Perkins had made of me.

"Can I get you anything?" Ivy asked as she opened the door to our house. I stepped into the foyer, and for the first time, it felt like home. This was where I belonged. I would have given anything to stay here.

With Ivy.

"Could you make me some hot chocolate?" I asked, my voice hoarse.

The request took Ivy by surprise. I wasn't good at letting her take care of me. I'd never asked her, even in a little way, even silently, to be my mom.

"I'll make us each a cup."

I did us both the favor of ignoring the raw emotion in Ivy's voice. She went to make the hot chocolate.

"Don't do that again," Adam said quietly. He'd joined us on the ride home, but like Bodie, he'd remained mostly silent, fading into the background under the roar of the connection between Ivy and me.

"Don't do what?" I said. "Ask for hot chocolate?"

"Don't let bad things happen," Adam said, pulling me suddenly into a hug, his words sounding more like a prayer than an order directed to me. "Not ever. Not to you."

"I'll get right on that," I replied into his chest.

He held on to me for a few seconds longer, and then the front door opened. William Keyes hovered in the doorway, his gaze frozen on Adam and me.

"Make yourself at home," Bodie told the old man dryly. "No need to knock."

Bodie's words snapped all three of us out of our reveries. The kingmaker stepped over the threshold and shut the door behind him, and Adam turned, one arm still wrapped protectively around me, to face his father.

"I was told my presence was required," Keyes informed Adam. There was a note of challenge in his voice, but he was the one who broke eye contact first, transferring his gaze from Adam to me.

"You are unharmed?"

Keyes had been updated on my condition, but this was the first chance he'd gotten to ask me for himself. I could only imagine how frustrating he'd found waiting—and the fact that the FBI had let Ivy in to see me but not him.

"I'm uninjured," I said. "But I'm not okay."

Ivy picked that moment to return. She handed me a mug of hot chocolate and kept the other for herself, positioning herself directly to my left. With Adam on one side and Ivy on the other, I should have felt safe.

I should have felt protected.

Three hours and fifty-four minutes.

I didn't have time for dread or guilt or fear.

"I'm not going to be okay until this is over," I said, looking from one face to the next. "And this isn't going to be over until we give them what they want."

"I didn't tell the FBI everything."

The five of us were settled around Ivy's conference table now—Ivy, Adam, Bodie, the kingmaker, and me.

"Why not?" Adam was the one who issued the question.

I answered it. "Because I was told not to."

Until I was sure that there was no chance of word getting back to Senza Nome, I couldn't take the risk. If the terrorists had two operatives planted at Hardwicke, I couldn't rule out the possibility that they had someone in the FBI, too.

"Besides," I said out loud, looking around the table at each of them, one by one, "this part of the message was for you."

You're a resourceful girl related to some very powerful people. I could still see the exact glint in Mrs. Perkins's eyes. *I have every confidence that you'll work this out.*

"The United States government does not negotiate with terrorists," I said. "That's a problem. We need the vice president to agree to release Daniela Nicolae. The authorities are going to have to send her into the school to get anyone else out."

That statement was met with momentary silence.

"That is a problem," Ivy admitted. "The situation at Hardwicke has already gained national attention. The vice president can't be seen negotiating with terrorists. Unless we want to encourage future threats, his hands are tied."

"Then you need to untie them," I said. "I don't know how. I don't care how. But this has to happen."

"Why?" William Keyes asked bluntly. Now that he had eyes on me, he was not particularly inclined to give the terrorists what they wanted.

"Because," I said forcefully, "if we can't get the vice president to release Daniela, people die. *Kids* will die."

"Why does this group care so much about securing Daniela Nicolae's release?" The tone in my grandfather's voice reminded me that he had a very personal stake in this. "Who is she to them?"

"A soldier?" Bodie suggested. "Left behind enemy lines."

Adam stared straight ahead. *He* was a soldier.

"They let her get caught," Adam said slowly. "Didn't they?" The question was rhetorical, and if any part of him had expected an answer, it was from Ivy, not me.

I answered anyway. "They planned on Walker tipping his father off. The hospital was never a target."

"The Nolans were," Ivy inferred. "It was a PR attack from the beginning." She paused. "Her superiors had to know there was a good chance Daniela was going to be apprehended."

Was she expendable? Or did they always have a contingency plan for getting her back?

"You've talked to this woman," William Keyes told Ivy, folding his hands on the table and leaning forward, looming over all of us. "Do you think she knew she was going to be apprehended? Do you think she's a good little soldier, caught behind enemy lines?"

Ivy's expression became a fraction more guarded. My gut said that to her ear, the kingmaker sounded a little too interested in the answer to that question, even if she didn't know why.

"I got a call while Tess was talking with the FBI," Ivy stated, taking her time with the words. "Homeland was interrogating Congressman Wilcox about his connection to Senza Nome. The congressman was on the verge of breaking."

Was?

"Congressman Wilcox was killed in custody shortly before the terrorists released Tess."

I took Ivy's statement to mean that Senza Nome, peace-loving bunch that they were, didn't respond well to the idea of their people talking.

"Daniela's not a soldier to them," Ivy continued. "She's a liability."

Ivy had told me that some of Daniela's interrogators believed that her feelings for Walker were legitimate. They'd questioned whether her loyalties could be changed—and if they already had.

If the people Daniela worked for were questioning them, too, she wasn't just a liability. She was a threat.

"If they could have gotten to her already, they would have," Adam commented. "Just like they got to Wilcox."

"Captain Obvious is right." Bodie leaned back in his chair. "If Daniela's terrorist buddies can't get to her where she's being kept, it's no wonder they want us to tie her up with a bow and send her back."

The kingmaker's jaw twitched slightly. Ivy and Adam didn't know that he was Walker's father. They didn't know that the terrorist was carrying *his* grandchild—and I could see in his eyes that he wasn't going to tell them. They already knew the woman was pregnant. They thought her child was a Nolan. They were closer to the Nolans than they were to him. He wouldn't tell them the truth.

And I couldn't shake the belief that this wasn't my secret to tell.

"We have less than four hours to get Daniela Nicolae released," I said, concentrating on that. There would be time later for me to decide what, if anything, to tell Ivy and Adam about Walker Nolan. Right now, I couldn't afford to forget that we were on a deadline here, and I couldn't let them forget it, either. "If she doesn't walk into Hardwicke in three hours and forty-six minutes, they start shooting. Talk to the vice president, talk to the Pentagon—blackmail, bribe, or steal, I don't care. Find a way."

I directed those words at all of them. The kingmaker was the first to reply.

"And you think," William Keyes said sharply, "that if we give them Daniela Nicolae, they'll just let everyone go?"

Clearly, he didn't see that as a likely scenario.

"No," I replied tautly. "I think that if we give them Daniela Nicolae, and someone leans on the secretary of state to start calling in favors with foreign governments about the overseas prisoners on their list, and twenty million dollars is transferred into their account, and we arrange an exit strategy for them, *then* they will let everyone go."

That wasn't all. That wasn't even half of it. But it was all I could say in this room, in front of all four of them.

"I don't mean to be insensitive to what you've been through," William Keyes said, "but given that my granddaughter has already been released, I do not feel particularly inclined to pay a ransom of any kind."

"So don't pay," I told him, my voice low. "Persuade the other parents to do it. Their children are still in danger. Some of them have deep pockets." I let that sink in. "You're always talking about the art of influence," I told Keyes, "about strategy and manipulation—so make it happen. Coordinate the transfer of the money, and make sure the police can't trace it."

For some reason, Senza Nome had believed the kingmaker might have some level of expertise in the kind of money transfers that couldn't be traced.

"That would be a risk," Keyes said. "It might mean opening myself up to scrutiny I would rather avoid."

I didn't ask him to do this *for me*. I didn't say *please*. The kingmaker would have been the first one to tell me: *A Keyes doesn't beg.*

"Does it bother you at all," Adam asked his father, his voice carefully, dangerously neutral, "to think of someone else's child in danger?"

I studied the old man's face in response to that question. *It bothers him more than he wants to admit.*

"You'll do it?" I asked quietly.

He stood. "I will." He looked at Ivy. "When it comes to getting the vice president to release a known terrorist, however," he continued, "you're on your own."

Keyes let himself out of the conference room, and twenty seconds later, I heard him let himself out the front door.

"What aren't you telling us, Tess?" Ivy's question took me off guard, just as she'd meant it to.

Ivy Kendrick had a sixth sense for when she was only getting half of the story.

"They had another request," I said. "For you."

Still not the whole story. As much as I can give you. As much as you can know.

I kept those thoughts from my face as best I could, pushing back against the black hole of emotion rising up inside me—the desolation, the knife twist of guilt, the white-hot fear at the thing I couldn't and wouldn't tell her.

The thing they had asked—demanded—of *me.*

"They want your files," I said, sticking to what I could tell Ivy. "The program that releases your client's secrets if you go offline. They want it, they want your client list—they want everything."

"How do they even know about the program?" Bodie asked.

My insides twisted as I tried not to think about the fact that Henry had known about the program.

They just asked for money at first. Then information.

Henry had asked me to access Ivy's files.

Before that, on the day that someone had broken into Ivy's office, Henry had volunteered to drop me off.

"Senza Nome has eyes and ears everywhere," I said.

"You can't give them the program," Adam told Ivy softly. "If that information got out, it would be devastating. Dangerous. For this country and for you."

Ivy wasn't looking at Adam. She was looking at me.

"They have Vivvie," I told her.

Ivy didn't flinch, but I saw the moment my words landed.

"They have Henry."

She didn't know what Henry had done, what he was. She knew the Henry I'd known—and that boy was worth fighting for.

"There might be a version of my files that I could give them," Ivy said. "Enough secrets for them to think it was the real thing, not enough to do more damage than I can fix."

Adam clamped his jaw down in a way that told me he wasn't happy with the idea of giving the terrorists anything. My stomach twisted for a different reason.

"Whatever you give them," I told Ivy, "make sure they think it's real. Pretend it's *my* life that depends on it."

Ivy stood and came to stand behind me. She ran a hand lightly over my head, assuring herself that I was still here, that I was fine.

She'd do what I'd asked of her. I had to trust that—because ultimately, my life *did* depend on it.

That was what had made this homecoming so impossible. That was why it hurt to be here with Ivy, why I couldn't bring myself to drink the last of my hot chocolate.

Of all of Mrs. Perkins's demands, the last one was the only one I couldn't tell Ivy.

After I'd done what they'd sent me out here to do, if I wanted my friends and classmates to live, I had to do one last thing.

I had to go back.

CHAPTER 56

Two hours and twenty-two minutes.

Ivy had gone to talk to the vice president. Adam had gotten an appointment with the secretary of state to see what wheels she could grease with respect to the release of foreign prisoners. Bodie was working on Ivy's files. And I was waiting—for the kingmaker to make good on his word, for the next stage of the plan to go into effect.

The doorbell rang. Bodie answered it with a gun.

"I come in peace!" Asher announced on the front porch. "Your friendly neighborhood rogue, recently suspected of murder!"

Bodie lowered the gun.

"Tess," he yelled, "you have company."

As I came to stand face-to-face with Asher, I didn't question the fact that in the midst of a terrorist attack, he was making jokes. Humor was Asher's first, best, and last line of defense against the world.

I met his eyes, and that defense crumbled. Even Asher couldn't manage a smile now.

"Emilia saved me," I told him. I was aware, on some level, that my face was wet, but it took me longer to realize that I was crying. I told Emilia's twin about the way she'd walked out into the line of fire, her head held high.

"It would take more than mere terrorists," Asher said, "to keep my sister down." He choked slightly on the words but kept talking. "I think we both know she's probably composing a college essay about the whole experience in her head as we speak."

I nodded, the edges of my lips pulling up. Nodding hurt. Smiling hurt. Thinking about Emilia hurt.

"Henry is probably lecturing someone," Asher continued. "And Vivvie is winning them all over with her best sad-puppy-dog eyes."

Vivvie is facedown on a floor somewhere. Henry might be the one holding the gun.

"I'm sorry," Asher blurted out. "I know it wasn't . . . I know you're not . . ." I'd never heard Asher at a loss for words. "I should have been there," he said finally.

If he hadn't been suspended . . .

If he'd been in school today . . .

If, if, if . . . It was a thought pattern I knew all too well.

If I'd told Henry the truth about his grandfather's death, if he'd heard it from me, instead of from Dr. Clark . . .

If I hadn't upset Vivvie, if she hadn't run, if I'd had her with me . . .

If I'd been the one to turn myself in, instead of Emilia . . .

"I have to go back," I told Asher, my voice as lifeless as I felt inside. "Either I go back in with everything they asked for, or they start shooting students."

His face pale, Asher turned his back on me. He bowed his head. I waited for him to say something, but instead, when he did turn around, it was to launch himself at me. He hugged me, as fiercely as Ivy had.

"If you get yourself killed," he whispered, "you'll never get to see the interpretive dance I plan to create based on this experience."

Asher was crying. He was crying and joking and dying inside— and I knew, in that moment, that I couldn't tell him the full truth of what had happened back at the school.

I couldn't tell him about Henry.

I hadn't told the FBI. I hadn't told Ivy. I wouldn't tell Asher. If I spoke the words out loud, that would make them true. If I said Henry was with the terrorists, there was no going back.

His hands on mine. His lips on mine. That subtle half smile.

I knew, deep down, that there was already no going back. Not ever. Not for me.

"What can I do?" Asher asked. I recognized the helpless tone in his voice. Telling him that I had to hand myself back over to the terrorists hadn't been fair of me. Expecting him to sit here and do nothing—that wasn't fair either.

"Actually," I said, "there is one thing."

"Anything." Asher spoke without emphasis, without frills.

I glanced down at my watch.

Two hours and fourteen minutes.

"I need you to deliver a message for me," I said, "to Vivvie's aunt."

CHAPTER 57

"I take it Ivy doesn't know what you're playing at here." That was how Priya Bharani greeted me an hour later when I picked up her call. She'd placed it from a blocked number, most likely a burner phone.

"You got my message," I replied, lowering my voice and shutting the door to my room. If Bodie knew what I was planning—if he told Adam or Ivy what I was planning—they'd never let me go through with it.

And if they didn't let me go through with it, someone would die, and then another and another, until the terrorists got what they wanted or the FBI decided to risk a high rate of casualties and take Hardwicke back by force.

"I also received another message."

That statement brought me back to the present. I didn't know what the terrorists had asked Vivvie's aunt to do, or how they had passed along their instructions. All I knew was that I'd been told to wait until Ivy had been gone for two hours to get in touch.

"It seems I am to help you make contact with Daniela Nicolae prior to her release," Priya continued. "That is assuming, of course, that her release is somehow secured."

"Ivy's working on it," I said.

One hour and twenty-one minutes.

"Is that all they asked you to do?" I asked Priya, trying to focus on Vivvie's aunt and not the ticking clock. "Getting me in to see Daniela?"

"No," Priya said shortly. "I am to ensure that both you and Daniela are delivered to them." She paused. "And I am, of course, to hand myself over as well."

I paused. "What do they want with you?"

"I made many enemies before I came here."

She'd come here for Vivvie, left her old life—whatever that entailed—behind for Vivvie. I didn't have to ask whether she would hand herself over to these people for Vivvie, too.

"What will they do to you?" I asked Priya, leaning my back against the door to my room, my heart battering my rib cage as I remembered Dr. Clark killing Anna's Secret Service agent and the offhanded way Mrs. Perkins had put a bullet between Headmaster Raleigh's eyes.

On the other end of the phone line, Priya answered my question with silence.

I slid slowly down the door until I was sitting on the floor, my legs pulled to my chest. "What will they do to me?"

I'd tried not to ask myself that question. I'd tried not thinking about Ivy's relief that I was home safe, or Adam's request that nothing bad happen to me ever again.

"If they get what they want?" Priya said, taking her time replying to my question. "They will do nothing to you. They will let you go."

And if they only get part of what they want? If they realize the program Ivy plans to give them is a fake? If the kingmaker can't arrange for the $20 million transfer? If the secretary of state isn't inclined to pull any strings to secure the release of Senza Nome operatives abroad?

"You do not have to do this, Tess."

I got the feeling that saying those words had cost Priya more than I could fathom.

"They asked *you* to bring me," I said.

If Priya didn't do what they asked of her, Vivvie would be the one to pay the price. I couldn't let that happen, no matter the icy chill that seeped into my skin at the thought of going back in.

"Women like this Clarissa Perkins," Priya said softly, "they excel at knowing where the tiniest pressure can create the most pain."

Vivvie was Priya's weak spot—and one of mine.

"I take it that Ivy is not aware—"

"She wouldn't let me out of her sight if she was," I said. I was Ivy's weak spot. I always had been. "I'd find myself knocked unconscious and on a plane to Aruba before I got within five miles of the school."

Ivy had thought, when she'd agreed to let her parents raise me, that lying to me was necessary. She'd thought it was the right thing to do.

I wondered now if that lie had hurt her, the way letting her believe that I was safe and that I was staying hurt me. If I went back in and never walked out of Hardwicke alive, she'd know that I'd chosen to go. She'd know that I had lied to her, and that I'd chosen to leave.

I'm sorry, Ivy. I don't want to go. I don't want to leave you.

I wished, for the first time, that I *could* be the daughter she wanted. The one she deserved.

A knock on the door jarred me from that thought.

"Just a second," I called.

Priya must have heard both the knock and my response because she saved me the trouble of ending the call. "I'll be in touch."

The line went dead. I took two seconds to try to wipe the remnants of our conversation from my face, and then I opened the door to find Bodie standing on the other side. I took the serious expression on his devil-may-care face.

"There's news," I said.

Bodie snorted, the way he always did when I jumped to a conclusion and found myself on solid ground. "Yeah, kitten, there's news."

I thought about Ivy and what she was trying to do—what I *needed* her to do. "Good news or bad news?"

"Depends on who you ask," Bodie told me. "I just got a call from Ivy, who got a call from Georgia Nolan."

The First Lady. My brain took that piece of information and scrambled to fit it into the whole.

Bodie saved me the effort. "President Nolan just woke up."

CHAPTER 58

Three minutes. In three minutes, someone dies.

President Nolan waking up was good news. It was also bad news because President Nolan didn't have a daughter at Hardwicke. He had no personal incentive to negotiate with Senza Nome, especially given that the terrorist whose release they were demanding had targeted his son—and was carrying what the president believed to be his grandchild.

Two minutes.

I hadn't heard from Priya since she'd hung up the phone. In contrast, I had heard from Ivy, who'd told me she had a plan.

I stared at the clock on my phone, willing the phone to ring, willing someone to tell me that the situation was under control.

One minute.

The time stared back at me, a brutal reminder of the promise I'd been made. *Every hour on the hour, I will put a gun to one of your classmates' heads. And, Tess? I'll enjoy pulling the trigger.*

The phone rang. I answered it. "Priya?"

"No." Mrs. Perkins turned my stomach with a single word.

I had to convince her we needed more time. I had to do something. "The president woke up—" I started to say.

"All the more reason to move quickly," the terrorist replied. "Once Nolan's doctor has ruled him physically and mentally fit to return to office, the game's rules change—and not in your favor."

Not in your favor, either, I thought.

"I'm waiting," I said, rushing the words out so she wouldn't interrupt me again. "I did everything you asked. Ivy, Keyes, Priya Bharani—everyone is doing what you asked."

"And I appreciate that," Mrs. Perkins replied, an odd undertone to her voice, a hum of energy that hit me like fingernails on a chalkboard. "But it's important," she continued, "for you to realize that I am the kind of person who keeps my word."

No. I couldn't seem to push the word out of my mouth. When I finally managed to, there was no one on the other end to hear it.

She hung up.

My grip tightened around the phone as I slammed it and my hand into the wall.

My time was up.

I closed my eyes. They burned beneath the lids. I forced a breath into and out of my lungs, shaking with the effort.

The phone buzzed in my hand.

With tortuous effort, I forced my wrist to turn, forced my eyes to open and stare at the screen. My whole body pounding, each breath scalding my lungs, I opened the text message I'd received.

A video.

My mouth and throat and lips went dry. I could feel my heart beating in the tips of my fingers as my shaking hand hit the *play* button.

"Let me go!"

Two pairs of hands forced a struggling boy to his knees. The last time I'd seen him, Matt Benning had exuded a quiet power. *Careful. Restrained. Protective.*

There was no one to protect Matt now.

"I'll do whatever you say," he promised on-screen, his naturally low voice rising to a pitch that was painful to hear.

"Say hello to Tess." The instruction came from off-screen. The voice was female. The two pairs of hands holding Matt in place were male.

"Hello, Tess."

He was ugly-crying. Part of him thought that if he did as they asked, they might let him go. Another part of him knew better.

"Tell her to help you," Mrs. Perkins instructed off-screen.

Matt's Adam's apple bobbed as he swallowed. He stopped struggling against the hold of the guards, going deathly still. "Help me."

His voice was lower now. He sounded like the boy I'd talked to at the party, the one who kept his head down.

"Say it again," Mrs. Perkins said, stepping into frame. She knelt next to Matt and pressed the barrel of her gun to his head.

Matt began struggling wildly against the hands that held him in place, jerking against their grip as if there were an electrical current running through his body. "Help me! Tess—"

The second he said my name, Mrs. Perkins pulled the trigger. The gun went off. The guards held Matt's body a moment longer, then let go. I watched as it fell to the floor.

Not Matt. Not anymore.

Mrs. Perkins addressed the camera. "You have one hour."

The video cut off. I dropped my phone. It clattered to the floor, and I stood there, frozen in place, anchored by dead-weight limbs that wouldn't move.

Help me.

My stomach lurched, and I lunged for my trash can.

Help me. Tess—

I threw up, and I kept throwing up until there was nothing left, my entire body racked with spastic shudders that wouldn't stop. Beside me on the floor, my phone rang.

It rang again.

Pick it up. My brain managed to form the words. *Pick it up. They'll want to know you watched it. If you don't pick it up, they'll—*

Somehow, my hand made its way to the phone. Somehow, I answered. "You *monster*."

"Tess." On some level, I recognized that the voice on the other end of the line wasn't Mrs. Perkins, but the words kept pouring out of my mouth.

"I'll kill you," I said, my voice as hollow as my stomach. "I will find a way, and I will—"

"Tess," Priya said again sharply.

Help me. Tess—

My body shuddered, but there was nothing left to throw up. I didn't sob. "We have to move," I told Priya.

Fifty-nine minutes. Fifty-eight. The countdown had started again.

"When I told you that you didn't have to do this, I meant it." Priya's words barely even penetrated my brain.

"We've been through this," I said. "I do, and I am, and you are wasting time that we do not have."

There was a pause, saturated with the questions Vivvie's aunt was asking herself—Could she do this? Could she allow *me* to do this?

"I'm outside." Priya's words answered the question for both of us. "If you can get out of the house without anyone noticing, I can get you in to see Daniela."

I pushed myself to my feet. I hung up the phone and dragged the back of my hand roughly over my mouth.

It was too late for Matt—but not for every other student held captive in my school.

Help me.

I would. If I had to die trying, so be it.

CHAPTER 59

I didn't know how Priya had located the facility where Daniela Nicolae was being kept. I didn't know what kind of favors she'd had to call in or who she'd had to kill—possibly literally—to get us in. All I knew was that we'd somehow successfully navigated both fingerprint and retinal scans, and the armed guards outside the door stepped aside when we arrived.

Inside the cell, a small woman sat with a hand resting protectively on her protruding stomach. Her dark hair was limp and lifeless, framing her face like a shadow.

Without moving her head, she shifted her eyes up toward Priya. "You, I expected," she said, her voice rough from lack of use. "But I will admit to being surprised about the girl."

Daniela Nicolae, the woman who'd infiltrated Walker Nolan's life in the most intimate ways imaginable, didn't move to get up from the bench on which she sat. She didn't flinch when Priya took a step toward her.

"Your people have seized control of the Hardwicke School."

Daniela's head snapped back, as if Priya's words had hit her with physical force.

"They've given us an ultimatum," Priya continued. "Either we hand you over to them, or they start shooting students."

They've already started, I thought, unable to stop myself from remembering Matt's face in those last seconds.

Daniela's left hand joined her right on her stomach. There was meaning woven into that gesture: she had a child to think about, too.

Whether that helps us or hurts us . . .

I needed to find out. "Could you give us a minute?" I asked Priya.

Vivvie's aunt and the terrorist both turned the full force of their powerful stares on me.

"I was told I had to talk to Daniela alone," I said.

With each second of silence that followed, I became more aware of the fact that I wasn't supposed to be here. No matter what strings Priya had pulled, all it took was the wrong person discovering our presence, and I might find myself in a facility exactly like this one.

Twenty-seven minutes. We didn't have time for complications, and we didn't have the luxury of getting caught.

"You can't get me out of here, can you?" Daniela pulled her gaze from my face and resumed studying Priya. "If you could, we'd already be on the move."

Vivvie's aunt returned the stare. "You aren't leaving here without an executive order." Priya's tone gave no hint to the pressure we were under, but my mind went to what would happen if that executive order didn't come through.

Twenty-six minutes.

"I need to talk to Daniela alone," I repeated. I had to trust that Ivy would come through. She would secure Daniela's release. She had to. And before that happened, before Daniela walked out of this room, I had to deliver the terrorists' message.

And one of my own.

"Let the girl deliver her message," Daniela told Priya. "She won't come to any harm by my hand."

Priya showed no signs whatsoever of moving.

I gave her a look. "She's *really* pregnant," I said. "I'm pretty sure I can take her."

Priya snorted. "I am fairly certain you cannot."

Nonetheless, after tossing another assessing gaze in Daniela's direction, Priya turned to leave, telling us she'd be right outside. Clearly, Daniela was meant to take those words as a threat.

I waited until the door closed behind Priya before I considered what I was getting ready to say—and whether or not it was worth saying it at all. "Walker Nolan is not the president's son."

In all likelihood, that statement—and all the ones that followed—would mean nothing to Daniela. In all likelihood, what I had to say would have no effect on her at all.

"Georgia Nolan had an affair," I continued, "with a man named William Keyes."

It didn't matter that this probably wouldn't work. I had to take the chance that the interrogators were right, that Walker Nolan meant something to the woman in front of me.

"This is the message you were asked to deliver?" Daniela raised an eyebrow to aristocratic heights.

"No," I said. "That's not the message. I'm not telling you this for them. I'm telling you for me. Walker doesn't know. The president doesn't know."

"But you know?" There was a clear note of challenge in Daniela's voice.

"My father died before I was born. His name was Tommy Keyes." I took another step forward. "He was Walker's brother."

Daniela said nothing. I took one step forward, then another. After a long moment, I turned and lowered myself onto the bench next to her. She tracked my movements, hyperaware. On the bench beside her, I stared straight ahead at the wall that Daniela had probably been staring at for days.

"Why tell me this?" Daniela asked finally, breaking the heavy silence that had fallen between us. "What could you possibly expect to gain?"

I didn't turn to look at her. "My name is Tess."

She hadn't asked. She probably didn't want to know.

"My mother's name is Ivy. She doesn't have any siblings. And Adam, Walker's other brother, he doesn't have any kids."

I didn't stumble over referring to Ivy as my mother. There was too much at stake.

"Your daughter," I said, bringing my hand slowly to Daniela's stomach. "We share the same blood."

We're family.

I willed her to see it that way, to see me that way, if only for the most fleeting of moments.

"And if you are telling the truth, if you and my daughter share blood, what does that make me?" Daniela asked.

A terrorist. A criminal.

"Someone who wants to protect her daughter," I said, my quiet voice cutting through the air like a knife. "And hopefully, someone capable of believing that I might want that, too."

Daniela stared at my hand on her stomach. She kept staring until I removed it.

I wanted her to trust me. I wanted her to at least try to convince me that I could trust her, too.

Nineteen minutes.

I knew in the pit of my stomach that we weren't going to make it back to Hardwicke before the hour was up. I knew what would happen when we didn't.

Stop, I told myself. I had to believe that Ivy would come through, that Daniela would be released. And if I believed that, if I could *make* myself believe that, then I needed to know what we would be walking into once Ivy had secured Daniela's release.

For that, I needed someone who knew how Senza Nome operated. I needed Daniela on my side, not theirs.

"You said that you had a message for me." Daniela's voice was even, without emphasis. I had no idea if she believed what I'd told her about Walker's parentage, or if she cared. I had no idea if she saw even a hint of him when she looked at me. "It would be in your best interest," Daniela continued in that same deadly, even tone, "to deliver that message."

What if the interrogators were wrong? I thought, unable to block out the hint of fear slithering its way up my spine. *What if Daniela hasn't been emotionally compromised? What if she's one of them in every sense of the word?*

What if they have no intention of silencing her at all?

For the first time, I truly processed the fact that the woman sitting beside me was Senza Nome. Like Mrs. Perkins. Like Dr. Clark.

"You want the message?" I said. "'The dove has always wanted to fly to Madrid.'"

I saw the moment the words landed for the woman.

The dove has always wanted to fly to Madrid. What did that mean? What could that possibly mean?

Beside me, Daniela climbed to her feet. I stayed sitting, tracking her movement. She turned back to face me, and I returned her stare.

"You are quiet," Daniela said finally, after a full minute had stretched by with us in silence.

I shrugged, my leg muscles tense, ready to propel me to my feet the second it became necessary. "I told you everything I came here to say."

The woman opposite me smiled slightly. I didn't know whether to be warmed by the expression—or chilled.

"If I asked you to," Daniela said, a slight, lilting accent creeping into her voice, "would you tell me what else my people asked you to do? Their other demands—the things that were not a part of their message for me."

I wasn't sure if this was a test or a trick or even just a request—but I was here, and she was asking. If things went as planned, Priya would be delivering both of us through the gates of Hardwicke. Honesty was a chance I had to take.

"They want you, and they want Priya, and they want me." That was just the start of their demands. In as few words as possible, I communicated the rest. Daniela listened in utter silence, one hand creeping to the small of her back, her eyes sharp as she digested my words.

"May I ask who issued your orders?" Daniela inquired once I'd finished.

I told her about Mrs. Perkins.

I told her about the armed men in the halls.

I showed her the video Mrs. Perkins had sent me. I didn't watch it. I couldn't. But even when I turned my head away, I wasn't able to block out the sounds. I closed my eyes. I pressed back against the strobe-like images that battered against the halls of my memory.

Help me!

I bowed my head, my arms curving around my torso.

Daniela let the video play to the end. When she looked up, her eyes were dry, but I could see a glint of emotion lurking in their depths.

Guilt? Sorrow? Rage?

"Why you?" Daniela asked me, her voice still even, still controlled as she paced to the far corner of the room. "Why let *you* go? Why send *you* these videos? Why send *you* here?"

I gave her the only answer I had, the only one I'd been given. "I'm a resourceful girl, related to some very powerful people."

Daniela looked at me and into me, like I was a clock, and she was a clock maker preparing to take it apart. "You care."

I do. For some reason, I couldn't admit that out loud.

"Walker cares." Daniela turned her head to one side, allowing her matted hair to fall into her face. "He's always cared too much."

About you, I thought. *You mean that he cared too much about you.*

This was the moment—the one I'd been waiting for, the only one I was going to get.

"I'll die to protect the people I love," I said. I let my gaze fall down to her stomach and let a question form on my lips. "Will you?"

Daniela walked slowly toward me.

"Congressman Wilcox was killed in federal custody," I told her. "He was a liability." The terrorist drew herself to a stop directly in front of me. "Are you?" I asked her. "A liability to Senza Nome?"

When the government hands you over, what are the terrorists going to do? To you? To your child?

Do they have your loyalty?

Do you have theirs?

Those questions never made their way from my mind to my lips.

"A liability?" Daniela repeated after an elongated moment. "To the people you have been dealing with, let us say that I am a *concern*."

She knows she's a threat, I thought. *And she knows what they do to threats.*

Once upon a time, Daniela Nicolae might have been a true believer in Senza Nome's cause. But right now, in this cell, looking at the possibility of confronting her own people, she was also a mother.

I knew from firsthand experience—from Ivy—what a powerful motivation that could be.

"The message you brought me—'The dove has always wanted to fly to Madrid.' It was an order to kill the woman who brought you here." Daniela Nicolae stood over me. "Priya Bharani. She's the dove."

I stood up, trying to process that statement. "And Madrid?" I asked, my tongue like sandpaper in my mouth.

"I know people," Daniela replied, "who have been to Madrid. I know what it is they refer to."

"Murder," I said.

"Execution," came the correction. "They don't just want the dove dead. They want it sudden and public, and they want the blood on my hands."

Priya had been ordered to give herself up, to deliver Daniela, to deliver me. She'd known that, in all likelihood, she would be surrendering her life.

"When we make it back to Hardwicke," I said, trying to process the reality of the situation. "When we go in . . ."

"I'm to make an example of her."

"With the FBI and SWAT team watching?"

Daniela gave a slight nod.

"Won't they shoot you?" I asked.

Daniela looked at me with an expression somewhere between detachment and pity.

That was when I realized: "They won't shoot you if you have me."

I could see how this would have played out, if Daniela hadn't told me the meaning behind the message. I'd have been prepared for an attack, but I wouldn't have expected it to come from her.

Neither would Priya, I thought.

The dove has always wanted to fly to Madrid.

"Why tell me this?" I asked the woman Walker Nolan had loved, the terrorist operative he'd never really known.

"You told me your truth," Daniela Nicolae replied. "You wanted my trust. You claim that we are family, of sorts." She let that sentiment hang in the air a moment longer than the ones that had come before. "My people, the organization I work for—they have been my family. I was taught, from the cradle, to protect that family." She laid a hand on her stomach. "I would have died for our cause. But I will not allow my daughter to do the same."

There was a noise in the hallway—footsteps, then a shout.

"Do you have a plan?" I asked Daniela.

She smiled again, that same subtle, chilling smile. "Do you?"

CHAPTER 60

Two minutes later, the door to the cell opened.

Priya stepped in and shut the door behind her. "We've got company," she said. "Tess, you and I need to get out of here. Now."

"What kind of company?" I asked.

Priya grabbed my arm, and as she pulled me out of the cell, she met Daniela's eyes. "You stay here."

I'd known that it wasn't my job, or Priya's, to get Daniela out. But after the past fifteen minutes—and especially the last two—my gut rebelled against the idea of leaving Daniela behind and *hoping* things went according to plan.

We need Daniela. Without her, we don't stand a chance.

"Stay behind me," Priya said softly, as she guided me down the corridor. "And do exactly as I say."

The two guards who'd been there when we arrived were still just outside the door, but they'd been joined by a third—and all three were slumped on the floor. Unconscious.

What happened? I bit back the words, suddenly sure that I didn't want to risk making any unnecessary noise.

Priya caught the look on my face as she glanced back over her shoulder at the men. The look on *her* face clearly said, *Don't ask.*

We rounded the corner, walking at a brisk pace. We continue at that pace until a group of men turned the corner at the end of the hall, walking toward us.

Not good.

There were four men. At least three of them were armed.

So not good.

"Head down and keep walking," Priya murmured. She slowed her pace slightly, and I matched mine to hers.

"You!" I heard a voice say to my left.

Priya tensed, ready to launch herself into action.

"Tess."

The sound of my name drew Priya up short, and for the first time, I looked past the guns to the men's faces. Three of them appeared to be guards of some type. The fourth was the vice president of the United States.

Where's his Secret Service detail?

"It is Tess, isn't it?" the vice president said. Beside him, one of the men's hands hovered over his weapon.

"Yes," I told the vice president, turning to face him full-on. "It is."

"They say you saw my daughter. They say you saw Anna." The vice president didn't say a word about my presence here. He didn't seem capable of registering surprise or suspicion or anything other than a haunting mixture of sorrow and fear. "She's okay?"

"She was screaming," I said, unable to keep the memory from coming to life on my tongue. "I saw them knock her unconscious, but they weren't trying to hurt her. They needed her intact."

They need her to get to you.

"They won't need her much longer," the vice president said, the words getting caught in his throat.

I realized, then, why he was here.

He turned to Priya. "I never saw you," he said gruffly.

"Nor we you," Priya returned. She started walking again at that same brisk pace. After a moment, I followed.

He's here for Daniela, I thought. *The same as us.*

The difference was, the vice president—the *acting president*—had the authority to let her go.

Priya and I made it to the surface. Somehow, I wasn't surprised to see Ivy waiting outside. Adam stood slightly behind her.

They were very surprised to see me.

"What—" Ivy started to say, but then she changed her mind. Instead of asking me what I was doing here, she turned on Priya, the look on her face promising dire consequences.

"She had a message," Priya told Ivy. "For the prisoner. I assure you—"

"I assure *you*," Adam countered, stepping forward, "that you do not want to finish that sentence."

Adam and Ivy hadn't been happy when Priya had used me to send a message to them. And now that she'd brought me to see a known terrorist? Put me in a room with that terrorist?

This wasn't going to be pretty.

"She didn't have a choice about bringing me," I said, trying to get Adam and Ivy to focus on me. "Just like I didn't have a choice about coming."

They have Vivvie.

I willed Ivy to remember that, willed Adam to ask himself what lengths he and Ivy would have gone to if the terrorists had still held me.

"Get Tess out of here," Ivy told Adam, clipping the words.

"Is it done?" I asked, stepping back and away from them before Adam could reach for me. "Daniela? The files? The foreign prisoners?"

Everything else Senza Nome asked for—is it done?

Ivy held up a USB drive. "My files," she said.

Or at least, the version she was giving Senza Nome.

Ivy inclined her head slightly. "It's done."

The door opened behind us. All four of us whirled in the direction of the sound. Daniela Nicolae stepped out into the evening air, her hands cuffed in front of her body, an armed guard on either side.

"President Nolan will be sworn back in within the hour," one of the guards told Ivy. "You need to move."

Priya was the one who heeded that instruction, stepping forward to take the USB drive from Ivy. "I've received an ultimatum of my own," she said, her voice steady. "I have to be the one to deliver their demands. I go in."

"You won't come out," Ivy told Priya. The resulting silence indicated Priya's acceptance of Ivy's words, both as truth and as inevitable.

Stone-faced, Ivy nodded to the guards. They transferred Daniela Nicolae to Priya's custody. Seconds later, the guards were gone.

They were never here. Vice President Hayden was never here. This exchange never happened.

"Come on, Tess," Adam said, stepping up beside me.

I swallowed. "I can't."

Ivy understood before Adam did. She always thought three steps ahead. "No," she said fiercely. "Tessie. *Theresa.* No—"

There was a blur of movement, and Ivy crumpled. Adam caught her just before she hit the pavement. Priya stood over them. She'd knocked Ivy out, and now she had a gun in her hand.

"I am sorry," she told Adam. "Truly. But Tess comes with me."

Adam lowered Ivy's prone form to the ground. He stood. Priya fired a warning shot to one side.

"Tess." Adam addressed me, ignoring Priya, ignoring her gun. "Come to me."

My throat tightened. "I can't."

Adam saw now what Ivy had seen instantly: Priya wasn't taking me against my will. He saw in my face that I'd known all along that it would come to this.

"I'm sorry," I told Adam. "If there was a way . . ." My words came at an uneven pace, my breathing ragged. "I wish there were a way, Adam, but I can't just step back and let people die. Tell Ivy—"

"Tess—"

I spoke over his objection. "Tell Ivy that I forgive her. For leaving me in Montana, for lying to me—for everything. Tell her I'm sorry. Tell her that I had to do this, okay? Tell her . . ."

I love her.

He could hear it in my voice. They all could. I stared at Ivy, lying prone on the pavement, her face peaceful.

"Tell her," I said, "that I am my mother's daughter."

I nodded at Priya, and she stepped forward, placing herself between Adam and me, her gun still pointed directly at him. I turned to go. I heard Adam step forward. "You won't shoot me," he told Priya.

A second later, I heard his body hit the ground.

I whipped back around. *There was no gunshot*, I told myself frantically. *Priya didn't shoot him.*

Daniela stood over Adam's body, her hands still cuffed. "He was right," she told Priya. "You would not have shot him."

How did she—

Priya trained her gun on Daniela, and I remembered Vivvie's aunt telling me that pregnant or not, Daniela Nicolae could take me.

"He will be fine," Daniela said, stepping over Adam's body. "Now, are we doing this, or aren't we?"

I tried not to think, in that moment, that Priya didn't know—not really, not fully—what *this* entailed.

The dove. Madrid.

I couldn't let myself go there. I couldn't think about the plan—my plan.

Priya lowered her weapon, but never took her eyes off Daniela. "Let's go."

CHAPTER 61

"There's no way I'm letting a minor put herself back on the chopping block." The FBI agent who'd greeted me when I was released was the same one we needed to let us back through the gate now.

It had taken us twenty-three minutes to get to Hardwicke and another twelve to arrange this meeting. Feeling suffocated by that tally, I laid my phone on the table in front of us. "You don't have a choice."

I'd received another text on the way here. *Another video.* As I watched, the FBI agent hit *play.* I'd seen the video, but I made myself watch it again. *A girl this time. A senior.* I couldn't place her name, but I knew she'd applied early to Princeton.

She wouldn't be going to college now.

"Give them what they want," I told the agent, "and we can end this."

She had to avert her gaze—from me and from my phone.

"Homeland's cleared it," one of her colleagues told her. *It,* in this case, was surrendering Daniela to the terrorists' hands, not me. "Word is that the order on this one came down from the top."

The clock was ticking on that order, just like the clock was counting down to the terrorists' next kill. *Once the president resumes his office, once he figures out what the vice president has done . . .*

We had a window, and we were wasting it.

"This is my choice," I told the hostage negotiator. "If nothing else, it will buy you time, and they won't hurt me, not right away."

We can't stand around debating this. We need to move.

"We've got the girl's guardian on the line." Someone held out a phone to the FBI woman. At the mere mention of Ivy, I snapped into motion. The FBI hadn't patted me down for weapons this time.

That was a mistake.

Priya had refused to give me a gun, but she hadn't left me defenseless. We'd had time to talk about how this would go down on the drive here. Before we'd left the car, she'd given me a knife.

"Put the phone down," I said. It took a single beat for the agents to process the fact that I was holding a blade. That was all the time it took for me to angle it at my own throat.

"*Put the phone down,*" I repeated.

"Tess." Hostage negotiators specialized in sounding reasonable.

I dug the tip of the blade into my own neck. I felt a sharp pain. Blood tricked down and over my collarbone.

They put the phone down.

"You have two choices," I said, stepping back. "You either send me in with Priya and Daniela and you risk that something *might* happen to me in there, or I swear to all that is holy that something *will* happen to me, right here."

They might be able to take the knife from me, but not before I did some serious damage to myself.

"Am I bluffing?" I asked the female agent.

She took in my posture, the expression on my face. "No."

My gut said that they *wanted* to send me in. They *wanted* to buy themselves time.

I just had to give them an excuse.

When Priya, Daniela Nicolae, and I walked through the gates of Hardwicke, I could just barely make out the silhouettes of the snipers on the roof. Behind us, the SWAT team and the FBI stood in a formidable line.

One wrong move, and it was all over.

Step after step after step, we walked away from the safety of the outside world and toward the main campus—toward the armed men and Mrs. Perkins and the bodies already littering the Hardwicke halls.

We'd made it two-thirds of the way there when Daniela spoke. "You can lower the knife."

My arm had held the blade in position long enough that for a second, it didn't want to move.

Closer to the front doors of Hardwicke. Closer.

My hand shaking, I managed to lower the blade to my side.

"Drop it," Priya told me, her voice guttural and low, as we approached the main building. I followed her gaze and saw the red dot on my chest.

The snipers.

I dropped the knife. It clattered to the pavement. For an elongated moment, the sound echoed all around us. The world was still. Calm.

And then Daniela Nicolae bent to pick up the knife.

Dove. Madrid—

Within a heartbeat, Daniela was holding Priya from behind, the knife at her throat. Daniela turned to face the SWAT team, to face the *world*.

"My name is Daniela Nicolae," she shouted, her voice high and clear. "And the time for waiting is *over*."

The blade slid over Priya's throat. One second, Vivvie's aunt was standing beside me, and the next, Daniela pushed her body aside and made a grab for me. She held the blade to *my* throat.

"Breathe," Daniela murmured into the back of my head, using my body as a shield as she backed away from the SWAT team's raised weapons, away from Priya, sprawled out on the ground.

The dove has always wanted to fly to Madrid.

I did as Daniela Nicolae instructed. I forced air into my lungs and I forced it out. But all I could see, in the world in front of me and in my mind, was blood.

CHAPTER 62

I'd known the plan. That was what I told myself as Daniela jerked me through the front doors of Hardwicke. I'd known that for us to do what needed to be done, the terrorists had to watch Daniela do as she'd been told.

They had to watch her kill Vivvie's aunt.

"Ms. Kendrick," Mrs. Perkins greeted me as we stepped inside the building. "So nice to see you again."

An armed man slammed me against the wall. My face pressed flat, my heart thudding in my chest, I tried to ignore the hands on my body, checking me for weapons, lingering a second too long.

"She's clear," the man said, stepping back. I turned slowly to face them. Opposite me, Mrs. Perkins plucked the knife from Daniela's hand. "I'll take this," she said.

The blade was still smeared with red, still dripping.

Mrs. Perkins let the knife dangle from her fingertips as she led us down the hallway and up the stairs. One of the guards pressed the tip of his automatic weapon against the small of my back.

When we stepped out into the third-floor hallway, I saw a trio of bodies lined up against the wall. *The headmaster, two students.*

"This isn't who we are," Daniela said, her voice low, her eyes on the bodies.

Mrs. Perkins opened the door to the third-floor computer lab. "It's who you are," she told Daniela lightly. "It's all you'll ever be in the eyes of the world, thanks to your wonderful little performance out front."

That was the point, I thought. Like the kingmaker, Mrs. Perkins played the long game. This was strategy. A carefully laid plan.

She's not treating Daniela like a traitor. She's treating her like competition.

"Now," Mrs. Perkins said, turning her attention back to me. "Let us see how our little fixer did, shall we?"

Anxiety and adrenaline shot through my body. Ignoring it as best I could, I scanned the occupants of the room. Dr. Clark was sitting in front of a computer. Including the guards who'd escorted us up here, there were a total of four. And standing in between two of them was Henry.

Don't look at him. Don't make eye contact. Don't feel his stare on your skin.

I focused on Mrs. Perkins and Dr. Clark instead.

"Money transfer came through," Dr. Clark told Mrs. Perkins. "Twenty million, untraceable."

I let out a shallow breath. William Keyes was a man of his word.

"Congratulations, gentlemen," Mrs. Perkins said to the guards. "You'll be getting paid."

Mercenaries. My chest tightened. *Guns for hire.* That had been my hope. I couldn't afford to show any visible reaction to the confirmation I'd just received.

"And what of Ivy Kendrick?" Mrs. Perkins asked me. "Did DC's most notorious fixer step up to the plate?"

"She got your prisoner released," I replied, glancing toward Daniela. "Didn't she?"

Mrs. Perkins made a *tsk* sound under her breath. "There's no need to take a confrontational tone, Tess. We're all friends here." She stepped forward and trailed the flat of the knife blade along my neck. "Now tell me, did Ivy happen to send us anything else?"

I nodded, as much as I could with a knife at my throat.

"Delightful," Mrs. Perkins declared, stepping back. On the other side of the room, Henry stared at her, his jaw clamped closed.

I won't let anything happen to you, he'd said roughly, his body less than a millimeter from mine.

"I believe you're looking for this," Daniela said, holding up the USB drive she'd taken from Priya. There wasn't an ounce of tension in her voice—nothing but the barest hint of challenge.

She's not afraid of them, I realized. *They haven't lifted a hand against her.*

There was a plan. Daniela and I had a plan—but the reason I'd put my life in her hands, *Priya's* life in her hands, was that I'd thought that our goals were aligned.

I'd thought she—and her child—were in danger.

Mrs. Perkins took the drive from Daniela and handed it to Dr. Clark. My former teacher plugged it in. A sequence of numbers and programming code appeared on the screen.

All eyes went to me.

"It has to be decrypted," Daniela spoke up on my behalf, leaning back against a nearby table as she did. "Would you expect anything less?"

She's on my side. She is. She knows the plan. She'll stick to it.

"For your sake, Tess," Mrs. Perkins said, her gaze lingering on my face, "let us hope it's decrypted quickly."

The sound of my own breathing was deafening in my ears, but somehow, I heard it—*a light, high-pitched whistle.*

Daniela eased herself off the table. The moment Mrs. Perkins attention was drawn to Daniela, I bolted.

Out the door, into the hall.

I made it two feet, maybe three, and then I was slammed into a wall. I heard a crack. *My jaw.* My teeth bit into my tongue.

One of the guards grabbed me roughly, my arms held so tightly behind my back that my shoulder threatened to dislocate. My eyes teared up. My vision blurred. I blinked.

Mrs. Perkins stepped out into the hall. She took her time and traded her knife for a gun.

My eyes found their way to Henry's. For a second, I let myself pretend that none of this had happened. That it was just Henry and me. That he was the boy I'd known, the person I'd thought he could be.

"Stop, Kendrick. Please."

I saw him say the words as much as I heard them.

Stop fighting. Stop taking chances. Stop.

I couldn't. I had to keep Mrs. Perkins looking at me. I had to keep her attention on me for just a few more seconds.

"The program won't work," I said. "Ivy would *never* give you what you wanted. If she gave you anything, it's a *fraction* of what she has."

Mrs. Perkins raised her gun. "Thank you for your honesty, Tess."

A second before she pulled the trigger, Henry threw himself forward. His body slammed into mine, curved around mine, shielding it, protecting it.

Protecting me.

I heard the gun go off. I felt Henry's body lurch forward with the impact.

No. I thought the word, and I screamed it. And all around me, the world exploded into chaos.

I sank to the ground with Henry. *Shot, just like John Thomas. Bleeding, just like John Thomas.*

Not Henry.

Traitor—betrayer—friend—

Please, not Henry.

His blood was on my hands. My fingers frantically searched for a bullet hole, combing his back, the weight of his body in my arms.

"Up!" one of the guards yelled at me. "Get up!"

"Or," a voice said behind him, "*you* could put your weapon down."

Priya Bharani pressed a gun to the back of his head.

The plan is working, I thought dully. We'd taken our chances that the snipers' attention would be on the FBI and securing the perimeter, not on the "body" killed within ten feet of the Hardwicke door. Priya was a trained operative. She could move quickly and silently. *The plan is working. This was the plan.* I should have felt a rush of victory. Relief.

I felt numb.

The guard lowered his weapon. Holding Henry, his blood thick on my fingers, I tried to stop the bleeding and took in the sight beyond us.

Mrs. Perkins was on the ground. There was a tiny, perfect bullet hole in the side of her head. *Priya's handiwork, thanks to my distraction.* Daniela had taken out one of the guards. She currently held another at gunpoint.

That just left one guard, and Dr. Clark.

The sole remaining guard trained his gun on the dead woman who'd appeared in front of him. He wouldn't make the mistake of underestimating Priya twice.

"Before you pull the trigger," Daniela told him lightly, "you might consider the fact that by now, that twenty million dollars has been transferred again—into one of *my* accounts." She smiled. "Were you hoping to get paid for this job?"

"You—" Dr. Clark couldn't get out more than a single word. She looked from Daniela to Priya.

"It was our understanding," Priya told Dr. Clark, "that what your colleague wanted was a very public show. So we gave you one."

The knife sliding across Priya's neck. The way she'd crumpled to the ground. The blood pooling around her wasn't hers. The blood on the knife wasn't hers.

It wasn't even blood.

I'd been told such sleight of hand wasn't hard, when the act was to be observed from a distance. I'd been told that people paid attention to threats, not bodies.

I'd known the plan. I'd *come up with* the plan. And still, it shocked me to see Priya standing there. She'd played her part well.

The blood.

The blood on the pavement hadn't been Priya's—but the blood on my hands was Henry's.

"Can you get us out of here?" the mercenary asked Daniela, his gun still trained on Vivvie's aunt.

"I have an exit strategy." Daniela's lips curved up slightly. "It will require some . . . sacrifices," she said. "Are all the men here loyal to you?"

Are you loyal to all the men here? That was what Daniela was really asking.

The mercenary stared at her for a moment. "No."

"Well, then," Daniela said, "perhaps what I'll need from you won't be so much of a sacrifice after all."

There was a beat of silence and then the mercenary lowered his gun. "I believe I speak for the men on *my* team," he told her, "when I say that we would like to be paid."

"Congratulations." Daniela lowered her own weapon, her eyes alight. "You now officially work for me."

CHAPTER 63

The United States did not negotiate with terrorists. Now that Daniela had seized Hardwicke, that left her attempting to come to terms with someone else.

"You're fine?" Ivy asked me, her voice shaking on the other end of the phone line.

"I'm fine," I said.

"You're . . ."

"I'm fine."

I heard Ivy suck in a breath. Even with a phone line between us, I could practically *see* her summoning up her composure with an uncanny level of emotional control. "You're grounded until you're forty."

"We're willing to accept those terms," I retorted, exerting the same control of my emotions that she'd shown over hers. "All you have to do is provide transport."

Across the table from me, Daniela tilted her head to the side, considering the phone, which I'd set to speaker.

It's not over, Ivy. I willed her to see that. *It won't be over until we come to terms.*

Daniela had taken control of Hardwicke. She was amenable to finding a peaceful solution—but that peaceful solution could not entail her going back into federal custody. The woman sitting across from me hadn't engineered this situation. She hadn't escalated it. But she held the reins now, and she wouldn't hand them over until she was sure that it was in her best interest to do so.

Our prior alliance could only carry this so far.

"Transport?" Ivy repeated, after an elongated silence. "The whole world is watching. This doesn't end with a cease-fire. This ends with a surrender. It has to."

"A student was shot," I said, feeling a bit like I was standing outside my body, watching myself dispassionately say those words. "He needs medical attention, Ivy."

There was silence on Ivy's end of the line.

"*Henry* needs medical attention," I repeated, my grip on my emotions slipping finger by finger when I said Henry's name. *Please, Ivy. You're supposed to be a miracle worker. Give me my miracle, just this once.* "Daniela," I continued, my voice remarkably steady, "needs safe transport out of the country for herself and a handful of men."

"And if I'm going to make *anything* happen," Ivy countered, "I need a surrender. I need terrorists in cuffs."

Daniela leaned forward, folding her hands on the table. "Perhaps," she said, "there is a way for all of us to get what we need."

• • •

I ended up sitting on the floor of an empty classroom. Dr. Clark sat beside me, tending Henry's wound.

"Don't worry," she told me, her voice oddly calm, given the circumstances. "Shoulder wounds are rarely lethal."

He's lost a lot of blood. I didn't say that, couldn't let myself say that. So instead, I said, "Why?"

"Unless the bullet hits a major artery—"

"No," I said forcefully. "Why agree to turn yourself in?"

"Because," Dr. Clark said softly, "it's for the greater good."

The United States government needed terrorists in cuffs. They needed a face for this horror. They needed to win.

Mrs. Perkins was dead. And the moment Daniela had asked, Dr. Clark had offered herself up. *In penance?*

No, I thought, watching her tend Henry with an unnatural calm. *With purpose.*

Even now, even after everything, Dr. Clark did everything in the name of Senza Nome.

Ivy would get her surrender. She'd get Mrs. Perkins in a body bag and Dr. Clark in handcuffs. She'd get two-thirds of the mercenaries.

The remaining men—the ones Daniela had struck a deal with—would get out of this alive and much richer, so long as they helped take down the rest. It was amazing how easy it was to find men willing to turn on their cohorts when there were $20 million and charges of treason at stake.

I heard the first gunshot.

The subset of the mercenaries Daniela had offered to Ivy on a platter wouldn't go willingly. That was why Daniela had stationed two of her men at my door—and more at the doors of the other classrooms.

More shots. Coordinated movement.

Daniela had brought the snipers down. She'd allowed the SWAT team in, and now they were doing what SWAT teams did.

"She'll make it out of this?" Dr. Clark spoke suddenly. "Daniela?"

That was the plan—and based on the tone in Dr. Clark's voice, that was what she wanted. That was *all* she wanted.

"Are you really doing this for the greater good?" I asked. "Or for her?"

"We're clear!" I heard someone shout from the hallway.

That would be the sign for the remaining mercenaries—Daniela's men, the ones she'd struck a deal with—to leave. *Daniela gets away. A small subset of the men get away. The government gets their body bags and their arrests.*

And no one would ever know the difference.

"Not just for her." Dr. Clark's answer came on enough of a delay that I'd stopped expecting her to reply to my question at all. "I'm doing this for the man who recruited me. The one who recruited all of us, trained all of us."

This was the first I'd heard a mention of a man, the first clue I'd been given that someone *was* in charge of Senza Nome.

"Daniela proved herself tonight," Dr. Clark said. "She's worthy."

"Worthy?" My stomach twisted sharply. Daniela had been the devil I knew. She'd been the lesser of two evils.

But she was still a terrorist. *My people, the organization I work for—they have been my family.* Daniela's words washed back over me as the door burst inward and SWAT officers poured in. *I was taught, from the cradle, to protect that family.*

"Worthy," Dr. Clark repeated as the men threw her facedown on the floor. "She's his daughter."

"We've got one wounded!" a woman shouted, kneeling over Henry.

"Secure!"

Amid the shouts, my concentration was wholly absorbed in Dr. Clark.

"His daughter?" I asked.

To the people you have been dealing with, Daniela had told me, *let us say that I am a* concern.

Dr. Clark's face pressed into the floor, her hands cuffed behind her back, she smiled. "His daughter. And now that she's proved herself," she said, every inch the true believer, "his heir."

CHAPTER 64

The occupation of Hardwicke made international news. So, too, did the takedown. All the terrorists had been either apprehended or killed.

Or at least, that was how the story went.

As far as the world was concerned, Daniela Nicolae had served as a double agent, helping the SWAT team infiltrate the building and take down her cohorts inside. Both she and her unborn child had been killed in the process.

The United States government had their victory. The Hardwicke parents had their children back. And I had another truth—another secret—I didn't want to know.

I wondered if it was the weight of secrets like this, as much as the fact that they served as a protective measure, that had made Ivy start keeping her files. She uploaded her secrets to the program. Maybe that meant she didn't have to carry them inside.

"Raise your arm over your head. Now rotate it away from me."

Grinding my teeth, I did as the doctor asked. I had a hairline fracture in my jaw, one hell of a headache, and a shoulder that the doctor subsequently informed me had not been dislocated, but that wasn't very happy either.

I felt it. I felt all of it—all the pain, all the terror, all the ways this could have gone differently—now that the ordeal was over.

"What's the verdict, doctor? Will our patient live?"

At some point, when I'd been caught up in the treacherous tangle of my own mind, Adam had entered the exam room. The doctor narrowed her eyes at him.

"Are you her father?" she asked.

Ivy was off running interference with the media, keeping them away from the hospital—away from Henry, away from Anna Hayden, away from me. If she'd had her way, Ivy never would have left my side.

"Uncle." Adam answered the doctor's question about being my father. I could see the woman on the verge of telling him she could only speak to my parent or legal guardian.

I spoke up. "Close enough."

Adam kept his face carefully blank as the doctor rattled off the details of my condition, but I knew him well enough to see the emotions underneath. He was the closest thing I had to a father, the closest thing I would ever have, with Tommy dead.

Soon enough, the doctor left the two of us alone. Adam came to stand in front of me. After a long moment, he sat beside me on the exam table. He didn't yell at me. He didn't ask me how I was doing. He just sat there, and I leaned into him.

His arm wrapped around me, and I cried—deep, bone-shuddering sobs that racked my body and his. He held on, held me, and when I stopped crying and straightened, wiping the back of my hand roughly over my tear-drenched face, he didn't say a word.

"I'm sorry Daniela knocked you out," I said, beaten at my own game by his steady silence.

In reply, Adam raised an eyebrow at me. "Are you?"

"Not really," I admitted, managing a small smile. "But I'm sorry it was necessary."

Adam snorted. "I hear you're grounded until you're forty," he said, pushing back any urge he might have felt to tear into me himself.

"I'm pretty sure Ivy was exaggerating," I said.

Adam's other eyebrow joined the first. "Are you?"

The door to the hospital room opened. I expected it to be Ivy or Bodie, who'd promised to bring me a snack, but instead, William Keyes stood there. He hadn't changed clothes since the last time I'd seen him. His thick white hair was disheveled. He'd aged a decade in a day.

"You are unharmed?"

Those were the exact same words he'd said to me before, but this time, there was more raw emotion woven through them than I'd ever heard in his voice. I wondered if he believed, as the rest of the world did, that Daniela and the baby had been killed. Given everything I knew about the man, if he hadn't uncovered the truth yet, he would soon.

"I'm going to be okay," I said. I meant it. I *almost* meant it.

"If I thought I would not be murdered on the spot," the king-maker said, coming toward me, "I would turn you over my knee for going back into that building."

I wasn't sure if Keyes was concerned about being murdered by Adam or Ivy or me. Beside me, Adam glowered.

I felt a grin tug at the edges of my lips. "You sound like my grandfather," I said. "My other grandfather."

William Keyes had never liked being reminded that Gramps had raised me and loved me and made me the person I was, but this time, he seemed to take the reference in stride.

"You're a horrible girl," Keyes said, coming to stand right in front of me. "A reckless, stupid, irresponsible, *horrible* girl. And I . . ."

He looked at Adam, then back at me.

"I could be a better man," he said hoarsely. "For you."

CHAPTER 65

The hospital didn't hold me. I was released into Ivy's custody. The first thing I did was ask about Henry. She knew me well enough to know I wouldn't back down. And—apparently—the hospital staff knew *her* well enough not to turn us away from the ICU.

Henry's mother was standing in the hallway, her back to the wall, her fist pressed to her mouth, her face crumbling around it. My throat and stomach constricted.

"Tessie," Ivy said softly, but I was already off running.

"Is he . . ." I asked Henry's mother. I couldn't get further into the question than that. Pamela Abellard-Marquette looked up. It took her a moment to register my presence, to look at me, instead of through me.

Her entire body shuddered as she bit back a sob.

"He's going to be okay." The words undid her, even as she tried to pull herself together. "He's out of surgery, and they say . . ."

Ivy came and rested a hand on Henry's mother's shoulder.

"I'm sorry," Pam said. "I can't fall apart right now. I know that, and Henry's going to be *fine*. He'll need physical therapy, but he'll be *fine*, and I don't know why I'm crying like this—"

Another sob racked her body.

I know. I knew why she was crying like she'd lost him. Because in the hours since Hardwicke had been taken over, she'd been down that road again and again. Grief was like a set of stacking dolls, and the woman in front of me had lost her husband. She'd lost the father-in-law who'd been her rock in the wake of that loss. She had a daughter who woke up screaming at night, terrified that Henry or her mother might be next.

Pam shook her head and pulled herself to her full height. She forced her breath to even out but couldn't stop the tears from streaming down her face. She was as strong a woman as I'd ever seen. And she was broken.

Life had *broken* her.

And still, she stood. She carried on. Standing there, looking at her, I saw so much of Henry. I saw that she would do anything to protect her children. I saw that she would be horrified by the idea of Henry carrying the weight of the world to protect her.

"Can I see him?" I asked.

"Tess." Ivy said my name in a way that meant *no*, with a side of *stop asking.*

"He saved me," I told Pam. "He took that bullet for me."

He betrayed me.

Pam must have heard something in my voice because she looked at Ivy. "It's fine," she said. "I'm not sure he'll be awake," she told me. "But you can go in."

I slipped into the room and left Ivy with Pam. Hopefully, between the two of them, they could hold the nurses off long enough for me to say what needed to be said.

To do what needed to be done.

I stood beside Henry's bed, looking down at him. Tubes covered his face. As I stood there, he opened his eyes. I saw the moment he registered my presence and the moment he remembered everything that had passed between us.

Everything he'd done.

"You used me to try to get to Ivy's files," I said quietly. "You let them make you a terrorist."

Henry closed his eyes, his face taut beneath the tubing, then opened them again. He forced himself to listen, to hear this.

"If you'd told me about Dr. Clark days ago, if you'd told me what you knew, we could have stopped it. The takeover, the executions—we could have told someone, and we could have stopped it."

Henry stared at me. His green eyes were familiar. Too familiar. I didn't want to feel what I felt when I looked at him, when he looked at me.

"I don't forgive you," I said, my voice low. "I understand how they got to you. I understand what it must have been like when they told you there was a fourth conspirator. I know you didn't mean for any of this to happen." Henry hadn't known that Senza Nome would take over the school. He hadn't known there would be guns or men or bodies. Dr. Clark had convinced him, the way she'd tried to convince me, that they were the good guys. "I know you would take it back if you could. I know you took a bullet for me." I stared at him, at those green eyes. "But I do not forgive you."

The expression on his face told me that Henry Marquette didn't expect forgiveness.

"You're going to do something for me," I told him.

He gave a slight nod under the tubes.

"I want your word, Henry Marquette," I said, my voice shaking. "Whatever I ask, you'll give."

He nodded again, slower this time, his face never leaving mine.

I bent down, until my mouth was very close to his ear. And then I told him my request: "Don't tell anyone what happened in there. Don't confess."

Henry jerked back, but there was nowhere for him to go.

"You gave me your word," I said. "I don't forgive you. But you're not going to confess."

It was written on his face that he'd planned to. He would surrender himself to justice without another thought.

"Your family doesn't deserve that," I said, my thoughts going to his mother, to the sister who woke up screaming at night. "The mercenaries are dead, or they're gone with Daniela. She swore to me that you'll be safe, that you're out, that you'll never hear from Senza Nome again." That was the one thing I'd asked of her, in exchange for the deal I'd brokered with Ivy. "Dr. Clark won't breathe a word to the police about your involvement. The headmaster knew, but he's gone, and Henry? I haven't told."

Now it was my turn to close my eyes.

"I didn't tell the FBI. I didn't tell Ivy." I forced my lids open. "Did anyone else know? Any other students?"

Henry didn't want to answer. I waited. And eventually, he spoke a single word around the tubing in his mouth, choking it out. "No."

No, he hadn't told anyone.

No, I couldn't make him live with this guilt.

"You gave me your word," I told him, my voice rough. "You know, and I know, but what we know doesn't leave this room. Not when you give your statement. Not ever."

Henry had been vulnerable. He'd been angry and powerless and alone, and Senza Nome had found him. They'd told him a truth he should have heard from me.

"I'm not doing this for you," I told Henry. "I'm doing it for Asher and for Vivvie and Emilia and everyone at that school who will never be the same." I pressed my lips together. "I'm doing it for your mom, and for Thalia, and for *me*."

I didn't forgive him. But he was Henry. And for the briefest of moments, he'd been mine.

"I'm doing this," I said, "for a boy I used to know."

A boy who'd been lied to. A boy who'd lost too much. A boy who had wanted justice. A boy who'd believed he was protecting the people he loved.

"This secret stays with us," I said, trailing my fingers over his jaw one last time. "But, Henry? You and I are done."

CHAPTER 66

Of all the things I expected to see when I exited Henry's hospital room, the First Lady wasn't high on the list.

Georgia Nolan was talking quietly to Ivy until she saw me. She murmured something to Ivy, then hung back as I approached.

"You okay?" Ivy asked.

I nodded. I wanted to mean it.

Ivy smoothed a hand over my hair. "If you're up for it," she said, "there's one more person who wants to talk to you."

The president of the United States was awake, aware, and fully vested with the power of his office. He was also still confined to a hospital bed. Unlike Henry, President Nolan was free of tubes. Beneath his hair, I could make out a long line of stitches that cut across the side of his head. The collar of his shirt revealed an expertly wrapped bandage underneath.

His shoulder? His chest? I tried not to imagine the bullet hitting the president.

I tried not to think about Henry and the moment he'd taken a bullet for me.

I forced my gaze up to the president's face. His wife went to stand beside him, and that was the only cue that President Nolan needed to start speaking.

"I understand this country owes you a great debt," the president told me. For someone who'd been in a coma, his voice was steady and strong. "I also understand that in my official capacity in this office, I can neither know the truth of what happened today, nor express my thanks for any role you may have played in it."

If it wasn't for me, Hardwicke might still be under terrorist control.

"The vice president will be resigning tomorrow," President Nolan said, reminding me that if it wasn't for the vice president's actions, Daniela Nicolae might still be in federal custody, too. "He'll cite family reasons. I suspect he and Marjorie will be anxious to take Anna home to New Hampshire."

I'd spent enough time on the periphery of the political game to read between the lines of the president's words. The vice president hadn't resigned for family reasons, and he almost certainly hadn't *chosen* to do so.

They'd forced his hand because he'd authorized Daniela's release.

The vice president knew, I thought, thinking back to Anna's father's demeanor in that hallway. *He knew this was how it would end.*

The official story might be that Daniela Nicolae's loyalties had flipped, that she'd died working for our country, but the president almost certainly knew the truth. He knew that Daniela was still a part of Senza Nome. That she was still out there, still pregnant. *He won't acknowledge that he knows. Officially, he can't know.*

But he did know. And given that he believed the baby she was carrying to be his granddaughter, I had to wonder if he was already *unofficially* looking for Daniela Nicolae, for that child.

"I don't have to tell you," the president said, "how important it is that you . . ."

"Keep my mouth closed?" I got the feeling that the president of the United States wasn't used to being interrupted. "I know what I have to do," I told the president. "And I know how to keep a secret."

I was starting to believe that was what our country ran on—secret upon secret upon secret.

"There will be a press conference," the president told me. "In addition to the occupation of Hardwicke, I will also address the attack on my life." A shadow flickered over the president's features. I wondered if he was flashing back to the moment he'd been shot, the feel of the bullet as it had entered his chest. "Thanks to the hard work of a trusted few," the president told me, shooting a brief look in Ivy's direction, "the shooter was apprehended less than an hour ago."

The shooter. As in the person who'd taken aim at the president and pulled the trigger.

"Unfortunately," the president continued, "the shooter resisted."

Resisted. The hairs on the back of my neck stood up the moment the president said the word.

"He's dead," I said, reading between the lines again.

"We've been able to connect the shooter, financially, to the same people responsible for the death of John Thomas Wilcox and the hostile takeover of the Hardwicke School."

Suddenly, I felt less like the president and I were having a conversation, and more like he was issuing a statement. This was the press release he would be giving shortly. This was the whole ordeal, wrapped up with a neat little bow.

My stomach twisted sharply. "The assassination attempt—that wasn't Senza Nome," I said. "Daniela, Dr. Clark, Mrs. Perkins . . . they all maintained the organization had nothing to do with the attempt on your life."

The attack on President Nolan might have disturbed one plan, but it gave us an opening for another. I could hear Mrs. Perkins, could remember the way that when I'd said that Senza Nome had claimed responsibility for the attack, her response had been, *Did we? Did we really?*

"People like this," Georgia said, her voice full of compassion, "organizations like this—they get inside your head, Tess. They tell you what they want you to believe."

I knew that. But I also knew that Mrs. Perkins hadn't been concerned with making me believe anything, other than the fact that she could and would execute the entire student population of Hardwicke, one by one, if I didn't do as she asked.

"Tess, darling, it's over." The First Lady rested her hand lightly on the president's shoulder. The president winced.

"Your shoulder," I said softly. Like Henry, the president had been shot in the shoulder.

A muscle in the president's jaw tensed slightly, but he didn't allow himself to close his eyes. "It's fine," he said. "I'm fine—grateful for my life. I'm ready to heal and to lead this country as they do the same."

"The bullet," the First Lady said softly, trailing her hand lightly over her husband's stitches, "did less damage than the fall."

"Apparently," the president joked, taking his wife's hand in his own, "my head is not as hard as I've been led to believe."

There was something intimate in the exchange between the two of them, something that made it easy to see how America had fallen in love with this first couple on the election trail.

Ivy put a hand on my shoulder. "We should go," she said.

President Nolan turned his attention back to Ivy, back to me. "Get some rest," he ordered. "And this time, Tess?" He smiled. "Try to stay out of trouble."

CHAPTER 67

Hot water beat against my body. I closed my eyes and stepped farther into the spray. This shower was the only thing standing between me and Ivy.

I'd risked my life.

I'd lied to her.

And we both knew that given the same circumstances, I would do it again.

Eventually, the hot water ran cold. I turned off the spray and stepped out of the shower, wrapping a towel around my body. I slipped on an oversized T-shirt.

Ivy was waiting for me in my room. With her hair wet from her own shower, I could see the resemblance between us. She was dressed nearly identically, in an oversized USAF T-shirt—one of Adam's.

It was two in the morning. I shouldn't have even been vertical. And all I could think about was how different Ivy's life might have been, if it weren't for me.

Ivy picked up the brush on my nightstand. She sat on the edge of the bed. I sat on the floor. Wordlessly, she began brushing my hair. As she worked her way through the tangles, I felt my throat tighten.

Every time I closed my eyes, I saw the headmaster. I saw Matt Benning. I saw Henry, drowning in tubes. I heard John Thomas Wilcox's gasping last words.

I couldn't close my eyes anymore.

I didn't realize that Ivy had stopped brushing until she lowered herself to the floor and sat beside me. I remembered leaning into Adam and crying into his chest. I didn't have any tears left for Ivy.

I pulled my legs to my chest and wrapped my arms around them. It took me a few seconds to realize that beside me, Ivy had done the exact same thing.

"Did Adam give you my message?" I asked her.

I'd asked Adam to tell Ivy that I forgave her, to tell her that I was sorry for what I'd had to do. I'd asked him to tell her that I was my mother's daughter.

"He did," Ivy said, the volume and tone in her voice an exact match for mine: soft and hoarse and hesitant.

Ivy and I had lost so many years together that sometimes it felt like neither one of us knew how to just *be* in the other's presence.

"I meant it," I told Ivy. "I'm tired of being angry with you. I'm tired of holding on to old hurts."

"I know I hurt you—again and again. But, Tessie, hurting you is the last thing I ever wanted to do. I never meant—"

"It's okay," I said.

She shook her head. "No. It's not."

"What you did—when I was born, when Mom and Dad died, when you left me in Montana—it's okay."

Twenty-four hours ago, those words would have been unfathomable to me. But I'd walked back into Hardwicke not knowing if I would walk out. I'd *chosen* to do so, and if I could choose to do that, I could choose to change things with Ivy.

I could choose to stop expecting her to hurt me again.

"I lied to you your whole life, Tessie. I don't expect you to forgive that."

I straightened my legs and leaned my head onto her shoulder. I closed my eyes. "We're all liars sometimes," I said.

I heard her suck in a ragged breath.

"Do you forgive me?" I asked, murmuring the words into her shoulder. "For going back in there? For lying to you? For not being the kind of daughter you want?"

Ivy took me gently by the shoulders. "You are exactly the kind of daughter I want." A lump rose in my throat as she continued, "You always have been."

CHAPTER 68

The next morning, I woke up in Ivy's bed. I watched her sleep, remembering the last time the two of us had shared a bed. *You'd just been held hostage*, I told Ivy silently. *I'd bargained for your release.* The symmetry between that situation and the one we'd found ourselves in the day before did not escape me.

Every family had their traditions.

I woke up in the middle of the night, I continued, watching the rise and fall of Ivy's chest. *And you were gone.* That time, Ivy had been the one who couldn't sleep. I wondered if she'd watched me, the way I was watching her now. *I went looking for you. I found you in the conference room. You couldn't stop going back over what had happened. You couldn't stop thinking about the fact that the Secret Service agent who'd held you captive had been in the middle of surrendering when he was shot and killed.*

Ivy had been convinced that wasn't an accident. It was too neat, too clean, too convenient.

Unfortunately, the shooter resisted. The words the president had spoken to me the day before echoed in my head.

Too neat. Too clean. Too convenient.

"Morning, Tessie." Ivy turned over onto her side. "How did you sleep?"

I woke up thinking. I can't stop thinking.

"Yeah," Ivy said softly, taking in the expression on my face and the dark circles under my eyes. "Me too." She pushed a strand of hair out of my face. "How about I attempt to channel Bodie and make us some pancakes?"

Ivy was many things, but a good cook wasn't one of them.

"Don't give me that look," Ivy said. "I'm a professional. I fix problems for a living. I'm fairly certain I can handle some pancakes without causing our kitchen to explode."

The kitchen didn't explode, but the pancakes did. Ivy called Bodie to undo the damage. When he walked through the front door, he wasn't alone.

"Look who I found lurking on the porch," he said.

Vivvie hovered in the doorway for four or five seconds, her big brown eyes fixed on mine. Her lips trembled, and I thought of the way we'd left things in the hallway.

You're supposed to be my friend. My best *friend—*

Before I could finish the thought, Vivvie launched herself at me, jackrabbiting across the room and flinging her arms around me. She pressed her face into my shoulder and hugged me hard. My arms curved slowly around her.

Bodie and Ivy exchanged a glance, then made their way into the kitchen. I barely noticed. All I could think was that the last time I'd seen Vivvie had been on the security feed. Her hands had been bound behind her back. She'd been trapped, terrified.

"I'm sorry I got mad at you!" Vivvie blurted out, pulling back to look up at me. "When everything happened, and I didn't know where you were, and people were getting shot, and—"

"Hey." I kept my voice soft but caught Vivvie's attention before she could progress to full-on babbling mode. "You had a right to be mad, Vivvie. You had a right to be upset. I knew something— something big—about what happened with your dad, and I kept it from you."

"I'm glad you didn't tell me," Vivvie said fiercely. "I don't want to know, Tess." She swallowed, her thumbs worrying at the sides of her index fingers. "That's what I realized, when I had a gun pointed at my head. I love what we do. You and Henry and Asher and me."

The way Vivvie said Henry's name, wedged between mine and Asher's, was a knife to the gut.

"I love helping you fix things," Vivvie continued. I could hear the tears in her voice before I saw the sheen of them in her eyes. "I like making people happy and righting wrongs. I like being *us*. But I'm okay with letting someone else handle conspiracies and terrorists and things that can get people killed. I don't need answers." Vivvie pressed her lips together and offered me a teary, apologetic smile. "I'm not like you, Tess. Or Henry. Answers don't matter to me. *People* do. And if not knowing is the cost I have to pay to keep *any* of us safe—I don't need to know."

There was so much I couldn't tell Vivvie—about Henry and Senza Nome, what had really happened in that school, the fact that Daniela Nicolae was still out there, alive.

"Okay," I told Vivvie. She was giving me permission to protect her. I loved her for that.

"I'm going to hug you again now," Vivvie warned me. Before she could make good on the threat, the doorbell rang. Vivvie glanced out the window, then grinned. "You might want to prepare for a group hug."

A second later, she flung open the door, and Asher bounded in. "Did I hear someone say 'group hug'?" he asked, throwing an arm around each of us. "What's next on the agenda? Might I suggest either an impromptu dance party or an epic battle of pillow fight proportions?"

"No."

The answer to Asher's question came from behind him. I looked up and saw Emilia standing in the doorway. For a second, as our eyes met, I saw her in the library. I saw her stepping out into the aisle. I saw her thrusting her chin out and facing Dr. Clark head-on.

"Asher's been banned from pillow fighting." Emilia's voice gave no hint to whether or not her thoughts in any way mirrored mine. "Trust me," she continued dryly, "when I say it's a kindness to all involved."

You gave yourself up for me. You risked your life for me.

"What?" Emilia shot back, staring me down. "Do I have something in my teeth?"

She didn't want a thank-you any more than she'd given me one for taking on John Thomas for her.

"I could be wrong about this," I told Emilia, "but I'm pretty sure they call it a *group* hug for a reason."

I saw a flicker of raw surprise cross Emilia's features before she hid it. Asher latched a hand onto his twin and pulled Emilia to the rest of us. Vivvie wasn't one to question a hug, so within seconds, she had one arm wrapped around Emilia and one around me. Asher kept hold of his twin and pulled me tight.

A little too tight.

We started to topple. Asher threw his whole body into it and brought all four of us to the floor. Vivvie started giggling.

"The bat is in the belfry!" Asher told her, falling back into code.

Emilia tried to pry herself out from underneath her brother. "We are not related," she told him.

Asher was unperturbed. "All we need is Henry," he declared, "and some borderline illegal fireworks, and all will be right with the world."

This was what it would be like, I realized, as I weathered the sound of Henry's name. This was what I'd signed up for, when I'd decided to keep Henry's secret—to make him keep it.

"Have you been to see him yet?" Asher asked me, propping himself up on his elbows. "The nurses didn't want to let me in, but I can be very persuasive." He wiggled his eyebrows.

"I saw him," I said, my throat tightening around the words.

Asher sighed. "I still can't believe Henry got himself shot. Even I can't one-up that." He sighed. "Now I will never win the heart of Tess Kendrick through acts of derring-do!" The teasing undertone in his voice—the one that said that he wasn't interested in my heart, but he thought that Henry was—cut into me with almost physical force.

Emilia rolled her eyes at her brother's dramatics. "And I," she added, "will never win the student council election." She sighed and leaned back on the heels of her hands. "My campaign is dead in the water. Do you know what heroically surviving a terrorist's bullet does to someone's approval rating?"

I stared at her.

"Kidding," Emilia clarified. "Mostly."

Emilia's taste in humor wasn't the reason I was staring at her.

Do you know what heroically surviving a terrorist's bullet does to someone's approval rating? My mouth went dry, my heart pounding deafeningly in my chest. *Too perfect. Too neat. Too clean.*

Suddenly, I was back in my World Issues class. Dr. Clark was at the front, lecturing about flashbulb memories. She was asking what people would remember about the day that President Nolan was shot. She'd asked if they would remember Georgia Nolan's rousing speech about her husband, the fighter. She'd asked if we would remember the record number of voters who turned out at the polls.

Going into midterm elections, the president's approval rating had been at an all-time low.

I hadn't paid much attention to the outcome of the elections. But I knew, in my gut, what I would find when I pulled the information up on my phone.

Before the president had been shot, the outlook for his administration had been dire. His party almost certainly would have lost its majority in Congress. The chances that the president would get a second term in office were next to nothing. That was *why* Congressman Wilcox had been working with Senza Nome. The revelation that Walker Nolan had impregnated a terrorist had been *meant* to devastate the Nolan administration at the worst possible time.

And then, the day before midterm elections, the president had been shot—and suddenly, President Nolan wasn't seen as complicit in Walker's ordeal. He was a victim, a soldier on the front lines of the war on terror.

Senza Nome had already gotten what they wanted. The thought solidified in my mind. *They had no reason to shoot him. None.*

I pictured the president in his hospital bed, telling me that the shooter had been connected to the terrorists. I pictured him telling me that he was ready to heal and to lead this country as it did the same.

There were good guys, and there were bad guys, and everything was tied up with a neat little bow.

The shoulder, I thought. *He was shot in the shoulder.*

I could hear Dr. Clark, tending to Henry: *Shoulder wounds are rarely lethal.*

I could hear the First Lady: *The bullet did less damage than the fall.*

If the president hadn't fallen, if he hadn't hit his head just right, there wouldn't have *been* a coma. He would have been rushed to the hospital, rushed into surgery.

Do you know what heroically surviving a terrorist's bullet does to someone's approval rating?

"Tess?" Asher's voice pulled me back to the present.

As I covered and picked up the conversation with the three of them, all I could think, over and over again, was that if it wasn't for the head injury, President Nolan would have been *fine*.

CHAPTER 69

Two days later, I got an invitation to dine at the White House. I hadn't said a word to Ivy about my suspicions. The president was a friend. I couldn't ask her to investigate the possibility that he'd arranged his own shooting until I was sure.

Sure that there was something to investigate.

Sure that it was worth it.

So I accepted Georgia Nolan's invitation to brunch, and I went to the White House, uncertain what I expected to find there.

Something to tell me I'm not crazy. Or, better yet—something that would tell me I was wrong.

I'd had forty-eight hours to think about Dr. Clark telling me that the Nolan administration was corrupt. She'd convinced Henry that the president was the fourth player in the conspiracy to kill Justice Marquette. The one who'd brought the other men together. The one who'd walked away scot-free.

Over the past two days, I'd found myself wondering if that was true.

The president's *doctor,* Dr. Clark's voice whispered in my memory as I took my seat opposite Georgia Nolan. *A Secret Service agent on the* president's *detail. That doesn't strike me as a coincidence.*

It shouldn't strike you as one, either.

If President Nolan was the kind of man who could arrange to have himself shot for approval ratings, what else was he capable of? *Could* he have been involved with the assassination of Justice Marquette?

Brunch was served in the family dining room. The residence was different from the public face of the White House, but I couldn't forget—even for a second—where I was.

President Nolan was out of the hospital and back to work. Ivy was off doing damage control for a famous philanthropist who had apparently gotten caught up in some not-so-philanthropic things.

It was just the First Lady and me.

How well do you know your husband? I thought, as Georgia dished out the food. *If I told you what I suspect, would it shock you? Would you turn around and tell him what I'd told you?*

Georgia speared a piece of fresh fruit with her fork and assessed me across the table.

"How are you doing, Tess?" she asked. "Truly?"

I considered my answer. "I'll survive."

"I have no doubt of it," the First Lady replied. "Ivy is one of the strongest women I have ever met, and you, my dear, are very much your mother's daughter."

I am.

That was why I was here. That was why I would watch and wait and look for patterns, hints that no one else would think to see.

"I'm so glad we were able to sit down like this," Georgia said. "I must confess, I did have an ulterior motive for asking you here today."

I'd told the First Lady—told the president—that the terrorists had said, again and again, that they weren't responsible for the attack on the president. *Did you ask me here to figure out what I know? What I suspect?*

Georgia gave me a considering look. "I understand that your grandfather may have told you certain . . . truths, shall we say?"

My heartbeat evened out. "Truths," I repeated. "About Walker." *That's what this is about. That's why you called me here.*

"My Walker," Georgia told me, "is very much like you, very much like his father."

Had we been overheard, an observer would have assumed she was talking about the president. I knew better.

"I know my son must be struggling," the First Lady continued. "I know that his heart is broken. But he doesn't say much. Not to me. Not to his father."

This time, she *was* referencing the president. He was the man who'd raised Walker. In the ways that counted, he *was* Walker's father.

"It would hurt them," Georgia said, "both my husband and my son, if certain truths were to come to light."

"I know how to keep a secret," I told Georgia.

She smiled slightly. "I suspect that you do."

Not long ago, I'd put my life in Daniela Nicolae's hands. I'd chosen to trust a known terrorist because Walker Nolan was her child's father. Because family mattered. Because we were connected by blood.

Sitting there, opposite Georgia Nolan, I thought about the connections between us. She'd had an affair with my grandfather, the result of a relationship that went back decades. Georgia treated Ivy like a daughter. I was a Kendrick, and I was a Keyes, and in some twisted way, that made me hers.

"What would you say," I asked the First Lady, my heart thudding in my chest, "if I told you that I thought there was a chance that your husband had himself shot?"

To mitigate the damage done by the Daniela Nicolae scandal. To protect himself from the fallout. To play on people's emotions on the eve of midterm elections.

"Tess, darling," Georgia said, "don't be ridiculous." She wasn't looking at me like a threat. She wasn't looking at me like a target. She was looking at me like a child. "The president simply is not capable of something like that." Georgia's tone was as polished as ever, but beneath the gentle Southern accent, I could hear a thread of sincerity.

A thread of steel.

"I've been married to the man for nearly forty years, Tess. I know him as well as it is possible to know anyone in this world, and I am telling you, he could no more arrange for his own shooting than he could kill our children in their sleep."

Everything in me wanted to believe what Georgia was saying. But I couldn't help thinking: *Do you know what heroically surviving a terrorist's bullet does to someone's approval rating?*

I couldn't help thinking about the Supreme Court justice, murdered by the *president's* doctor and an agent on the *president's* detail. *They could have been working for him.*

"You've been through a very traumatic event," Georgia told me. "It's understandable that there would be some lingering aftereffects." Georgia softened her voice. "Have you talked to Ivy about any of this? To Adam, or your grandfather?"

She said the words like they were a suggestion, but part of me couldn't help wondering if they were a probe.

"Ivy knows Peter," Georgia continued. "Almost as well as I do. She knows he is not capable of something like this."

This time, when the First Lady said the word *capable*, I heard it in a different way. What if *capable* wasn't a value judgment, a comment on the president's moral compass? What if it was a statement of fact?

The First Lady was the one who held the press conference after the president was shot. She was the one who made it a call to action.

From things I'd overhead here and there, I knew that Georgia Nolan took an active hand in her husband's administration. I knew that Ivy and Adam and Bodie considered her a force to be reckoned with.

I knew she was a woman with whom the kingmaker had fallen in love.

When I asked the headmaster why he took down the photo of the Camp David retreat, I thought suddenly, *he said that someone had told him it was a bit gauche.*

That photo connected the three men who'd conspired to kill Justice Marquette. There was a chance—a good one—that the fourth conspirator had been there, too.

I was told displaying that photograph so prominently was a bit gauche. That didn't sound like something the president would say. The word *gauche* sounded polished. Female.

I was told displaying that photograph so prominently was a bit gauche.

I was sure, suddenly, irrevocably sure that *someone* was Georgia Nolan.

Why would Georgia tell the headmaster to take that photo down?

She held a press conference after her husband was shot, rallying support for him, for the party.

"You really should talk to someone," Georgia told me, "about everything you've been through."

Even now that I'd put my initial suspicions on the table, Georgia wasn't treating me like I was a threat. She wasn't telling me to keep my suspicions to myself.

"Everything," Georgia repeated softly. "Including the truth about Henry Marquette."

Slowly, I registered the meaning behind those words. *Georgia knew.* Somehow, she knew that Henry had betrayed me. She knew that he'd been working with the terrorists.

Just like I knew that she was the one who'd had her husband shot.

"I care about you, Tess," Georgia told me. "You're very dear to people who are very dear to me."

People who would scorch the earth to find the person responsible if anything ever happened to me.

The First Lady wouldn't attack *me*. But she knew about Henry—and whether I was family or not, whether she cared about me or not, she'd come at him to get at me.

You really should talk to someone about everything you've been through.

I could tell Ivy what I suspected. I could tell the kingmaker. I could start them down the path of tying the First Lady to the attack on the president, maybe even the assassination of Justice Marquette.

Everything. Including the truth about Henry Marquette.

This was what it looked like to play five moves ahead. This was strategy. This was power.

I stood. Georgia came over and pressed a kiss to my cheek. All I could think, as I made my way out of the residence and was escorted onto the White House lawn, was that William Keyes had been right.

The queen is the most dangerous piece on the board.

CHAPTER 70

In the weeks that followed, I found myself going back over the conversation I'd had with Georgia Nolan: every word, every nuance, the expression on her face. There were days when I found myself wondering if I'd imagined the subtext to our exchange, the underlying threat. Georgia had admitted nothing. She'd said nothing incriminating. She'd told me I should talk to Ivy, to Adam, to the kingmaker. She'd done nothing but express concern.

And let me know that she knows about Henry.

She'd threatened me, so subtly that I couldn't even use that as evidence against her. She had a light touch. She played to win. I could picture her, using that light touch to draw together three men, to plant the idea in their heads that together, they could get away with murder. I could see her pulling their strings. I could see her doing it all without leaving even a trace of evidence behind.

Months ago, I'd told Georgia that a dead Supreme Court justice was a problem, and she'd corrected me. *Theo Marquette's death is a tragedy*, she'd said. *And, quite frankly, it's an opportunity, tragic though it may be.*

I couldn't prove anything. I couldn't tell anyone. But in the pit of my stomach, I knew.

The First Lady was the most dangerous player in this game.

"In the past weeks, each and every one of you has demonstrated the qualities that the Hardwicke School values above all else: integrity, perseverance, courage." The new headmaster spoke from the front of the chapel. "With the start of the new semester," she continued, "we are looking forward, as a community, as a family, as a school. You are all survivors. I feel awed to be standing here in front of you, with you, as we move into the future."

Beside me, Vivvie slipped a hand into mine. Asher sat on my other side, folding what appeared to be an origami flamingo. He bumped his shoulder into mine. On his other side, Henry eyed the flamingo with some level of distrust.

Henry's eyes flitted briefly toward mine. I looked away.

"You are all changed," the headmaster said. "What happened at this school will never leave you. You will carry it with you— but it isn't a burden that any of you have to carry alone. You are part of a long tradition of excellence, a family of scholars, a community that will come through this stronger than ever. *You*," the headmaster said, emphasizing the word, "are the leaders of tomorrow."

Leaders. My mind went to the president, to the First Lady, to everything I suspected and knew and couldn't tell.

"To that end, next week, we will begin anew with a fresh round of student council nominations. I hope that many of you will run, that your pride in your school—and yourselves—is stronger than ever, for what you have survived."

My gaze found its way to Emilia. She was sitting a few rows in front of us, between Maya and Di.

Stronger than ever, for what you have survived.

Emilia deserved to win.

As chapel let out, and we began to walk back to the main campus, Henry fell in step beside me. "I won't run," he told me.

I heard what he didn't say: *Emilia deserves it. I don't. I'm not what they think I am. I'm not what I thought I was. I don't know who I am anymore.*

I heard all that in those three words of Henry's. I also heard the underlying assumption: that if he ran, he would win.

"Go ahead," I told Henry. "Run."

Emilia would beat him. Somehow, some way, I would make sure of it. Just like somehow, some way, I would find a way to prove what I suspected about Georgia Nolan.

Power. The First Lady had it. I didn't. But I was Ivy Kendrick's daughter. I'd been raised by Gramps and taught strategy by the kingmaker. When I saw a problem, I solved it.

I wouldn't stay powerless for long.

ACKNOWLEDGMENTS

The Fixer books, more than any of my others, are stories that have been made in revision. I am incredibly grateful to Catherine Onder for her feedback and guidance as we zeroed in on Tess's adventures in *The Long Game*. Special thanks also go out to Nick Thomas, who helped see this book from start to finish. As always, I'm indebted to my agent, Elizabeth Harding, who has fought incredibly hard for this series at every step along the way. Thanks also to Holly Frederick, Sarah Perillo, Kerry Cullen, and Jonathan Lyons at Curtis Brown, as well as the fabulous Ginger Clark, who's been a huge advocate for *The Fixer* since day one. I'm incredibly grateful to everyone at Bloomsbury who has worked on these books and owe a special thank you to my publicist, Courtney Griffin.

This book could not have been written without the lovely Rachel Vincent, who kept me company (and kept me sane) as I wrote it! Rachel, I appreciate how many times you listened to me say "I just need to get the [spoiler] into the [spoiler]!" I truly could not have written this book without you.

I also owe a huge debt to my mother, Marsha Barnes, who took over planning my wedding (and made it the most incredible, perfect day) when I was on deadline. Thank you to my dad for spending nine hours stuffing invitations, ordering a flower girl dress, keeping track of RSVPs, and doing all of the table and menu arrangements, so that I could write and revise (and revise!) this book. I am truly blessed to have such a wonderful family and am grateful for each and every one of you.

Finally, thank you to my husband, Anthony, for constant support, always being there to listen, and making me laugh every single day.